Nightshade City

Nightshade City

HILARY WAGNER

Holiday House / New York

HOLIDAY HOUSE is registered in the U.S. Patent and Trademark Office.
Printed and bound in June 2010 at Maple Vail, York, PA, USA.
www.holidayhouse.com
First Edition
1   3   5   7   9   10   8   6   4   2

Library of Congress Cataloging-in-Publication Data
Wagner, Hilary.
Nightshade City / Hilary Wagner.—1st ed.
p. cm.
Summary: Eleven years after the cruel Killdeer took over the Catacombs
far beneath the human's Trillium City, Juniper Belancourt,
assisted by Vincent and Victor Nightshade, leads a maverick band
of rats to escape and establish their own city.
ISBN 978-0-8234-2285-2 (hardcover)
[1. Fantasy.   2. Rats—Fiction.]   I. Title.
PZ7.W12417Nig 2010
[Fic]—dc22
2010002474

To my husband,
Eric

Contents

Acknowledgements   ix

Prologue   1

Chapter One: The Catacombs   3

Chapter Two: Nightshade City   31

Chapter Three: Hard-Core Beliefs   74

Chapter Four: The Feast of Batiste   100

Chapter Five: Alive!   139

Chapter Six: More Flies with Honey   170

Chapter Seven: A City of Devils   202

Chapter Eight: Most Evil of Creatures   232

Chapter Nine: Home   252

Acknowledgments

THIS BOOK IS FOR MY husband, Eric, the man who dared me to write this story! He put up with my craziness and found his way through the early drafts, giving brilliant insight along with unwavering love and support. There would be no *Nightshade City* without him.

This book was inspired by my son, Vincent—my smart, funny, and strong-minded boy, who is the essence of Vincent Nightshade, and by his sister, Nomi, my clever little girl, who was with me the entire time I wrote *Nightshade City*, born the week the novel was finished.

I am forever grateful to Marietta Zacker and Nancy Gallt. Marietta and Nancy stood behind this book and were absolutely vital in making it happen. From day one, Marietta has championed my writing; she has been nothing short of an inspiration. I could not ask for a better agent or friend and do not know what I'd do without her to keep me sane!

Many, many thanks go to everyone at Holiday House. Julie Amper, my extraordinary editor, did unqualified wonders with the book, not to mention that she taught me a great deal. I know I'm a better writer for it, and I can only hope to work with her in the future.

Last, but by no means least, this book is for Craig Virden. He called me on a Tuesday, forever changing my life. He took a chance on my book, and he took a chance on me. Without a doubt, a small part of his spirit dwells within the corridors of *Nightshade City*, burning brightly for one and all to see.

Prologue

JUNIPER SLEPT like the dead, his infant son curled next to him, murmuring peacefully. The boy's miniature tail and feet were snugly tucked under Juniper's dense winter fur. The fire smoldered softly, infusing the room with a warm caramel glow, the ideal setting for a midday nap. Juniper had earned his rest. The battle was over, and for the first time in a long time, life underground was calm.

A noise interrupted Juniper's sleep—a dull scraping against the planking of his chamber door. "Who is it?" he called out. Juniper sluggishly looked up from the rocking chair, hoping that the anonymous knocker would go away and that his much-needed nap could continue. He listened for a reply; no answer. It appeared that the stranger at the door had given up. Letting his muscles once again relax, Juniper settled back into his slumber, his substantial arm cradling the tiny boy.

A low, raspy voice whispered, "Juniper. Juniper, wake up."

Juniper half opened his eye and for a second time looked towards the door, now a bit bothered. "Whoever is there, please come back tomorrow. I'll be more than happy to talk to you first thing in the morning. I promise you will have my undivided attention." He waited for a response; again no answer. The stranger had gone. "Thank the Saints," Juniper said. The room was silent, apart from the baby, who squeaked softly as Juniper shifted in the chair and once again drifted off.

"Juniper!" railed the voice, jolting him from his tranquil state. Juniper bolted from his chair, and plucking up his son, he reached into the fire pit for the hot poker, but it had vanished. He looked frantically for a weapon, quickly grabbing a knife off the table. Trying to follow the voice, he blindly swung the dull blade into the shadows.

There was a crash. Juniper jerked around. His leather satchel had been ripped from its hook and had fallen to the hard dirt floor, its contents sprawled everywhere. Unable to see in the hidden corners, he spun wildly in a confused circle. He hollered angrily into the dark. "Come out! Come out and face me, coward! I *know* why you've come!"

Finding a match, Juniper swiftly lit the wall torches, illuminating all things unseen, and still clutching his sleeping boy, he scoured the room.

No one was there.

CHAPTER ONE

The Catacombs

THE TWO BLACK RATS kept running. The Nightshade brothers coiled swiftly around a dimly lit corner as a tenpenny nail grazed Vincent's ear. It only nicked the tip but burned like hot coal. He shook his head, ignoring the searing sting, and kept running. Major Lithgo and two senior lieutenants thundered behind them, leaving a cloud of powdered earth in their wake.

As they galloped through the dark winding corridors of the Catacombs, Vincent wondered how High Major Lithgo could move so swiftly. He could actually hear the stout major's ample belly skidding through the dirt. Even through his panic, Vincent couldn't help but find this amazing. Belly or not, Major Lithgo grunted madly at their heels, intent on catching them.

"Another!" said Lithgo, commanding a soldier to hurl a second tenpenny.

"Catacomb Hall," huffed Vincent to his brother, "father's corridor behind Ellington's."

"Agreed," said Victor. The tenpenny impaled the dirt wall, just missing Victor's flank, as they took a sudden turn.

The Nightshades deftly took a sharp left, knocking an old toothless rat to the ground, his bag of candlenuts tossed into the air and scattered about the corridor. A lieutenant promptly stumbled over a nut, forcing the other soldier and Major Lithgo to skid violently through the dirt, landing atop one another in a muddled heap of tails, claws, and ears.

Lithgo scrambled to his feet and peered down the empty corridor. Nothing but gloom; no sign of the Nightshades. "They're gone! They could be anywhere by now!" Picking up a candlenut, he whipped it at the old rat's head, who cowered and shook, blocking his face from the blow. Lithgo growled contemptuously, "Useless old one, I should kill you for interfering with Kill Army business! I'm within my rights if I so please!" He stomped the ground like an overgrown child, kicking dirt at his lieutenants. "We should have finished off the last of the Nightshade Clan long ago—when we had the chance!"

Lithgo dropped to the ground, grunting loudly. His chest felt as if it might burst, and vomit rose in his throat. The soldiers stood silent as he gathered himself.

The old rat left his candlenuts and softly scuttled out of sight, hiding a shriveled grin. He was dumbfounded that he was alive.

Lamenting his large dinner, Lithgo leaned against the wall for support as sweat trickled down his thick russet brow and steam wafted from his now-filthy coat. The two young lieutenants stood without a sound, waiting for the major's orders. All that could be heard in the dusky corridor was Lithgo's weighty breathing.

* * *

The Nightshade brothers kept up their fevered pace, racing side by side through the Catacombs, their limbs ablaze. Lithgo and his soldiers were gone from both sight and sound, but that meant little. Deep beneath the congested metropolis of Trillium City, the Catacombs went on for miles, a swarming maze of hollowed dirt corridors. Kill Army soldiers could be hiding anywhere within its bleary depths.

Vincent and Victor reached Catacomb Hall, the epicenter of the Catacombs, an expansive public square. After long hours of drinking at the Ministry-run pubs, the only rats about were a few inebriated males, still on the prowl for female company. Stumbling about the cobbles in a stupor, they paid the brothers no mind.

The pair made their way to Ellington's Tavern, a decrepit old pub at the end of the horseshoe-shaped Catacomb Hall. Behind the tavern, hidden by trash and rusted signs, was an abandoned corridor. The brothers quickly squeezed under the debris, pulling themselves up into the arcane hole, which stank of toadstools and insect leavings.

Their father, Julius Nightshade, had taken Vincent there as a child and had met with assorted rats in the hidden passageway. Vincent didn't know what the meetings were about; he just remembered that the voices were always hushed and deadly serious. "Run as fast as you can," he told Victor. "Don't stop until we've hit Topside, all right?" Victor grunted in response, heaving his tired body up the steep tunnel.

The brothers' gait did not slow, and they panted harder as they neared the city's surface. With each stride, Vincent grew more troubled. Once they were Topside, they'd be able to disappear into Trillium's confused labyrinth of alleys and sewers, finally free from the grips of the Kill Army but still facing great danger. Rats were not welcome in the world of the Topsiders—the world of the humans—but Vincent and Victor could not risk one more second in the

Catacombs. Their guardian had died, making them wards of High Minister Killdeer's Kill Army. It was the Kill Army's right to take them, and Major Lithgo had come to collect them.

Glancing Victor's way, Vincent smiled confidently at his brother. Victor need not be worried about the Topsiders just yet. That would come soon enough.

They heard a sharp yelp as they clambered up toward the surface. One of them had stepped on an earthworm. The neglected corridor was overrun with them.

Lazily picking a scrap of roast hen off his distended stomach, Killdeer idly flicked the oily meat across his den. The mammoth rat slumped down further in his silver-chalice throne, only his limbs, potbelly, and snout visible to an onlooker. He had been the self-appointed High Minister of the Catacombs for eleven long years. Life had become unexciting and mundane.

Staring blankly at the ceiling of his den, Killdeer rolled his eyes in absolute boredom, crudely scratching his huge abdomen. His legs draped over his silver throne like mounds of heavy velvet, leaving his immense feet hanging over the side like two dead gray rabbits.

Massively built, Killdeer resembled more of an overfed house cat than a rat. Trillium's unusual rats were known for their extraordinary size, but Killdeer's proportions had grown considerably in recent years. The indolent Minister delegated most of his duties to Billycan, his second-in-command, which left the High Minister with nothing much to do but indulge his vices: eating, drinking, sleeping, and mating.

Incredibly, despite his ever-widening waistline and at times questionable hygiene, Killdeer proved entrancing to females. His smoky gray coat shimmered. His slanted eyes, black as pitch, gleamed like polished onyx. Pointed white teeth glistened in a smarmy smile that oozed confidence and dripped charisma. Catacomb females pursued him, drawn to his power and intrigued by his rogue nature. Eager females fought to be chosen by the great High Minister.

He wore a heavy silver medallion around his neck. It had belonged to the Mighty Trilok, the original High Minister of the Catacombs and, if not for fear of losing their tongues, most rats would say the only true High Minister. Killdeer had taken over during the Bloody Coup, the conquest that changed the course of the Catacomb rats' history. Enraged and humiliated by his banishment years before, Killdeer ambushed the Minister, assaulting the aging Trilok with primordial fury, slashing his jugular and tearing off his silver pendant, proclaiming himself the new High Minister.

With lucky timing, he seized control during Trillium's Great Flood, using it as cover for murder, snuffing out Trilok's key defenders—the leaders of the Trilok Loyalists—claiming they had drowned. Most of the adult Catacomb rats had been searching for food Topside in Trillium City when the flood struck. Water levels reached the rooftops, and while the resilient rats treaded the muddy water for days, many perished, leaving scores of young rats orphaned in the Combs. Killdeer then artfully solidified his position by creating the Kill Army. Rounding up the stray children of the Catacombs, he and his faction sent males to the Kill Army and females to its kitchens.

Killdeer reached into the bedding of his throne and pulled out his bottle of Oshi berry wine. Predictably, the bottle was empty. "Texi!" he yelled. "Texi, come here!" His voice thundered down the halls of his den. "My Oshi is empty again!" Moments later, he heard his half sister scurrying down the hall.

Despite Killdeer's obvious foul temper, Texi arrived cheerful but out of breath. "Yes, Killdeer?" she asked, panting. Texi came into the world dull of mind, utterly devoid of trickery. She easily forgave her older brother his sins, unlike the rest of her sisters, who hated him with every shred of their beings, secretly wishing him an agonizing death at every opportunity.

"Where is my Oshi, Texi?" he asked crossly.

Texi spoke in a high-pitched, childlike voice. "It should be where it always is. I replaced the bottle while you were sleeping."

"Well, it's empty." He sneered at her, waving the bottle scornfully.

She grew confused, her face crumpling as she thought about the day's events. "I do remember swapping it for the empty one. Perhaps you forgot you drank it?" Texi suddenly gasped and covered her mouth, realizing what she'd said. Even Texi knew never to question Killdeer. Only Billycan could get away with that.

Killdeer flung the bottle against a wall, shattering it. He bounded off his throne and pounced on Texi, grabbing her by the throat and pinning her to the wall. Her tiny feet dangled above the ground like small fish flopping in distress. Killdeer glared viciously at his half sister, poking her in the face with his huge snout. She could smell his sour breath. It reeked of Oshi and sardines. "Are you questioning me, cherished sister?" Killdeer snarled, pressing his face into hers. "Is it *you* who commands the Catacombs? Are you the new High Duchess? Should I bow down to you?" Spittle dripped from Killdeer's teeth onto Texi's ginger fur.

She tried to break his gaze, but he locked her head in place as he tightened his hold. "No, Killdeer," she said. She began to shake. "You are right. I am mistaken." Texi tried not to sob. "I'm very sorry."

He kept his face pressed to hers and lowered his voice to a controlled rumble. "Understand, dear sister, the only reason I allow you to live another day is because you're feebleminded. You are dense, and I pity you. Any of your sisters would be long since dead."

He released her from his grasp, dropping her carelessly to the ground. He squalled at the top of his lungs as white froth spewed from his mouth. "Now, get my Oshi!" Texi picked herself up and darted out of the den. Tears streamed down her face. In her foolish heart, she knew she'd replaced the bottle. Killdeer knew it too, but tormenting her amused him.

The growing pressure between Killdeer's ears intensified. He let out a moan and climbed back onto his throne. He rolled on his side and pulled his wine-stained bedding over his aching head.

Vincent and Victor Nightshade finally reached Topside—the city of Trillium. They sprang up through the hole like bullets. Victor, unable to stop, slid across the boggy grass, drenched with autumn rain, and skidded through a puddle onto the sidewalk. Vincent quickly grabbed him by the tail and wrenched him back onto the grass, just before a chubby-cheeked Topsider could squash him under her rain boot.

"Of all the terrible luck," said Vincent, taking in their surroundings.

It was Hallowtide night. There were small Topsiders everywhere, clad in colorful costumes and painted faces, roaming the streets for Pennies-or-Pranking, stuffing as much candy as would fit into their pillowcases and buckets. The older children raced from door to door, their fathers chasing them down with umbrellas, while the little ones clenched their mothers tightly with one hand and their sweets with the other.

Vincent helped his brother back to his feet. "Steady, now," he said. "The Topsiders are too busy running after their children and trying to stay dry. They won't notice us in the dark." Victor nervously inspected the swarm of Topsiders invading the nighttime streets, so big compared to them. They sat in silence, not certain what course to take. The wind picked up. The rain pounded their licorice coats.

Looking from one side of the street to the other, Vincent regarded the colossal brownstones that lined it like brick sentinels. He noticed a particularly oversized one directly across from them. Two granite gargoyles loomed on its roof. They glared down at him with a look of disapproval.

The front door of the brownstone opened, casting an ocher glow. A red-haired Topsider, clearly female, stepped out and greeted her neighbors with a bowl of candy. She handed the bowl to the children, who greedily rooted through it like a pack of country buzzards as she settled against the doorway and chatted with their parents.

Victor started to shiver, soaked to the bone. Sitting up on his narrow haunches, he clenched his spindly tail for security, a habit he'd clung to since he was a baby. "We should have just gone into the army," he said miserably. "We'd be warm and have food. Can't we just go back?"

Vincent grabbed his brother by the shoulders. "No," he said firmly. "We fled a Kill Army High Major. Do you know what that means?"

"No," said Victor.

"It means we can *never* go back. Fleeing the army is treason. If they ever catch us, we'll pay with our lives."

"Then what are we going to do?"

"Listen to me," said Vincent. "The night of the flood, when the waves pulled us away from Mother and Father, I promised them I'd take care of you, and haven't I always done that?"

"Yes," said Victor softly.

"We've always held out hope that our family survived the flood, swept away by the water, far from home, but I think we both know better—our family is dead, all of them. I know you were too little to remember much of Father, but he would *never* want us to be in that army. Do you really want to be run day and night by rats like Major Lithgo? Forced to bully citizens, serving rats that murdered High Minister Trilok, the ones who made our city the wretched place it is now?"

"No," replied Victor.

"All right, then," said Vincent. "We've survived for eleven years in the Catacombs, taking better care of ourselves than old Missus Cromwell ever could, but now we need to do more than just survive. Our lives need to mean something. This is our chance! Major Lithgo coming for us was a sign. I know it. Father firmly believed in fate. He said Killdeer's sins would return to haunt him, whether in this world or the next. He told me the only way to change our fate is to change our lives. Only *we* can do that, Victor, no one else—then we'll find our true fate, just like Father said. Do you understand?"

Victor nodded silently. The two hadn't eaten in days. Vincent watched his brother's ribs tremble under his wet raven coat. "Victor," he said with authority, "pay attention. I know you're cold, but I need you to listen to me. You see that open door across the way?" He pointed to the brownstone. "You see it—the one with the Topsiders talking under the awning?" Victor nodded stiffly. "We are going to make our way inside it. Topsiders or not, the house will be warm and dry."

"What if there's a cat or dog inside?"

"We are soaked to the skin, and thus clean. Our dismal circumstances are of benefit, at least for tonight. It will be several hours before any creature can detect us. By that time we'll be long gone." Vincent grinned at his brother.

Victor trembled in response, too frozen to return the smile. "All right, then, let's go," he muttered, teeth chattering. He let go of his tail and wiped his eyes.

The Nightshade brothers glided across the darkened street and up the concrete stairs of the brownstone, right past the Topsiders. The rats slipped into the house unseen, quickly disappearing behind a white pillar.

Vincent sniffed the air for beasts. He smelled nothing more than houseplants, not the smoky, peppered smell of dogs, nor the briny, pickled odor of cat. *Dumb luck*, he thought. "All clear," he whispered to Victor. "Follow me." The brothers skirted along the edge of the wall, their black nails clicking across the checkerboard tile.

They came to a closed door. Emaciated from days without food, they easily wriggled under it. The room was some sort of art studio, complete with easels, canvases, and a desk, barely visible under the extensive assortment of paint tubes, bottles, and brushes. The studio, covered with a fine layer of dust, had clearly gone unused for some time. It was an ideal hiding place for the night.

A streetlight shone through the window, reflecting in Vincent's green eyes, turning them a gauzy white. Victor shook the water from his coat and headed under a leather wing chair in a dark corner. Without warning, Vincent grabbed him, jerking him back. Victor looked at his brother, bewildered. Vincent stared, perplexed by something in the corner.

"What is it?" asked Victor.

"It's a rat hole." Sniffing, Vincent caught a rat's scent, one that seemed familiar to him. It quickly faded. He smelled nothing.

Billycan ambled down the corridor of Sector 337, leering broadly. His red eyes flashed against the flickering torchlight, making the towering snow-white rat appear more maniacal than usual. He swung his beloved billy club as he raucously called for the High Ministry's weekly Stipend. "Billycan thinks you should be more generous to your Ministry! Don't try my patience. Billycan wants the Stipend paid now!"

Billycan served his Ministry well, holding the dual title of High Collector of Stipend and Commander of the Kill Army. He was dangerously clever and wicked to his core. His depravity and sadistic persecution of Catacomb rats were legendary. They claimed Billycan was possessed—supernatural even. The old ones told how he once drove a rat to stab himself, mesmerizing him with his eyes. The rat lived through the ordeal, claiming that Billycan's eyes glowed like galvanized rubies, two glass bulbs filled with a red vapory substance, commanding him to take his useless life.

The few rats that had dared to challenge the High Collector were either dead or missing their tongues, his favorite form of torture. He had a raised, black scar running across his face—the result of one such challenge during the Bloody Coup. The thick gash trailed from the corner of his left eye, continued over his long snout, and finally tapered off at the opposite corner of his mouth. Billycan didn't mind the scar; in fact, he giggled every time he thought about his opponent's grisly fate. A Trilok Loyalist had briefly gotten the upper hand, but not for long. Left bleeding, the fearless rat lay dying, one eye splattered against the corridor's dirt wall.

Rumors circulated through the Combs regarding Billycan's damaged brain. Everyone knew he had served as a lab rat at the Topsider pharmaceutical company, the infamous Prince Laboratories. He alone survived the torturous experiments. No other white rats existed in the Catacombs, or in all of Trillium for that matter. Since his liberation from the lab, he'd never seen another of his kind. Other than Billycan, the albinos were gone forever.

The Catacomb subjects assumed that the drugs given to him in the Topsider lab had eaten away part of his brain, leaving only the corrupt portions intact. Years of inbreeding, forced on the rats by the lab personnel, combined with the mind-altering injections, were most likely the culprits, but gossip concerning the roots of Billycan's wickedness propagated throughout the Combs.

The Topsiders' testing had caused Billycan's spine to grow coiled and elongated, making his neck and angled jaw jut out far in front of his body. His milky coat ended at the base of his extended tail, which trailed behind him like a hairless garden snake, revealing flaky skin that was a powdery, encrusted white, more reptilian than vermin.

Cursed with a nagging and insatiable hunger, no matter how much he gorged and gobbled, Billycan could not keep weight on his bones, giving him a lean, cadaverous look, like that of a half-stuffed scarecrow.

Stipends were collected weekly—one from each Catacomb rat. Stipends consisted of items useful to the Ministry—food, weapons, tools. Food had to be edible. Attempting to disguise compost as Stipend incurred a fatal consequence. Once, a desperate young rat tried to palm off a rotting pear as Stipend. Billycan chained him to a post in the center of Catacomb Hall, leaving him to die of hunger for all subjects to see. The boy's parents wailed as their son took his final breath.

"Stipends for Killdeer!" shouted Billycan. "Stipends for Killdeer! Everyone to their doors! Quickly, quickly—do not test Billycan's patience." With a piercing pitch, his voice blasted through the corridors. "Billycan's time will not be wasted. Have them ready. Billycan does not like to wait!" The Collector sauntered down the corridor, followed by three hulking lieutenants and his Kill Army aide Senior Lieutenant Carn, all four pushing rusty wheelbarrows in single file.

Billycan, with his hollow chest pushed out, looked like an under-fed rooster. He wore a crimson and navy blue sash, Kill Army colors, made specifically for his lanky frame by the High Mistress of the Robes. It looked fitting across his broad yet exceedingly lean chest. As he strolled, he swung his billy club from side to side, banging it on Catacomb doors and scratching it against the flimsy planking with an eerie resonance. The Ministry subjects knew the Stipend routine. Don't speak unless spoken to, have all items ready, and above all, don't look the High Collector in the eyes.

"Billycan waits for no one!" he snapped, hammering his club on another door. A sheepish gray rat opened the door, her eyes fixed to the floor as she timidly put her family's Stipend in a wheelbarrow. "Quickly, quickly, my dear! Billycan need not use his club today if you hasten your step. Good, good—mark her off the list, Lieutenant Carn."

Carn marked her clan's number off the register. He nodded his head at the girl. "Thank you, miss," he said quietly.

Billycan cocked his head and glared at Carn. "Thank her for what, lieutenant? She owes Stipend, and Stipend she shall pay. We do not thank our subjects for giving what they rightfully owe. Is Billycan understood?"

The coffee-colored Lieutenant looked vacantly at Billycan. "Yes, Commander," was all he said.

Billycan shook his head. "I swear, Lieutenant Carn, all these years serving Billycan and you still need correcting—useless, entirely useless. Off you go," said Billycan, shoving the girl out of the way.

Billycan and his soldiers made their way to the next set of doors, marked with sloppy whitewashed numbers, indicating the clan that dwelled inside. He stopped at door number 73. Billycan regarded the number coolly. He cracked his stiff jaw, scowling. Time now for some personal business for High Minister Killdeer. He disagreed with his assignment, but if nothing else, the pale rawboned rat's loyalty remained steadfast, at least when it came to Killdeer.

Clover was preparing the fire pit for an early dinner when she heard a slow, methodical scratching against her door. She hadn't heard Billycan calling down the corridor. Immediately recognizing the sound of his billy club against the wood slats, she sprang up towards the door.

"Get out of sight," she whispered. A tall, cloaked figure rose from the table and concealed itself in the shadows. "Stay back and stay covered. He only wants Stipend. I'll be back promptly."

She gathered herself, swallowed hard, and opened the door.

"My, my, running late today, aren't we, Miss Clover?" said Billycan, his voice acidic.

Clover kept her eyes to the ground and put her items into a wheelbarrow. "I'm sorry, High Collector. I'm making dinner. Lost in my recipe, I did not hear your call. It won't happen again," she said.

"Very well, very well. Billycan is sure it won't happen again. Mark her off the list, Lieutenant Carn," barked Billycan. Carn silently marked her off the list and stepped back in line with the other soldiers. "I have more pressing matters today, my dear—more pressing indeed." Billycan reached into a wheelbarrow and retrieved a stiff scroll. He unrolled the discolored paper, signed at the bottom with Killdeer's three-pronged mark.

Clover eyed the parchment and backed into her quarters. She prayed to the Saints for the Collector to move on. *Please,* she thought, *let the scroll be for another.*

"Not so hasty, little one," said Billycan. He beckoned her back, curling a gnarled claw. "Billycan has something to share with you." He gave a broad grin of yellowed teeth. "Something I think you'll be rather delighted with." He poked his mangled snout into her room.

Clover tried to block him, but he lurched over her like an oversized ivory sickle, examining her small quarters.

"Where is your guardian?"

"He's hunting Topside, High Collector."

He carelessly pushed her out of his way and stepped into her quarters with his scaly, hairless feet. "Pity, pity," said Billycan. He had spotted the hidden rat, whose feet were simply too large to conceal. "Billycan wants to know who that is, in the back." He pointed a spiny digit at the shrouded rat. "Who is that hiding shamelessly in the corner? Billycan would like to know, and he would like to know now." Clover stood speechless.

Billycan's blood began to pump as he imagined a potential conspiracy in his midst. Her clan could not be trusted. Abruptly swooping down to her level, he displayed his barbed, yellow teeth in a crooked scowl. "Now, for the last time, girl, who and why is this brazen rat hiding in your quarters?" His eyes bulged and his torso heaved. "Out with it!" he hollered.

Her heart thumped in her elfin-sized chest. Through her young life, Clover had told many tales to the Ministry, just not with Billycan towering over her, his teeth dripping with icy drool. A thought finally came. "I give you my word, High Collector, he is *not* hiding. This is my grandfather, my guardian, Timeron. He is stricken with plague, unsightly to behold, and highly contagious. The disease has left him ravaged—disfigured. Like you, grandfather is a proud rat, not wishing anyone to see him in such a dreadful state. I told you he was Topside so that you wouldn't look at him—to save what pride he has left—to keep *you* from catching it. I fear he will soon be at rest with the Saints, but as my late father always said, the living must do just that—live."

As much as Billycan wished otherwise, her explanation sounded reasonable. He composed himself. "Yes, they must indeed live, as must Billycan," he said. He took a step backward, wondering what ghastly deformities awaited under the mucky shroud. He resisted his urge to check.

Billycan held up the scroll for Clover to see. "Well, young Clover, it seems my purpose is quite a fortunate one for you. As your guardian will soon be meeting his maker, by right it's off to the Kill Army kitchens with you." He tapped on the scroll. "This saves you from that abysmal fate—at least for a time." He quickly changed his voice to a more official one. "Billycan has a sacred decree in his possession that he and only he can make official. It must be read to the Chosen One and read now, as mandated by the High Ministry."

On occasion, Clover had contemplated this day, but with the thousands of females the High Minister had to choose from, she had never really considered herself a likely candidate. She had grossly underestimated herself.

She was quite lovely, with smooth cocoa skin, and light fur, buff in color and downy soft, more suited for a snow hare than a rat. She had a short, rounded nose and a sculpted, refined muzzle. Eyes the color of citrine offered up varied hues of yellowy brilliance, round and open. Despite her beauty, she had an approachable sweetness, modest and shy.

Clover had been educated in secret, since school was strictly reserved for males by the Ministry. Well aware of the evils of the Catacombs, Clover did not dream of the High Minister like the other females. She thought Killdeer a swine, a fleshy pig masquerading in the pelt of a rat.

Billycan stretched out the rigid parchment. Clover knew the general substance of the edict. She had witnessed a reading as a child and remembered the excitement that whirled around the Chosen One. She had exclaimed innocently to her mother, "I want to be a Chosen

One when I grow up. I will be with Killdeer!" Without hesitation, her horrified mother yanked her by the arm and pulled her forcefully down a dark passageway. She explained to Clover exactly what a Chosen One embodied and what her so-called duties to Killdeer would involve.

From that day on, Clover's worried parents decided to teach her along with their boys. After their death, taken by the second wave of the Great Flood, her uncle continued the practice. The power of wisdom far outweighed Killdeer's law against the schooling of females.

Billycan cleared his throat and stretched his bristly chin from side to side. He stood rigid in military stance. "Gather round, one and all!" His shrill voice bounced down the corridors as he beat his billy club against Clover's doorframe and slapped his serpentine tail against the ground. "The High Ministry of the Catacombs is here to announce an official decree, signed and certified by the High Minister himself, the beloved Killdeer. Quickly, quickly, gather round!"

Placing a skeletal paw decisively on Clover's diminutive shoulder, Billycan pressed his nails into her skin, his prickly claws pinching like thorns. He had a dour feeling about the girl, but continued with his duty.

Rats ran to the scene, surrounding Clover and Billycan, anxious to hear the decree. Lieutenant Carn directed the onlookers, giving the High Collector space. With the crowd now thick, Billycan began. "I, Billycan, High Collector of Stipend and Commander of the Kill Army, hereby declare Clover Belancort a Chosen One, anointed by Killdeer, High Minister of the Catacombs. Upon consummation of this union, Clover and her family will be released of all Stipend for one year. Upon discovery of offspring believed to be the progeny of the High Minister, the Belancort Clan will be released from Stipend for the duration of Clover Belancort's life."

He turned and addressed Clover. "This is a great honor bestowed upon you, Clover Belancort. Along with this honor, Killdeer sends his wishes of hope, prosperity, and safekeeping for you and the entirety of the Belancort Clan." He eyed the grandfather. "What little there is left of it, that is." Billycan chuckled inside as Clover trembled under his grasp. "Do you, Clover Belancort, accept your title as Chosen One, as decreed by myself and the High Minister?" Billycan smiled wryly at the crowd, who looked blankly at Clover's stone face, waiting for her answer.

Clover fought her visceral reaction to rip away from Billycan and run for her life, but if she ran, it would be straight to her death. The growing crowd of rats gasped and gawked, awaiting her reply. Clover turned frantically towards her quarters, her eyes darting in all directions in search of the veiled rat. She struggled to move under Billycan's grip, trying in vain to get the rat in her sights.

"The silly girl is so very excited she can't stop fidgeting," said Billycan. He looked at the crowd with a bogus grin as he firmly pressed down on her shoulder. "I believe we can accept her enthusiasm as a 'yes'!" The crowd laughed awkwardly, still waiting to hear her reply.

Playing to the mob, Billycan looked down at Clover with an air of concern. "Oh, Billycan sees what your fuss and muss is about, poor little dear." He leered at Clover with a patronizing grin. "You would like permission from your poor ailing grandfather. What a respectful youngster you are. More of the Catacomb youth would benefit from your example. Look, everyone," he said, motioning to Clover's quarters, "our little Chosen One wants approval from her ill grandpapa." The crowd moved closer to the door, trying to see the sickly old one, resting against the back wall. Billycan called into the room. "Well, good Grandfather Timeron, do you endorse this union? Is the High Minister an acceptable match for your humble granddaughter?"

Clover's eyes widened in panic. She spoke smartly. "You'll have to excuse him, Collector. His speech has been destroyed by his malady. His throat is malformed, corroded by disease. He is mute."

"Of no matter," said Billycan. He toyed with her cruelly. "He can give us a motion, a wave of his crippled paw, perhaps a nod of his stately chin. That will do."

The masked rat steadily leaned forward, revealing a long, blackened snout with grizzled whiskers peeking out from his grimy cloak. The ominous figure held up a cragged paw, the color of tar, with thick purplish claws. Bushy, unkempt fur poked out from the edges of his sleeve. With a shaky digit, he pointed to the decree, still dangling from Billycan's bony fist. The old rat's head swiveled towards Clover. With a feeble nod, he confirmed his approval.

"He agrees!" shouted Billycan in an exaggerated ballyhoo tenor.

Applause filled the Catacombs. Well-wishers gathered round Clover, hugging and kissing her. Lieutenant Carn stepped in front of her, pushing them back. Clover felt sick. Her eyes drifted down a desolate corridor, oblivious to the noise exploding around her. She finally looked up. Carn was staring at her. They exchanged glances, but he quickly turned back to the crowd.

Bending down, Billycan got as close to her ear as physically possible, his paw still clutching her shoulder. The blood rushed to Clover's head as the cold from his mouth hit her ear. His voice purred with satisfaction, a smug whisper. "Clover, my dear, Billycan is speaking to you now. Listen to me and listen well. You will be summoned in the customary fortnight. Billycan must insist you keep yourself safe at home. There is no need for you to be outside your quarters. The Catacombs can be such a very *lethal* place. Billycan would hate to have something gruesome happen to such a pretty, unblemished face. I suggest you stay here and tend to your grandfather like a good little girl, but don't get too close—no, no. Billycan can't risk you catching that nasty plague. Then what would be the point of even keeping you alive? In that case, it would be much more merciful to simply end your life. As you said yourself, the living must do just that—live." Clover didn't need to respond. His threats were clear.

Billycan pulled up to a standing position, blanching his voice to suit the crowd. "Now, run along, dear—scamper back inside." He patted her head, feigning affection, before finally releasing her. "The High Minister would not want his precious Chosen One running about the Catacombs catching cold, now, would he? All right, then, good rats of the Catacombs, all is said and done. Billycan wants everyone back to their business. Miss Clover needs her dinner."

He waved the remaining rats away with a spindly arm. The rats headed back down their corridors, gossiping about the news. Billycan brusquely thrust Clover inside her quarters and shut the door behind her. Famished, he reached into a wheelbarrow and swiped a large chunk of dried pork, his favorite, promptly shredding it with his teeth.

Public spectacles made his normal hunger pangs intensify. He rarely took food from the weekly Stipend collection, but his emotions overwhelmed him, especially his annoyance with Killdeer. He thought the Belancort girl untrustworthy, a foolish choice for a mate. "The daughter of Barcus Belancort, filthy Trilok Loyalist," he mumbled as he chewed. "He may be dead, but his treacherous blood still runs through her veins." He growled angrily as he choked down the scrap of hog. "Lieutenant Carn, go with the others and finish the Stipend route."

Carn did not move; instead he looked intently at Clover's door. "What are you staring at?" demanded Billycan. He jabbed Carn in the spine with his billy club. "Forever dawdling. On with your duties, boy!"

"Yes, Commander," said Carn. He trotted down the corridor, caught up with the others, and vanished into the dark.

Alone, Billycan stood outside Clover's door. *What an odd young person*, he thought. It was obvious to him that Clover wanted nothing to do with her new title and station. He leaned on the wall across from her chambers and stared at the whitewashed number 73 splashed across the rotting wood. *This one must be watched closely.*

Strolling back down the corridor to Killdeer's den, he used a tarnished nail to scrape out a stray morsel of pig that had the audacity to get stuck between two of his yellowed teeth.

"How could you give your blessing? How could you, Uncle?" muttered Clover. She looked at her uncle dismally.

Juniper Belancort leaped off the ground and shook himself furiously, freeing his body from the sweaty black shroud. He walked towards the front door, stretching his muscles, which were sore from sitting so still. He listened intently. He heard nothing.

Juniper's looks were far from conventional. His coat matched that of Oshi wine, a rich mahogany. The broad-shouldered rat resembled a dog, with the strong, square muzzle of a Topside pinscher and the wiry fur of a terrier. Wide and open, his face resembled his niece's but was overtly masculine. He wore a weathered leather patch over one eye, which had been wounded long ago. His face was marred with deep scars, partially hidden under his purplish fur. Despite his wounds, his features were kind, even pleasant to regard.

Juniper had hoped this day would never come. He shook his head at the irony of the situation. Of all the females in the Catacombs, *his* little niece took favor with Killdeer. He should have known it would be only a matter of time; she possessed a beauty other rats could only dream of. It made him wish he could take her beauty away, if only for the time being.

"Clover," said Juniper, "I agreed so Billycan wouldn't drag you by your tail to Catacomb Hall and remove your very tongue while the good rats of the Catacombs watched you bleed to death on the cobblestone floor. Did you think Billycan would take no for an answer? Did you? I agreed to this farce of a union lest we both be executed. Had I another choice, surely I would have taken it. All we have left in this world is each other."

Juniper had been sneaking into the Combs, pretending to be her grandfather, Timeron, staying covered in his shroud, allowing himself to be seen only on rare occasions, but seen all the same. If it was found out that Clover was without a proper guardian, she'd lose her home and be forced into servitude in the Kill Army kitchen and barracks. The orphan girls were treated cruelly and always in constant peril. The young female population of the Catacombs dwindled at a rapid rate. Food in the Combs was a problem, and the kitchen girls could barely survive on the meager scraps the High Cook spared them. Clover did not belong there; no child did.

Juniper took Clover's small face in his paws. Billycan had terrified her. "No one in the Ministry thinks me alive, and for now it needs to stay that way, or all our plans will be for nothing. I *will* get you out of here. I need a little more time. Our hidden city is growing at a massive rate. Killdeer has no idea how many rats have already defected. We are bringing back the days of Trilok. I will soon bring you to a new home where you will never have to be afraid of Billycan, Killdeer, or anyone ever again. I promise it on my brother's—your brave father's—soul. Barcus is cheering us on from beyond. The Saints are on our side, little one." He smiled tenderly. "Clover, they aren't coming to collect you for a fortnight. That buys us some valuable time. I will be back in a week, well before the Ministry comes to claim you. I must meet with Oard and the Council. The Ministry will be watching you carefully, so we need to devise an escape route. As hard as it may seem, you must act as though nothing has changed, especially around anyone from the Ministry—Billycan in particular."

Juniper held his ear to the door as he shrouded himself once more so that only the tip of his snout was visible. He would make his way back through the west end of the Combs through Catacomb Hall. Behind a tavern, a forgotten corridor led Topside on the way to Juniper's covert city. It was once a secret meeting place for key members of Trilok's Ministry, who worked to make certain there were no conspirators in the Catacombs and Killdeer and other banished rats were kept out. The corridor was now run by the earthworms. With no place left to hide from the Kill Army majors, who tortured them for wagering and amusement, the earthworms had made the corridor their home. It was their last refuge.

Oard, leader of the earthworms, allowed Juniper and his rats the use of their corridor and his tribe's services in the clandestine battle against Killdeer. In exchange, the worms would be given their own habitat in the new city. The tribe neared extinction in the dry, failing dirt of the Catacombs, but Juniper's secret city had fresh, healthy soil, and the earthworms would thrive and multiply there.

Making sure not to disturb the position of his cloak, Juniper placed a shabby leather satchel across his chest, the strap barely holding on to the worn-out bag. He kissed his niece on the cheek and gently patted her head, tousling her soft fur. He looked into her eyes. *Warm marigold, same as her late father's,* he thought. "Clover, you *must* do as I say. Act normal. Be the strong rat I know you to be. We will survive this. A week, then I'll be back to collect you. I promise with my life."

"Well?" asked Killdeer indifferently, sliding further down in his throne.

Billycan entered the den, tossing the rolled-up decree on a table.

"She of course complied. I do find her a strange little thing. Billycan thinks she may be up to something—she and that wretched grand-father, Timeron, who is apparently riddled with the plague. There is something not quite right with him. Either the reaper is afoot as she claims, or he's scheming with the child. In his repulsive state, Billycan did not dare verify his affliction."

Killdeer grunted. "You worry too much. There is no conspiracy within the Belancort Clan—that past is long since dead and buried. All that's left is one girl and a sickly old one—Barcus, the wife, and sons, all in their graves." He snickered. "The second wave of the flood took care of them—and *you* took care of that bedeviling brother. Your years in the lab have made you paranoid, a good quality in many ways, but maddening none the less."

Billycan *knew* something was not right. Clover's intellect well exceeded that of the typical dithering female. She possessed some quality that set her apart from the other young ones. Billycan sensed something masked about her, something concealed from him other than fear, a controlled demeanor that went far deeper than simple fright. "You may be right, Minister, but given the Belancort history, it does make one wonder if, in this instance, my paranoia is warranted. I suppose it's of no matter now." The Collector's mood darkened. "We have bigger issues to attend to, I'm afraid. Minister, there has been talk. The soldiers have informed me they hear murmurs of sedi-tion. Just last night, a group of majors encountered a drunken rat in Catacomb Hall blathering on about liberation from the High Minis-try. He claimed to know about a faction of rebels, insurrectionists. He kept spewing about the days of Trilok and how he would be avenged. The majors pegged him for an unruly tippler and thrashed him to pulp, but later went to High Major Schnauss and reported the incident. Schnauss went back to take the rat in for questioning. He had disappeared."

"So," said Killdeer, "because a drunken lout with a loose tongue crawled away from the scene, I'm to believe we rule a city of traitors?"

Billycan scratched between his front teeth, still trying to release the stuck strand of pork. "Drunk or not, Billycan thinks this rat may have been telling the truth. High Major Lithgo informed me today that several clans from his sector have gone missing. He called upon our best trackers, but they have found nothing, no evidence of where they've fled. This is hardly paranoia. These are real defectors, and defectors lead to revolt, and then to full-scale revolution. Billycan does not need to tell you what that means. We must wrangle these rats back to the Combs and punish the fugitives accordingly."

Killdeer sat up in his throne, miffed with Billycan and his grim hypothesis. "How many families do we have living in the Catacombs—over a thousand, I would presume? You expect me to believe that we have a confirmed rebellion because a few have gone astray?" Killdeer pulled his great tail out from under him, slapping it against the side of his throne. "These truant families, from Lithgo's sector, eh? You are aware that our rats frequently go Topside in groups—security in numbers, I suppose. Couldn't a cluster from his sector have been snuffed out by Topsiders' toxins, traps, or perhaps been drowned in a burlap sack? It's happened before, and it will happen again. Our dim subjects have grown too careless Topside, more worried about their bellies than their necks. The Topsiders will forever attempt to lure us to our deaths, poisoning our blood and snapping our bones like matchsticks. That is why our subjects stay here, rather than up there—it's far more fatal."

"I suspect all that's possible, Minister, but there is one flaw with your theory—these rats were not signed out by our guards, the only way for them to leave the Combs. In other words, they've simply vanished."

Killdeer's face reddened as his blood pressure rose. He dug impatiently into the bedding of his throne, found his bottle, and chugged half its contents. "Make the proclamation for the Grand Speech. We'll have it early if you're so worried, on Rest Day, tomorrow at midnight. Have all the troops present. Our majors have grown lax and slack-jawed. It's about time we reminded our sulking subjects that living in the Catacombs is a privilege. It is by no means a right." Killdeer took another swig while his chest swelled with a forthcoming outburst. Billycan muttered to himself, not wanting to deal with Killdeer's brewing tantrum. Killdeer was proving more useless with each passing year, becoming more of a figurehead and less of a Minister. Killdeer continued to issue orders. "I want the Belancort girl in attendance at the Grand Speech and well turned out, as she will be standing by my side. She will be pleased to know she does not need to wait a fortnight to see me."

"Oh, yes, Minister, I'm sure the dear lass will be delighted," said Billycan. He smiled gleefully at the thought of breaking the news to her. His chalky skin prickled in anticipation.

"I haven't made myself visible of late. My subjects' memories have dulled." Killdeer grinned slyly. "With the girl next to me, a member of the Belancort Clan, a family of Trilok Loyalists—before they all died, that is—my subjects will once again warm to me. Have all your majors announce the Grand Speech to their sectors."

"Very well, Minister. I will go to the Belancort quarters myself. I would like to find out more about this grandfather, Timeron. There is something about him—"

Killdeer grunted. "Investigate all you desire, but just get it done."

The Minister jumped from his throne, landing on the floor with a heavy thud. He stomped out of the room, bellowing down the hall for Texi to get his bath ready.

Billycan stood alone in the den, scratching his pearly chin. He studied his reflection in Killdeer's silver throne, running a digit over his black scar. "Timeron, who are you? Why do you smell of deceit?" he asked, as if his mirror image might answer. Billycan seemed to be acquainted with the old rat's scent, but he could not place it. Perhaps it was the looming stench of death.

Be it an omen, good or bad, the two Nightshade brothers ventured into the hole they had uncovered in the Topsiders' brownstone. Their options were few, and this seemed a serendipitous course, perhaps a sign from the Saints, and if not a sign from above, at the very least somewhere to go. The trudge down seemed endless; the tunnel's angle severe. After some time, the ground started to flatten and the corridor widened. They found themselves entering an open space with a cavernous dirt ceiling, a rotunda of sorts. They stood in one of three arched entryways, all equidistant from one another.

Vincent whispered to his brother. "I smell that rat again. The scent is so familiar. The same one I picked up in the Topsiders' house. Why can't I pinpoint it? Something about it reminds me of father." Proud of his scent detection, Vincent ruffled at his inability to identify the rat. Julius had always told his son that he had a talent for the craft, and even now Vincent didn't want to disappoint him. "I know this rat. Who is he?"

"Whoever he is, he's in desperate need of a thorough cleaning," Victor said. He crinkled his nose at the heady odor. "Smells like mugwort."

They looked around them. The space could hold at least a

thousand rats, maybe more. It reminded Vincent of Catacomb Hall. During Trilok's reign, all the clans would gather there for events and holidays. The children would play, and the adults would dance. Vincent remembered his mother and father dancing as he ran wild with his siblings, laughing till it hurt.

Ordinary rats lived for only a handful of years, four or five at most. Catacombs rats lived decades upon decades, just like Topsiders. The extended years were thought to be a gift from the Saints, but Vincent had sometimes wondered if they might be a curse. Why should one have to live so long surrounded by misery and constant disappointment? He used to think it unjust, but now with their newfound freedom, maybe they could find some form of happiness. Even if they died as a result, at least they'd die free.

Etched deep into the wall, a marking accompanied each of the three passageways. "What is that symbol?" said Victor, pointing to one. They walked across the center of the rotunda and examined the emblem. It consisted of three jagged prongs, connecting at a pointed base.

Victor's insides twisted in dread. "Isn't that Killdeer's mark?" Shaking, he instinctively backed away.

"It is," said Vincent. Acid rose in his belly as he realized where the Topside hole had led them. He kept his composure for Victor's sake. "I don't know this place. I've never been here before, but I'm afraid we're back where we started. We're back in the Catacombs."

Vincent reached up and touched the mark, tracing Killdeer's crude insignia with his claw. The Minister had sentenced many a youth to death for offenses substantially less serious than dodging the Kill Army. Vincent could only imagine what their penalty would be.

He heard a loud, whiplike crack. Everything went black.

CHAPTER TWO

Nightshade City

Vincent awoke to a soft orange light. He tried to focus on the small torch affixed to the wall. With his head still buzzing from the blow, tiny flecks of white and gold swirled about his blurred vision. As his sight returned, he remembered what had happened. He and Victor had unwittingly returned to the Catacombs.

Bound to an iron ring protruding from the wall, Vincent twisted his limbs awkwardly. The ring dug into his spine as he tried in vain to writhe free from his shackles, contorting his body in every conceivable position. Pressing his feet against the wall for leverage, he clenched his teeth, straining, as he tried to wrench the metal ring from the wall. His efforts proved useless.

He listened intently for his brother's voice but heard nothing. He could smell other rats now, hundreds of scents overlapping, a jumble of males, but no one he could identify. *They must be Kill Army majors,* he thought.

Once again he picked up the pungent scent of the rat he'd smelled earlier. He must have been wrong about it. His father would never have associated with a Kill Army major.

His ears perked. Heavy footsteps neared the room, perhaps one of the majors, or possibly the High Collector. The tales of Billycan flooded his mind. Could they be true—could they? The stories had always been so hard for Vincent to swallow: the excessive malice, the unwarranted torture, incomprehensible even for the most savage of rats. Vincent's coat grew soaked with brackish sweat.

The door opened with a hollow groan. Vincent tried to gather himself, inhaling a deep breath and slowly releasing it. He would be steadfast, at least in the eyes of his executioner, as were all the Nightshades who had met an untimely demise.

A figure stood in the darkened doorway. "Vincent Nightshade," said a deep voice. "Vincent, don't be frightened, son. First off, your brother—he is all right. I didn't know who you were back there, and I simply can't take any chances with our city's safety. I am a friend. I knew you when you were a child. I knew your father—Julius." The rat entered the room, ducking under the small doorway.

Raising his sore head, Vincent sized up the substantial rat before him. His fur was dense, like steel wool the tint of blackberries—*An unusual color,* thought Vincent. He was not old but not young either; Vincent guessed him to be somewhere around his father's age. His head nearly touched the ceiling of the tiny cell. The rat dragged in a small crate and sat on it. As his face became clearer, Vincent noticed a ragged leather patch over his left eye, under which lay a profoundly scarred muzzle. The rat's visible amber eye looked distinctively friendly, almost merry.

The rat took a seat on the wooden crate and smiled gently at Vincent, who, though terrified, desperately tried to hide it. "I followed you boys the whole way down that tunnel from the Topsiders' brownstone," said the rat. "I could only guess you were Kill Army soldiers sent to find our location. I figured you were trackers from the High Ministry. I couldn't risk you reporting back. I'm sorry for striking you."

Vincent sat in stoic silence, not sure if this rat could be believed. The rat pulled the crate closer so he could get a better look. "Victor is fine, by the way, just fine. In fact, we can't get him to shut up!" The rat chuckled.

Vincent stared at his captor without expression or response. "Vincent, you don't remember me, do you? You were far too young, I suspect. Now I'm going to free you and bring you to your brother." The rat scratched around the edge of his eye patch. "I'm Juniper Belancort. Does that name ring any bells with you? Do you remember my clan—*Belancort*? My older brother, Barcus, was close with Julius, your father, as was I. You used to play with Clover, my little niece. Do you remember her? I don't see how you could—you were just a child." Vincent's face remained blank.

Bending forward, Juniper released a heavy sigh. "Vincent, we are deep in the ground, far deeper than the Catacombs. We are under the Reserve—miles under the hole you and Victor found. The High Ministry has no idea we exist, and for now, that's how it will stay. We are building up our city as fast as we can. Through our small group of Loyalists, rats are escaping the Combs every day." Juniper's voice grew in enthusiasm and his broad face brightened. "As soon as our numbers are strong, we are going to crush the High Ministry and the Kill Army majors. No further blood will be shed by Killdeer or Billycan. We are bringing back the days of Trilok. Killdeer's reign *will* come to an end. The unfortunate boys recruited into the Kill Army and the blameless girls they compel into servitude need to be freed, as do all the Ministry's subjects, harassed and petrified by Billycan and his loathsome majors for his blasted Stipend. Your father and Barcus would never have allowed any of this to happen if they were still alive."

Vincent looked at Juniper. Cocking his head, he studied the rat's unusual face, trying to remember. He thought of his father, trying to recall the secret corridor and his father's friends. He remembered the little things, the things that made him laugh and the things that made him feel safe. He thought of everyone he'd ever seen his parents welcome into their home with a warm smile and a fresh pot of tea. He remembered his seventh birthday, recalling a family party for him and his brothers and sisters. A tall, woolly rat came to mind: a high-spirited fellow who'd throw them all into the air till they almost lost their cake. His hackles suddenly tingled. He recalled riding atop the rat's shoulders and holding on to the rat's bushy fur...a funny purplish color. That rat had arrived with..."Wait," he blurted. "Your brother is—Uncle Barcus?"

Juniper smiled, glad to hear the boy finally speak. He stomped his foot on the ground. "Yes, lad, that's my brother, Uncle Barcus! I forgot you children called him that. He and your father were like family, like brothers, as close as you and Victor. As close as black is to night, we used to say!"

Vincent's grave face suddenly lightened. "I remember you now—I do. You would carry me and my brothers and sisters on your shoulders and toss us into the air till we all felt sick. I even remember your berry fur. I *do* remember you!" Vincent's body relaxed. He felt safe, at least for the moment.

"Yes, your mother scolded me many a time for roughhousing with you children! I was always at the heels of Barcus and your father, traipsing after them everywhere. Those two led the way in those days.

Did you know they were both close friends of the Mighty Trilok? They had audiences with him weekly, along with me, when I was finally old enough. Trilok had great admiration and respect for your father and Barcus. He attended your parents' nuptials. He and Duchess Nomi held you the day you were born. That's how much your family meant to Trilok, in fact to the entire Combs. Your father spoke for the Catacombs. He served as the voice for its citizens. The Citizen Minister, that's what they called him. They loved him. We all did."

"I remember people calling him that," said Vincent, "Citizen Minister. I had no idea what it meant. I didn't know he was held in such high regard, or *any* regard for that matter. He was simply Father to me."

"That's how all children think of their parents," said Juniper, chuckling, "Mother and Father, no identities other than that. Why, I was shocked the day I realized my parents had first names!"

Thoughts of his father and his family made Vincent's eyes well. He hadn't shed a tear in years and was not about to start in front of a grown male. He wiped his face on his shoulder. "Juniper, would you mind freeing me from these chains? My arms are getting sore."

"Oh, yes, let's get those off you, lad. Thoughts of the old days seem to take me away sometimes."

Juniper reached for the chains behind Vincent's back, taking the opportunity to discreetly check the boy's head for any serious injuries. A significant egg-shaped knob poked through Vincent's black fur. *Not so bad*, thought Juniper. The boy would heal fast.

Juniper took a key, one of many, from around his neck. He continued to speak as he unlocked the chains. "When I lost Barcus, I never thought I'd get past it, but here I stand. I'm glad you and Victor have one another. You should be proud of yourself. I know Julius would be. You've done an admirable job with your younger brother. Victor needs to grow a bit, but he'll be a fine leader someday.

"I see Julius in both of you. You, my boy, are the spitting image of him. I suppose I should have taken a closer look before walloping you on the head. I never could have missed the resemblance, even with those green eyes of yours. I remember them being much darker when you were a child. Eyes the tint of fresh clover—I've never seen that on a rat. I've only seen Topsiders with that shade, maybe a few of the more exotic cats, but never a rat—never." They exited the cell and began to walk.

Vincent stretched his sore arms as they traveled down the twisting prison corridor. "No one knows where my eyes came from," said Vincent. "A mutation of some sort, I suppose."

"Mutation," said Juniper, almost indignantly. "I'd dare say. Vincent, those eyes make you singular, like my strange coat, the color of wine and the texture of goat! Being different is a reward, not an affliction. You'll see. The Saints always have a plan for us. In fact, I think they planned our reunion tonight, the son of Julius Nightshade and the brother of Barcus Belancort. The Saints are watching over us—even when it doesn't feel that way."

Juniper reached out and put a solid paw on Vincent's shoulder, steering him down another corridor. The paw felt heavy and warm, just like his father's had.

Juniper pointed to a rounded doorway accented by torchlight. "Now let's go meet the others, shall we? And let's see about that grumbling stomach, which sounds to be in great need of some supper. I think you'll find making yourself useful comes easy around here, but not on an empty belly. C'mon, then."

Clover sat in the corner of her quarters on a tattered straw mat, her slender arms wrapped tightly around her legs, as she quietly rocked back and forth. She stared blankly at her parents' vacant nest where she usually slept. But sleep eluded her.

Until she left the Catacombs for good, officially out of Killdeer's reach, she would have no peace. She loved and trusted her uncle but questioned his ability to rescue her in time. She could never be sure where Juniper was—forever roving between the Catacombs and the world of the Topsiders—or even if he was still alive. For all she knew, he'd already been captured. Billycan could easily have been hiding in the dark, just outside her door, waiting and watching.

Juniper had intended to steal her out of the Catacombs much earlier but couldn't take the chance of being caught. If captured, not only would the last two survivors of the Belancort Clan be put to death, but it would surely compromise his promising city's success. On top of that, Clover's sector, commanded by Major Lithgo, had been vigorously patrolled of late. The soldiers on guard had doubled, and Juniper took a great risk every time he set foot in the Combs. After this last incident of nearly being discovered by Billycan, Clover worried her uncle had little time left on this earth. She knew that Billycan had his suspicions about her, and with good reason.

Clover spotted a piece of mirrored glass in her mother's sewing basket. She picked it up and gazed at her reflection. Her golden eyes stared back at her. A *Chosen One*, she thought. *How pathetic, how sadly funny.* She did see one bright spot. Her ghastly predicament wouldn't last long. Killdeer would quickly grow tired of her, as he did with all the Chosen Ones, and would promptly move on to another. Killdeer lacked loyalty in both politics and matters of the heart.

She tossed the mirror back in the basket and shoved it away. *Think like a rat,* she told herself angrily. *Stop sniveling!* Deciding she must eat something despite her lack of appetite, she forced herself up on her feet. If the Saints were listening, Juniper would be at her door sooner rather than later, and she needed to be fit to travel when they finally made their escape.

She lit the fire pit in the center of her small chamber, then rummaged through her supplies and retrieved a small piece of waterchip root. It was tangy and sour, and she adored its vinegary taste. Picking up the razor blade that Juniper had found her Topside, she began to scrape off the root's tough exterior. As she peeled away the leathery skin, she remembered helping her mother prepare the family dinners. Life had changed so much. A large clan had dwindled down to just her and Juniper.

As the bare waterchip browned over the flames, she noticed a shadow under the door. Clover instinctively froze. Her insides knotted as she heard the frosty sound of Billycan's club scraping systematically against the boards of her door. Her heart pounded as Billycan's craggy nails poked through the flimsy planking, his bristly white fur pushing through the cracks.

He leaned against the door. "Oh, dear Clover," he whispered. He spoke in a peculiar singsong manner, more frightening to Clover than his moments of shrieking rage. He rested his head on the decaying door. "Billycan is here to see you, dear. I come with word from your beloved High Minister. Open, open. I won't be made to wait."

Clover refused to let him spook her this time. She wasn't ignorant like the other females. She would not let him dominate her. She remembered the words of her late father. He told her liars and cowards never look you in the eyes. With that in mind, she opened the door and looked at Billycan directly, telling herself his eyes were no more powerful than her own. "Good evening, High Collector. What can I do for you?"

Her newfound confidence went unnoticed. He brushed past her and skulked into her quarters, poring over its contents. "Billycan thinks the more appropriate question would be what can I do for *you?*"

"Yes, do come in, Collector," she said, ignoring his strange comment. Billycan continued to sniff about her things, contorting his snout in disgust. "Sir, would you like some waterchip root? I've just smoked some over the fire."

"So, that's the horrid smell. Waterchip is a repugnant creation. Billycan does not take well to it, not well at all. Its scent could wake the dead, and its taste could kill them all over again. The root repulses me," he said. He waved his rangy arms, trying to force the odor out into the corridor.

Billycan nosed through the room some more. He checked every corner, making sure no more shrouded rats were hiding in the shadows. "Where is that mangy grandfather of yours? I want to speak to him now."

"I regret to say my grandfather has taken a turn for the worse. He left a short while ago. He went to a healer that lives Topside, somewhere in an alley of the Battery District. I asked him to stay so I could take care of him, but he's worried for my well being, not wanting me to take ill. He told me his trek will take at least three days or more. I fear he may die on his journey."

Billycan giggled, secretly glad for his absence. "I see. What a shame. My deepest of deepest sympathies. Well, let's change unpleasant subjects to happy ones." He smiled with ghoulish satisfaction. "I have more good news for you, my dear, very good indeed. It is with great pleasure that Billycan invites you to attend the next Grand Speech in Catacomb Hall, this very Rest Day. Why—that's tomorrow, isn't it? The gracious Minister is eager to address the Catacomb rats and has moved up the date for his Grand Speech, asking me to personally invite you."

Clover crinkled her brow and tilted her head in confusion. "Collector, I would never miss a Grand Speech. I am flattered by the

Minister's invitation, but you needn't have wasted your valuable time coming here yet again to tell me."

"But you're wrong about that, little one. Billycan never wastes his costly time." He waved a skeletal digit in the air. "I come with purpose!" Overwhelmed with fiendish delight, he became giddy. "You, my dear, have the distinct honor of standing at our inspiring Minister's side during the speech! *You* will be the highlight of the whole affair! You are expected to be clean and well groomed, making every effort to represent the High Ministry to the very best of your charming ability."

Clover's face twisted in panic. "High Collector, I don't know what to say. I—don't. May I please ask why the High Minister would bestow such an honor on me? I am an ordinary daughter of an ordinary clan. I have nothing special to offer the High Minister." For once, she need not pretend. Why would Killdeer want her by his side? Surely a Chosen One he had children with or, at any rate, one he already knew would be a more appropriate choice.

"My cherished little one," he said mockingly, "Billycan worries for you. You are not slow of mind, are you?" He grinned sharply, baring his ruddy gums and discolored yellow teeth. He bent down and picked up the piece of mirror Clover had been gazing at earlier. He knelt behind her on one knee, still towering over her. Holding up the mirror in front of her, he spoke in a low, throaty tone. "Do you see what I see in this reflecting glass, my dear? Do you see the diamond shape of your face, the contour of your subtle saffron eyes, the high bones of your cheeks? This is what the male rats of the Catacombs see every day as you walk down the corridors of our underground world. They see you in all your youthful perfection, like the freshest of cream. You have no idea, do you? What a pity, a pity indeed." He paused, examining their two faces in the mirror, gazing in silence, lost in his own twisted mind.

Clover did not wince or recoil. She would not make her discomfort evident. Her eyes reddened as she forced back tears. The more fear she gave away, the more torment she would receive. "Collector, surely you compliment me. I could only wish to be as striking as you imply. I do not see myself that way."

As if snapping out of a trance, he quickly returned to a full stand. He idly tossed the mirror to the ground. He spoke plainly. "That, my dear, is of no consequence to me. The High Minister *does* see you that way. Killdeer, chivalrous as he is, has waited till you were of an appropriate age, and now you are." The white rat squinted and stared coolly at Clover's face, as if mentally dissecting it. "You're quite the pretty little riddle, aren't you? Billycan sees something else in you, something that's lacking in the other female dullards. You have something in your diminutive head—a brain, perhaps?"

"My father always said I was a smart one."

Billycan cringed. "Speaking of your *dear* departed father, you know, he and Billycan went back a long way. In fact, we had many a meeting in the old days. Rather a shame he's no longer here to give his political speeches. Quite the eloquent speaker, your father was—and a loud one at that." Billycan could not hide his disdain. Barcus Belancort had caused many headaches to the then-new High Ministry. Barcus got away with his life, one of the few Loyalists to do so. Billycan's blood boiled hot when he thought of the infuriating rat. The one Killdeer forbade him to kill. Billycan fought with Killdeer, dead set as he was on slaughtering Barcus and the entire Belancort Clan, but Killdeer insisted he be kept alive, using his wife and children as leverage for his allegiance. The Ministry needed supporters with influence. Barcus, so trusted by the citizens, could sway them any way the Ministry desired. If he kept out of Ministry affairs, his family could keep their lives. After a mass killing of Loyalists and their families, Barcus agreed. He would not jeopardize the lives of his family. But then, a year later, they all drowned in the second wave of the great flood—all except Clover. Thinking of it, Billycan's whole body quivered with hilarity. The quirk of fate was almost too much—all that, and dead anyway!

"You knew my father?" asked Clover, feigning ignorance, but knowing full well her father's history with the Ministry.

"Oh, yes, he and I had many a dealing. It's such a pity he's not here to see your newfound fortune."

Not wanting to push his unpredictable temper, Clover changed the subject. "High Collector, when do you wish me to be ready for the Grand Speech?"

"I will be back to collect you at midnight on Rest Day. Be flawless to the eye, and mind your manners. Killdeer does not want you scratching and fidgeting while all the Catacomb subjects bear witness. You now represent the High Ministry." Twisting down like a snake, Billycan placed his nose to Clover's, tip to tip. He grabbed her muzzle with a hard, thorny paw. His voice lowered to a scratchy, uneven bass as his eyes flickered in the tawny reflection from the fire pit. He spoke harshly, leaving no room for uncertainty. "If you disobey my orders and are not present and accounted for tomorrow at midnight for the Grand Speech, that will be considered direct treason to the High Ministry. Do you know what the Ministry enjoys doing to traitors, young one? Do you, my sweet?"

Clover's mouth wouldn't move; it couldn't. She'd heard all the tales of Billycan's hypnotizing stare but never believed them. She lost herself, paralyzed by his unfaltering gaze. His eyes no longer had form. They churned and sloshed with splashes of red and light—electrified pools of rolling blood. "If your father weren't already dead, you could ask him. He could tell you what we do with traitors. Old Barcus knew firsthand."

Billycan released her and pulled up to his full height, instantly changing his tone to a much more agreeable one. "Be ready, my dear. You will not let your Ministry down. Incidentally, you will be fulfilling your Chosen One duties directly following the Minister's speech. Minister Killdeer is always wound up after a stirring speech to his subjects, and he is looking forward to his *time* with you." He grinned in warped amusement and exited her quarters.

Clover stood staring out the open door, spellbound. The fire made a loud pop, waking her from her daze. The truth hit her like a slap, and she dropped to the floor in a heap. Unless her uncle returned before midnight tomorrow, she was doomed.

Juniper led Vincent down the dimly lit prison corridor, lined with heavy wooden doors on both sides, each with a bulky iron bolt and a thin slot barely big enough for an underfed paw to slip through. Past the doors sat barren dirt cells.

"Are all these rooms for prisoners?" asked Vincent, surprised by the vast number.

"Well, we're going to need them. Vincent, this is a serious endeavor we're taking on. You know as well as I do the size of the Kill Army. Most of these rooms are intended for Kill Army majors. Those are the rats we're worried about. We feel the bulk of the foot soldiers will easily convert back to citizens once they realize the High Ministry has been dismantled. Most of the so-called lieutenants are simply scared young rats, such as you, conditioned to believe there is no real life for them without the Kill Army."

Vincent thought about Major Lithgo and how lucky he and Victor were to have eluded him. Vincent shuddered as he thought of the tenpenny just missing his head.

The brothers' guardian, old Missus Cromwell, had gone dotty, and in planning for her death had innocently brought Lithgo to see her wards. Her mounting dementia had rendered her judgment useless, and she easily fell for Lithgo's buoyant speech about a new family for her orphan wards. After her passing, the brothers managed to keep the death quiet for months, but eventually Lithgo found out.

"Did you ever think of escaping the Combs before?" asked Juniper.

"All the time," said Vincent. "It just never seemed the *right* time. I was eight at the time of the flood, and Victor was only four. After that night, the night we lost our family, he was terrified of everything. It took years before he'd even go Topside again. When he was finally brave enough to go with me, I grew worried. What if something happened to him Topside? I'd never forgive myself. Or what if something happened to me? He'd be alone, without anyone to look after him or teach him what Father had taught me."

"You are a good brother."

"I suppose," said Vincent. "I always dreamed of leaving the Combs. It was almost as though every time I saw an opportunity to leave, there would be some sort of sign to stop me—a warning. Years ago, Victor and I were leaving our sector to go Topside and collect Stipend. The major who always signed us out had fallen asleep at his post. I thought it was our chance. We could sneak out of the Combs, and the majors would never know. Our names would not be on the register—by the time anyone realized we'd even left the Combs, we'd be so far away they'd never find us. We made it unseen all the way to Catacomb Hall, just about to Father's corridor, ready to make a run for it, when it happened."

"What?" asked Juniper. "What happened?"

"Billycan happened," said Vincent. "Just at that moment, he came parading through Catacomb Hall with two pairs of soldiers, each pair carrying the carcass of a dead rat tied to a wooden post by its wrists and ankles. Billycan announced that the dead rats were caught trying to escape. They'd been signed out of the Combs and were secretly trying to leave with a sack filled with their belongings. A High Major seized them. Death was their punishment. They were two black rats, one older, like me, and the other younger, like Victor. I thought it was a clear sign from the Saints—don't go."

"That certainly sounds like a sign to me," said Juniper. "You were smart to wait."

"I don't know if I was smart or just afraid."

"I think you were both. You were smart for staying and afraid for Victor, which you should have been. After all, he was only a child. You were right to think of him first. It's much easier to throw caution to the wind when there's only yourself to worry about. You're both free now, not to mention alive! That's because of you, Vincent. Don't think otherwise."

Juniper led Vincent into a large gathering hall with high vaulted ceilings. "This is Bostwick Hall," he said as they walked through the rounded entry.

"Bostwick Hall?" asked Vincent. "Is Bostwick a rat, someone who knew my father?"

"Just someone I knew long ago," said Juniper. "Someone the Saints had other plans for. We can chat about that some other time. Now, then, there is someone here who is anxious to see you."

A round wooden table sat in the center of the room, surrounded by several mismatched chairs and stools. Seated at the table were five rats, all robust, looking to be about Juniper's age, all except for one— Victor.

He bounded from his chair and ran at Vincent like a freight train. Victor grabbed his brother in a tight hug, nearly knocking him to the ground. "Vincent! I was so worried about you, but you're all right, thank the Saints! I've told everyone about you and how you'd gotten us out of the Catacombs and away from that major and into the house and how you—" Vincent put a claw to his mouth, hushing his excited little brother. Victor stopped talking and caught his breath.

Normally such displays of affection in front of strangers would have embarrassed Vincent, but not this time. Before Victor could start up again, Vincent hugged him firmly, not caring that the rats were staring.

The older rats smiled silently. They resumed eating their meal, which consisted of a thick cut of reddish meat and pumpernickel bread, both doused in dark, savory gravy, along with a full mug of Carro root ale.

Juniper walked up between the boys and put a paw on their shoulders. "Now, Victor, let's get your brother something to eat. He must be starving. We have a lot to catch you boys up on. You've earned the right to be here, and your father would want it this way. You two could very well be vital hands in our fight—your father's fight. I think he would be honored to know his boys had a key part in finishing what he started."

Juniper walked Vincent to the table, pointing to an open spot. One of the other rats, a black and white mottled fellow, dished up a generous plate for Vincent. After so many days without food, Vincent's belly had started ratcheting in on itself, eating away at its own tissue. Smelling the aromatic sauce and spiced meat bordered on torture. He attacked his food, licking his nails clean with every bite, being sure not to overlook even a smidgen of meat or a drop of gravy.

The spotted rat poured Vincent a mug of ale and slid it in front of him. Vincent looked at the ale and then looked at Juniper. "Don't look to me for approval, lad," Juniper said. "You're definitely old enough to have a mug of Carro ale if you so please. Your father would not disapprove. You are of age, a grown rat now, not a boy. As for your brother, we collectively decided he could have half a pour. He didn't like it!" The rats laughed out loud.

Victor grinned sheepishly. "It tasted like Topsider sewer water, Vincent."

Vincent took his first mouthful, wincing at its bitter taste. His face knotted into a grimace. Juniper held back his grin, signaling with a glance at the others to do the same. Vincent took another drink. The suds stuck to his black whiskers, forming a frothy white mustache. The second guzzle tasted slightly better. "Well," said Vincent, "it takes a little getting used to, but it sure goes down easy enough!" Vincent choked as he said it, causing the others to erupt in wild laughter.

"It does knock back pretty easy," said Juniper. He held up his mug and gave Vincent's a hard clink. Vincent smiled. It felt good to be included with grown male rats.

Once everyone started talking, Vincent learned their identities. With no formal city government or even a city name, Juniper and his counterparts were simply referred to as the Council. These were Juniper's brothers-in-arms, his board of advisers, the four rats who would die at his side if necessary.

Juniper slapped the back of the black and white mottled rat, an odd-eye rat, with one lilac and the other a deep ruby. "Vincent, this is Cole, my second-in-command. He is a master strategist and is instrumental in our plan to overthrow Killdeer."

"I was in a similar boat to you and Victor," said Cole. "When I was a boy, my parents were taken from me too, killed by poisoned apples left out by the Topsiders in their efforts to exterminate our kind. So I too know what it's like to grow up without parents. My wife and I may not have little ones of our own, but our door is open to as many Catacomb orphans as we can squeeze in it." He glanced at both boys. "I had family to look after me when my parents passed on. Tell me, how have you two managed all this time?"

"Missus Cromwell, an old neighbor of my parents, took us in just after the flood," said Vincent. "Since then, we've tried to stay quiet and out of trouble. We've had our share of scraps in the Combs, but the Ministry didn't seem to take notice of us. Some rats would stare at us strangely sometimes, but Victor and I thought it was because of my green eyes."

"I'm afraid there was far more behind those stares than your eyes," said Juniper. "You look just like your father. I suppose the Ministry didn't need to worry themselves with two orphaned boys, no matter who your father was. Thank the Saints for that."

"In any case," said Vincent, "Major Lithgo heard a rumor of Missus Cromwell's death and came for us straightaway. We were just coming round the corner to our quarters, and there he was. When I saw the smug grin on his face, I knew we were found out. We turned and ran."

"He nearly caught us," said Victor. "But Vincent remembered Father's secret corridor in Catacomb Hall. That's how we escaped."

"We all know that corridor well," said Cole. "Many a meeting was held there, away from traitorous ears." He glanced at the Council. "Or so we thought."

"I thought you boys had surely been picked up by the army," said Juniper. "I remember thinking how heartbroken your parents would have been, knowing their boys were serving in Killdeer's army of orphans. The very rat who—" Juniper stopped. "Never mind that now. We've got other fish to fry, as they say. Our pasts can't be rewritten, but our futures can." He nudged the rat next to him, a tall fellow, with fur the shade of wheat. A ledger sat next to his plate, and a feather pen peeked out from behind his ear. "This here is Virden, our City Planner. He's in charge of our city's bright future."

"Indeed," said Virden, smiling at the boys. "I direct city planning and design, making sure we don't have cave-ins and the like. Quite the tricky business, but with a little bit of math and measuring, and a whole lot of praying, it *is* possible."

"You designed all this?" said Vincent, gazing up at the rotunda.

"He did," said Juniper. "Ol' Virden is also our resident expert on Oshi. We only serve the wine on special occasions, and Virden here makes sure our berries are of the highest quality."

"Well, what did you expect?" said Virden. "My father was born in a vineyard—taught me everything I know. We'll serve none of that moonshine the Ministry pushes on its subjects in its effort to numb their spirits. Might as well drink turpentine!" Virden chuckled. "Killdeer drinks so much of it himself, he's lucky he hasn't burst into flames within arm's length of a candle!" Everyone laughed as Virden topped off their mugs of ale.

"And last but not least, these are the twins," said Juniper, nodding at two identical rats of slate blue. "Quite the perceptive pair, they are. Ragan and Ulrich are in charge of our city's security. Questioning new city inhabitants is an essential role."

"Yes, sir," said Ragan with an excited snigger. "If anyone can sniff out a rotten apple, it's the two of us. Don't know where we got the knack, but we have it all the same—only been wrong once."

"Yes, indeed," announced Ulrich in the same quickfire manner. "Our mother had the gift. I suppose she passed it down to us."

Vincent looked at them, already unsure of which twin was which. "But how do you tell them apart? I've never seen two rats that look so much alike."

Ulrich jumped up and turned around. "This is how," he said with a grin. He wiggled his stubby excuse for a tail, causing the Council to snort with laughter. "Got my tail hacked off by a livid Topsider hausfrau wielding a meat cleaver!"

"Did it hurt?" asked Victor.

"It was so quick, I scarcely felt it," said Ulrich. "I'm lucky that's all she got. I reason my knack for sensing trouble doesn't work on irate Topsider housewives. Ragan yanked me out of the way just in time." He looked at Vincent and then back to Victor, smiling. "But I suppose that's what brothers are for, aren't they—saving each other's necks?"

"Absolutely," said Victor, gazing proudly at his brother.

Vincent's eyes wandered over to Juniper. He wondered why Juniper's eye was covered with that patch, and what sort of creature could make such deep scars. He inspected the others, Juniper's Council. All four rats were about Juniper's age. They seemed rugged, tough, and strong of heart—just like Juniper. They too were friends of Julius Nightshade. It seemed to Vincent that everyone was.

"It's a lot to take in," said Juniper, sensing Vincent's puzzlement. "I know you boys must be overwhelmed—all this history."

Vincent glanced at his brother. He always told Victor stories about their father. He tried to teach Victor what Julius Nightshade had taught him. "I knew our father was involved in Trilok's Ministry, but I had no idea how important he was. I'm beginning to feel like I never really knew him at all."

"You *did* know him, son," said Juniper, "just not this part. Julius tried to shield you children from politics, at least until you were old enough to decide things for yourselves, and I believe that time has come. Julius wanted you children to make your own choices, not follow blindly in his footsteps."

"A year or so back, I tried a few times to talk to rats in the

Catacombs," said Vincent, "asking why we never rose up against Killdeer, taking back what is ours. I was told to hold my tongue, or Billycan himself would have it. For Victor's sake, I stopped asking. I wish I could have met you sooner—someone not afraid to fight back."

"Well, then," said Juniper. "It seems you've already made your choice. Julius and Trilok, along with my brother Barcus and later myself, did our best to make the Combs a safe place to live. We instituted laws voted upon by the citizens and systematically banished rats who chose to break those laws, which included Killdeer and his disgraceful mob of majors...."

As the evening progressed, the boys learned about the plans to attack the High Ministry. "We are rallying behind the memory of Julius, Barcus, and Minister Trilok," said Juniper. "We will bring down Killdeer and Billycan once and for all. Our city is getting larger by the minute. Every day more families, entire clans, slip away from the Combs. We have a covert network of Loyalists, getting word to known followers of Trilok. Family by family, rat by rat, they trickle out of the Combs and into our city—"

"Juniper," said Cole, obliged to interrupt, "it's almost time."

"That it is," said Juniper.

"Time for what?" asked Victor.

"Time for a celebration," said Juniper, his eyes flashing with mystery. "Boys, it seems your timing couldn't be more fated. I don't claim to be devout, but it's as if your father and the Saints have intended our auspicious meeting. Our citizens have given me the great honor of naming our fair city. I've been racking my brain for a name that tells our citizens what we are all fighting for. We are having a naming celebration tonight—within moments. The guests, our new citizens, are scheduled to arrive—well—now!"

Juniper sprang from the table, grabbing a lit torch. He swiftly paced around the circular hall, lighting the remaining torches, which lined the chamber. The firelight made his violet coat glow, backlighting his wild hair as if he were smoldering.

Juniper ignited the final torch. "We'll start the merriment after we reveal our city's name." Juniper leaped on top of the round table, standing purposefully in the center of the expansive hall. "Open the doors," he said. Cole and Virden climbed atop the table on opposite sides of Juniper. Ulrich and Ragan went to the main entryway and slowly pulled opened the heavy wooden doors.

A sea of eager rats flooded the room. There were hundreds, maybe a thousand, maybe more; the Nightshade brothers could not be sure. Cole waved the boys over to him. He crouched on the table. "Just stick by us," he said, giving them a wink. "No need for panic."

The hall filled with muddled voices, bouncing off the vaulted ceiling. The citizens' rumble hushed to a dull murmur as Juniper held up his paw for silence. Once all had quieted, he began. "Brave new citizens of our unnamed city, the Council thanks you for coming. We hope you are all enjoying your new home, and that it's of great comfort to know you'll never pay a single Ministry-mandated Stipend again. No more will you provide lavish feasts for Billycan, Killdeer, or their greedy majors while your own family starves. Consider it a favor to the High Minister, as Killdeer could surely stand to lessen his waistline!" The hall rumbled with laughter. "Friends, citizens, we have gathered here tonight for one particular reason, the naming of our burgeoning city, but due to unforeseen events, we are now here for two. Something has occurred tonight which I never in all my years thought possible. I once again saw the face of someone I'd lost long ago. I sadly witnessed the fire extinguished in one great rat, but tonight that fire has returned to us in two others."

Juniper looked down at Vincent and Victor. "Boys, come up here." Vincent and Victor felt rather embarrassed being stared at by such a large audience, but they got up on the makeshift stage just the same, standing between Juniper and Cole.

All eyes were upon the Nightshade brothers. The crowd's faces turned from joyful to bewildered; the rowdy noise turned to deafening silence, then shifted to a low drone of whispers.

The boys heard one rat say, "I saw them in the Combs. I swore they were ghosts!" Others said "Julius lives" or "Nightshade has returned!" The brothers were terrified and exhilarated. Who *was* their father?

Juniper's voice turned serious. "My friends, you are looking at the only two known survivors of the Nightshade Clan—two brothers—sons of our beloved Julius, our Citizen Minister. It is with great pleasure that I introduce Vincent and Victor Nightshade." The crowd gasped. "At first, I was in disbelief myself, but fate is sometimes a remarkable thing. These two young rats have been surviving in the Catacombs, hidden in the populace and managing to avoid being drafted into the Kill Army. Choosing to make a bold escape, they started a search for a new home. Well, their search ends here—tonight! They have found that home! I welcome the Nightshades to our city!"

The crowd clamored, "a Nightshade, no less two Nightshades—alive!" Children climbed on one another's shoulders trying to catch a glimpse; their parents embraced, while the old ones wept.

"You'll all get to meet the boys momentarily," said Juniper. "Now let's address our original purpose. Good rats, you have asked me to name our city, and I have not taken the task lightly. After weeks of consideration, I have come up with what I think are a few good options." Juniper's voice surged through the hall. "Without further delay, the first choice is a good name, a strong name, a name that shows we will not be ruled by tyrants anymore! The first name that came to mind is—Loyalist City!" The crowd applauded, whooped, and whistled shrilly, all yelling in a vote of approval.

The rats settled yet again. Juniper walked with his hands clasped behind his back, circling round the edge of the table, making sure everyone could see him. "Now, the second choice I'd say is even better. This name shows our loyalty to our fallen leader, a rat among rats, devoted in his day to each and every one of us." Juniper smiled. "Are you all ready?" he asked, purposefully pausing, playfully teasing the eager crowd. The mass of rats shouted impatiently for the name.

"All right, then," his deep voice blared. "The second choice, good citizens—is Trilok's City!" Applause and cheers resounded through the hall. Rats thumped their feet in endorsement, the old ones especially pleased with the name.

As Juniper waited for a break in the noise, he nodded at Vincent and Victor, who looked at each other and shrugged their shoulders. He continued. "Now for the third choice. This name, good citizens, in my opinion, is the finest name of all, rather a bolt from the dark, I'd say. This name is one that combines our resistance to the High Ministry with the knowledge of what the word 'citizen' really means. A name Trilok would be proud for us to choose, a name he would *insist* we choose over his own!"

Juniper waited for silence, finally smacking his tail on the table, forcing the lingering voices to cease. No rat should chatter through this moment. Bostwick Hall fell completely still. "This is for our long-departed Citizen Minister, a rat who gave his life for everyone in this room! A name that meant everything to generations past and will mean even more to the generations of our future, standing for everything we hold dear—standing before you right now." Motioning to

Vincent and Victor, Juniper cleared his throat and bellowed with all the force his chest could push out, "From now on and until the end of days, we would be known as Nightshade City!"

The room exploded in earsplitting screams of approval and hundreds of feet stomping in support. Juniper kept talking despite the noise, his commanding bass resounding over everyone. "We survive by cover of night. We live in the shadows, waiting for our redemption! Our name must symbolize our burning spirit, kept secret for eleven years, but no longer! This is for Julius! May his vision be our certainty! Tonight and forever, we are Nightshade City!"

Juniper jumped down from the table. Vincent and Victor followed. A whirlwind of hugs and handshakes greeted them. Rats surrounded the boys, patting their backs and shaking their paws, the old ones touching their fur for luck. The boys were dizzy with the barrage of outstretched paws and new faces.

Vincent, standing with Victor and Juniper, assessed the room, soaking it all in. He felt exceedingly—good. Strangely, the invisible cloud that had hung over him for so many years suddenly dissolved.

The Council disappeared through various doors within Bostwick Hall, emerging with wooden barrels filled with Carro ale and Oshi wine, and rolled them towards the center of the room. Cole's wife, Lali, and some helpers darted round the room, carrying out small wooden crates filled with mismatched mugs and dishes. They then dashed to the open kitchen, which lined the back of the great hall, wielding heavy trays filled with salted meats, cheeses, and fresh-baked biscuits.

A group of older rats gathered in the center of the room. One whistled, another struck a drum, and the rest began to sing a jaunty song, a melody revived from the days of Trilok. Onlookers were stomping to the rhythm as couples started dancing in time with the lively vocals. The children chased one another, whizzing around the hall, tackling one another, and landing in a heap of legs and tails, giggling riotously.

A young female rat with pale blond fur and dark eyes approached Juniper, her gaze wandering toward Victor. "Why, Petra, how are you, my dear?" asked Juniper. She reached up to Juniper's ear, so he bent down and met her halfway. She cupped her tiny paw around his ear and whispered something in a soft little chatter. "Well, why don't we ask him?" Juniper looked in Victor's direction. "Victor, Petra would like to know if you would be so kind as to have a dance with her." Vincent snickered as he watched his baby brother turn to jelly, his charcoal skin turning a flushed indigo.

"Well—yes," he said, trying not to stammer. "I *would* like to dance. Petra, is it? I'm Victor."

"I know," said Petra in a high little voice. She grabbed Victor's paw quite confidently and pulled him out with the other dancing couples. Victor and Petra moved well together, despite the obvious size difference, her little blond head barely reaching his chin. Victor grinned from ear to ear.

"Now, Vincent, come walk with me," said Juniper. "There are a lot of important rats who want to meet you. Rats who knew your father well. Rats who will be expecting *you* to follow in his footsteps. Let's do some introductions, and then I'll give you a tour of our city. I *should* say Nightshade City, your father's city—and yours."

It was late. Clover lay in her parents' nest, agitated, twitching under the covers, unable to sleep after the distressing visit from Billycan. She'd lost all hope that Juniper could retrieve her before the Grand Speech. Her uncle had a whole city of rats counting on him, not just her.

Her thoughts shifted to Killdeer. She imagined standing by his side at the speech, wondering what his hot breath would reek of. She shivered, revolted by the thought. She twisted and turned, trying to force herself into slumber. Clover beat the covers in frustration. The Collector's threats echoed in her head, hounding her.

Jerking herself up, she leaned limply against the wall. She stared at an etching of the late High Duchess Nomi, the wife of Minister Trilok, carved into the opposing wall. Deeply saddened by her passing, Clover's mother had carved the picture as a memorial of sorts. They had been dear friends and confidantes. The aging duchess had no children of her own and showered affection on Clover, who was barely a toddler at the time of Nomi's death.

A rapid, determined knocking on the door startled Clover. Who could it be at this hour? She crept to the door, waiting for the scraping of Billycan's club, but heard nothing. "Who's there?" she whispered.

The rat on the other side of the door responded brightly, in a cordial, almost operatic tone. "Hello, dear, it's Mother Gallo, Mistress of the Robes to the High Ministry. I've been sent by Billycan to help spruce you up for the Grand Speech! Now, please, dear, let me in. I have my duties to attend to. I'm sorry to call at this hour, but as you know, the Ministry waits for no one when there is work to be done!"

Clover knew she could not refuse a member of the High Ministry, and Mother Gallo seemed pleasant enough. She opened the door, quickly jumping out of Mother Gallo's way as the plump Mistress of the Robes swooped in like a drunken pigeon, pushing an overloaded wheelbarrow, which she clumsily banged into the wall, rattling its contents. It was filled with ornaments and trinkets, a tangled mess of ribbons, piles of fabric, glass bottles filled with colored liquids, and a long, skinny mirror, which teetered precariously over the edge of the barrow. She plopped the rickety cart down and pulled out the mirror, leaning it against the wall. Rummaging feverishly through her supplies and mumbling to herself throughout the process, she eventually fished out a frayed measuring tape from somewhere near the bottom.

Mother Gallo had a welcoming disposition that suited her ample proportions. Her fur was a soft ash gray, and there was a bold flicker in her eyes. Around her full waist, she wore a sash of royal blue, stuck with pins, scissors, and other tools of her trade.

"All right, then, dear, let's have a look at you, shall we?" Firmly grabbing Clover by her shoulders, she positioned her in front of the looking glass. She looked Clover up and down in the reflection, finally focusing on her face. "Well, my, my, you *are* a pretty little thing. No wonder why Killdeer is so taken with you. What a wonderful canvas I have to work with. You are as lovely as a budding flower, my dear. Now, let's see if we can put you into full bloom." She began measuring Clover from head to toe.

As Mother Gallo measured, Clover thought she'd try to find out what the High Mistress knew. "If you don't mind me asking, High Mistress, do you know why the High Minister would like me to stand with him during the Grand Speech?"

"First things first," said the seamstress. "Please don't bother to call me High Mistress. I think the title snooty and ridiculous." She twirled the tape measure around Clover's waist. "Frankly, I prefer Mother Gallo. I have little ones of my own, not to mention no less than thirty-three godchildren spread throughout the Combs. I think I've earned that title much better than Mistress of the Robes, don't you? For goodness' sake, I merely have a knack for sewing and color, nothing more, nothing less." She continued to measure Clover, wrapping the tape around her shoulders.

"Now for your question, my dear, why would the High Minister want you to stand next to him during his Grand Speech?" Mother Gallo twisted and turned around Clover, assessing every inch of her. "Well, I think that answer should be obvious to everyone—everyone but you, it seems. Why, you're stunning, my dear, plain and simple. You don't seem the type to put on airs, and from what I hear from talk around the Ministry, you're sharp-minded to boot. The *real* question should be why the Minister *wouldn't* want you to stand next to him?" She patted Clover on the back reassuringly and flashed a quick smile at her in the mirror.

Mother Gallo, surprisingly agile for her size, hopped over to the barrow and took out a wide ribbon the color of raspberries. She layered it around Clover's waist and pulled one end up over her shoulder to form a lovely satin sash. Grabbing a needle and thread, Mother Gallo swiftly sewed portions of the ribbon together, hiding her handiwork with a perfectly sized bow and draping the two ends of the ribbon down the center of Clover's slender back.

Mother Gallo looked at Clover contentedly, quite pleased with the result. "Well, now, that's just lovely, I would say; near perfect, I think. What do *you* think, my dear?"

Clover regarded herself in the mirror. Nothing so fine had ever touched her small frame. "It's like nothing I've ever seen," she said. Clover turned around and looked at the bow trailing down her back. As a slight smile emerged on her face, she looked almost happy.

"I'm so glad you're pleased," said Mother Gallo. "Now let's see how we can top that!" Mother Gallo went back to her wheelbarrow and pulled out some red and pink baubles. "No, no, none of these will do; too garish," she said. She shook her head disapprovingly and dropped the items back into the barrow.

She set one paw on her waist and tapped her chin with the other. "Those delicate golden eyes—so unique—what should we pair them with? You certainly don't need much in the way of frippery. Your beauty speaks for itself." Her eyes sparked in revelation. "I know!" She dove headfirst into her wheelbarrow, practically losing herself in it. "Here they are," she said. Slightly out of breath, she retrieved some green stones. She polished them with the end of her sash. She repositioned Clover in front of the mirror and placed a sparkly emerald on a short silver chain around her neck. She then placed a delicate silver circlet adorned with more emeralds atop Clover's head.

"Ah, that's it," said Mother Gallo. She sighed with satisfaction. "Now, that's loveliness in its purest form, if I do say so myself. You know I found these stones locked away in an old storeroom of the Ministry? They had been sitting there for years, covered in layers of dust and grime. It took hours to polish them back to their full brilliance. These emeralds are rumored to have belonged to none other than Nomi, the High Duchess. They are perfection on you. Nomi would be proud. This is a great honor, my dear—treasure this moment always."

She looked at Clover fondly, but with a slight sadness. She had known the duchess well. Mother Gallo sighed deeply. "Back to business," she said. "Now, my dear, what do you think of our finished creation?"

Clover regarded her reflection in the looking glass. Even she could not help but notice the change in her appearance. Out of the corner of her eye, she saw the wall carving of Nomi, who seemed to be staring at her. Did the duchess approve? Did her parents approve, or were they looking down at her, shaking their heads in shame?

Mother Gallo approached Clover and placed a soft paw on her shoulder. "What is it, my dear? What on earth could you have to be so sad about? This is a happy day for you. If Killdeer is pleased with you, your family will never go hungry again; your future children will never lack for anything. Most Chosen Ones are elated to have the chance to unite with the High Minister."

Clover balked at the mirror, abruptly crumbling into unrestrained tears. Mother Gallo hugged her close. It was then she noticed the carving of Nomi on the wall. Maybe the girl had a special fondness for the duchess, and all her ridiculous talk about what an honor she'd been granted had set the poor thing off. Perhaps the grandfather caused her distress; Billycan had mentioned he was deathly ill. That would certainly warrant the tears.

"My darling, what could be so awful?" asked Mother Gallo. "You're young, beautiful, and have just received the honor of a lifetime—one most will never know." She smiled sympathetically and patted Clover's cheek. "Now, dear, tell me what is bothering you?"

Clover whispered, scarcely audible. "I don't want to be a Chosen One," she mumbled.

"What did you say? I'm afraid I didn't quite hear you."

"I don't want to be a Chosen One." Clover's voice grew louder, angry. "I don't want to be with the High Minister, a rat old enough to be my father. Why did he pick me? What have I done to deserve such a revolting fate? Who have I offended?" She looked up defiantly. Regardless of the consequence her words might bring, it felt liberating to finally speak the truth.

"Quiet, dear. You must stay quiet," whispered Mother Gallo. She looked around Clover's quarters as if a Kill Army soldier might be hiding in a corner. Such slanders led to dire penalties. "Look at me," she said sternly. She held Clover by the shoulders. "Clover, it is imperative that you answer me candidly. I may work for the Ministry, but that doesn't mean I condone everything they do. Now, you must tell me again with certainty, lest you be making a grave error in judgment." Clover nodded. "Clover, are you telling me you do *not* want to be a Chosen One? You do *not* want to be with High Minister Killdeer?"

Stiffening her body, Clover looked into Mother Gallo's eyes, answering without hesitation. "I do *not*." She walked over to her parents' bed and flopped down on it like a rag doll. She carefully removed Nomi's tiara and necklace, and stared at the silver's intricate floral pattern. "I wanted to say no, but I thought Billycan might cut my tongue out."

Stunned, Mother Gallo sat down on the stool Clover kept by the fire pit. "Clover, you did the right thing by accepting. Billycan surely *would* have cut your tongue out—or worse. Here I thought you wanted this. I thought you were happy. All the others seemed to be so thrilled by the idea. It never occurred to me...I'm bewildered." Mother Gallo tapped her foot nervously. "What to do? What to do?" she mumbled to herself. She needed to tread lightly. No one in the Ministry could be trusted. She'd always thought the Minister a bullying degenerate with the character of a cockroach—cockroaches not being known for their strong moral fiber. She'd known Killdeer as a boy, well before Trilok banished him from the Catacombs. Even as a lad, he was a detestable bounder who exuded an air of entitlement.

"My dear, what does your grandfather think of all this? Does he know of your unhappiness? Surely he wants the best for you."

Clover shifted awkwardly. With no one else to turn to, she had to take a chance. For now she'd keep quiet about Juniper. She needed to be sure she could trust the seamstress first, without endangering her uncle or his hidden city. "Mother Gallo...my grandfather is long dead," she said plainly. "He did take care of me at first, but he died a year after my parents. A family friend pretends to be my guardian, my grandfather Timeron, so the Ministry still thinks he's alive, insuring I won't be sent to the Kill Army kitchens. For now, Billycan thinks my grandfather has gone Topside in search of a healer."

"And this family friend?" asked Mother Gallo. "Has he been looking out for you all this time?"

"He occasionally walks through the Combs in my grandfather's cloak. That way, at least others will see him, but mostly I take care of myself."

"You've been alone all this time? My goodness, how did you manage to survive on your own for so long?"

Clover removed the sash from around her waist. "At the time my grandfather died, I didn't know what to be scared of, so I suppose being so young was a good thing. Even the loneliness became ordinary, and I got used to looking after myself."

Amazed and impressed, Mother Gallo began to gather her things. Any female clever enough to concoct a story that Billycan believed, or at least accepted, deserved her freedom. She headed towards the door, thinking how much better her children had it. Her title in the Ministry had given them an easier life, if such a thing existed in the Combs. With Mr. Gallo dead six years back, killed instantly when a corridor collapsed, she'd had no choice but to accept Killdeer's offer to employ her. The well-being of her children forced her to stick with a job she loathed, working for the despicable Killdeer.

She touched Clover's chin with the tips of her paw, and leaning in close, she spoke softly. "I need time to think. The Grand Speech is a day away, just barely. Hear me, now, we *will* find a way out of this. Clover, most would call this an impasse, but it's simply a crossroads. We will find the right path. I promise you that."

The party lingered on well into the morning hours. Rats were stuffed and happy, full and then some. Victor and Petra sat together on the floor, worn out from dancing. They leaned against the wall of Bostwick Hall, deep in conversation. Wobbly at first, Victor shortly found his footing, handling his newfound romance surprisingly well.

Vincent reveled in his brother's good fortune. He knew his time would come. His father always told him he'd know when love struck, for it would feel like the beginning and end of his world all in the same breath. He found Petra endearing but a bit too giddy for his taste, which made her a perfect choice for his excitable brother.

Juniper stood chatting with a group of old ones. When he noticed Vincent, he politely excused himself from the conversation. He put a paw on Vincent's shoulder and navigated them through the noisy crowd, exiting Bostwick Hall down a snaky corridor. Vincent welcomed the silence.

Lined with doors, the passageway's layout was identical to the Catacombs, but the doors were stained with various earthy tones and adorned with dried plants and other ornaments. Such décor was strictly forbidden in the Combs. There were chairs and stools along the length of the corridor, even a few children's toys scattered here and there. A welcoming torch flickered every so often, giving the corridor a warm pumpkin hue, making Vincent's eyes glow a sharp bottle green.

As they reached the middle of the corridor, Juniper stopped in front of a door freshly stained the color of stewed tomatoes. "I think it's high time you and Victor had a proper place to live, no?" He opened the door, exposing a space of four dirt walls with a small wooden table, a cupboard, and a fire pit.

Vincent looked in. "Well, go ahead," said Juniper. "It's yours and Victor's now." Juniper sized up the space. "We'll get you some bedding and necessary items for cooking and such. You two can do anything you want with the place, make it your own. We believe all creatures have a right to their own unique expression, unlike the High

Ministry, who think free expression will eventually lead to rebellion. In truth, it's the lack of that freedom that leads to uprising. Your fire pit is over there, and a cupboard for your supplies is to the right of it. Ulrich and Ragan can get you some stain if you two want to color the place up a bit, unless of course you're at home with these dirt-brown walls." Juniper tapped a bare wall with his knuckle. "I dare say your time in the Combs has almost certainly made you sick of this particular shade of dry earth."

Vincent didn't know what to say. He twisted clumsily, embarrassed. Generosity was a hard thing to come by in the Catacombs. "Thank you, Juniper," he said awkwardly. "It's more than anything I could imagine. This whole day has been beyond words. Thank you for your charity." Vincent turned in a full circle, admiring the room.

"It's not charity I'm giving you—it's your due. I feel like part of Julius has been brought back from the dead. I'm only giving you what would have rightfully belonged to him. Now it's yours." Vincent's eerie likeness to his father still haunted Juniper. He hoped in the end the boy would meet with a happier fate.

"Let's go," said Juniper, pulling a small iron key on a leather loop from his rucksack and locking the door behind them. He placed it over Vincent's head. "This is yours now." Vincent stared down at the key. It felt comfortable on his chest. "A new key for a new beginning," Juniper said.

They walked silently, passing more and more corridors, curving and coiling this way and that. The growing city had more new vacancies than residents, but not for long. With the help of the Council and their network of Loyalists inside the Combs, families were slipping out from under Killdeer's control. The sector majors had grown lazy, not paying attention, which allowed families of rats to sneak away in the night. Nightshade City would soon be just that—a city.

As the two walked, Vincent took in the enormity of Nightshade. He couldn't believe how much Juniper and the Council had accomplished already. He felt so comfortable in Juniper's company that he thought it all right to ask him a delicate question, one that had been nagging at him since they met. "Juniper, I hope you don't mind my asking, but what happened to your eye?"

"I don't mind at all," said Juniper. "It's rather a timely story, I suppose." They walked into the hall that Vincent and Victor had first come through, the rotunda with the three entrances and the unusual symbols.

"What is this place called?" Vincent asked.

"We were going to name it after the city, it being our main gateway and all, so I assume it will be Nightshade something or other," said Juniper. "What would *you* call this place?"

"Well," said Vincent, looking thoughtfully around the hall, "how about Nightshade Passage?"

"He's a genius, just like his father!" said Juniper. He gave Vincent a good-natured slap on the back. "I like it!"

"I like it too," said Vincent, studying the room. "The symbols posted at each archway, what do they mean?"

"As you can see, each symbol is different. If you look at the carving by the entry you boys first came through, you'll see it looks like a Topsider's house—a bit crude, mind you, but a house all the same. It indicates the Topside corridor. Now, this entrance, the one you and I just came from, has the mark of Mighty Trilok, an *M* with the *T* centered through it. It honors the original Ministry and marks the passageway to our fair city. Last but not least," said Juniper, walking towards the third entrance, "this is the mark of Killdeer, those three jagged scratch marks, rather childish for a grown rat, if you ask me. His infamous mark obviously represents the Catacombs."

Juniper gazed down the unfinished corridor, then went on. "The Catacomb tunnel is not yet complete. That will be done the day of the invasion. When the time is right, we'll swiftly excavate the remainder of the corridor that leads to the many quarters of our supporters still in the Combs. With the Ministry and its army none the wiser, we'll break through the ground of these quarters, which lie scattered all over the Catacombs. I'm hoping for one mind-boggling surprise. I want that crusty white rat's mouth to drop," he said firmly. "It won't be long now."

His voice lightened. "I believe I cracked you on the cranium at this very doorway," he said, regarding the scuffle marks on the floor. "I followed you boys the whole way down from the Reserve."

"I *knew* I smelled someone familiar," said Vincent, "someone from Father's time."

"That you did! Now about my eye. That, my boy, is a classic. Come sit with me on this hard and uncomfortable floor, and I'll let you in on the particulars." They sat in the center of the rotunda. "Well, now," he said, "just so you're aware my eye is not damaged, dead, nor simply crossed, the fact is, it's gone, carved unceremoniously out of my head and coldly splattered against the wall of some dark, lonely corridor in the Catacombs some eleven years back now. This happened just days before the Bloody Coup, staged by Killdeer, Billycan, and their unseemly band of miscreants, who, apart from Billycan—who was a Topside lab rat—had all been expelled from the Combs, banished years prior by Trilok."

"Why were they cast out of the Combs?" asked Vincent.

"Many, including Killdeer, had committed murder. Trilok banished the lot of them for terrorizing citizens. He thought banishing them Topside would be enough of a punishment, even though we all pushed for imprisonment. Ragan and Ulrich predicted they'd be back to claim their revenge, and—of course—they were.

"Your father, Julius, my brother, Barcus, and I fought constantly to keep Killdeer and his growing splinter-group at bay. Not counting a few broken ribs and a scratch or two, Julius and Barcus got out unscathed, at first anyway. I, on the other hand, did not. The three of us had been planting booby traps in and around the entrances of the Combs, basically anywhere we thought Killdeer or someone from his circle might try to slip in. Trilok had the entire Catacombs on lockdown, nobody in or out. We had stockpiled food so no one needed to leave nor risk getting killed by the teeth of our deadly traps.

"As it turned out, we had a traitor in our camp, a saboteur—Jazeer Newcastle. Jazeer told Billycan of everyone's whereabouts, what sectors of the Catacombs we patrolled, and that I had constructed the deadly traps. It seems Billycan had promised Jazeer a title in the new regime, but instead he killed him as soon as he had the information he needed and, from what we know, the entire Newcastle Clan."

"So that's what Cole meant," said Vincent. "When he spoke Father's secret corridor, he said it was away from traitorous ears, 'or so we thought.' He was speaking of Jazeer. And Ragan mentioned that he and Ulrich had only been wrong about one rat—Jazeer Newcastle—that's who he meant."

"Yes," said Juniper, nodding. "We believe Jazeer snuck Billycan in to kill me. With me dead, Killdeer and their troops could easily gain access."

"But even if you were out of the way, wouldn't the traps still be waiting at every entrance?"

"Jazeer was intelligent. He showed Billycan how to deactivate the traps, allowing their troops to invade from all sides. The Bloody Coup took place in concert with the first wave of the flood. With so many of our citizens trapped Topside, fighting for their lives in the Great Flood, we never stood a chance." Juniper sighed. "Your father was especially heartbroken about Jazeer. Never once had we been so wrong about another. Jazeer had been a good friend to all of us. He and I were especially close friends. He knew you as a child, same as me. In fact, you played with his children."

Vincent tried to remember back. He remembered the unusual name—Jazeer. "He was a tall brown, wasn't he?"

"Yes. It's remarkable you remember that. The entire Newcastle Clan was dark brown from head to tail." Again Juniper sighed. "You can never really know someone, I guess." Juniper looked tired.

"Do you still want to talk about your eye?" Vincent asked. "You don't have to—"

"Of course I do! That's the meat of our tale. Every fellow loves a good gruesome yarn!" Juniper readjusted on the floor. "That night, Billycan lay in wait like a specter, tucking himself in the shadows of the sector I patrolled. He jumped me as I came round a turn, striking me square in the throat, rendering me unconscious. When I came to, Billycan was thrashing me in the face with his claws and his blasted billy club. My nose gushed with blood, coating my eyes, so I was blind to his rage. I reached up and dug into his face as he dug into mine. Regrettably, I only

caught the corner of his eye with my claw. I gouged in as hard as I could, hooking my nail under his skin. I ripped the flesh from the corner of his eye, across his muzzle, finally ending at his mouth, where my claw broke free, which is how he got that striking black scar he's so proud of.

"Blood gushed from his wounded face, soaking his white fur. The demented ghoul laughed at the sight of his bloodied coat. He started cursing me and struck my face with such power I cannot describe. Billycan was a ferocious opponent, his attack sadistic, his fury primeval. The most disturbing thing about the encounter was his demeanor. He wasn't just trying to kill the enemy; without a doubt, he reveled in my agony. To this day I will never forget the crazed delight, the laughter.

"That's when he dropped his club and went straight for my eye with those needle-sharp nails. He sliced my skin to ribbons, as if carving out a Hallowtide pumpkin. He threw my eye against the wall of the Combs with such force it splattered everywhere. I was so jolted, I didn't even feel the pain. That would come later. I raised my arms and clasped my paws around his bony throat. I dug my claws in deep, squeezing as hard as I could. Billycan started to struggle, so I just kept pressing, rallying all the strength I had left. That's when I saw it—I saw the fear, even through the cloud of blood. I saw his terror. Though it was brief, I saw it—sheer terror.

"After that, I thought I was done for, so far gone I kept fading in and out. Sometime during the scuffle, a citizen saw the attack and alerted Ragan and Ulrich. They made it to me just before Billycan bashed my skull in with that hellish club of his. As they raced to my aid, he fled down a corridor, disappearing before anyone could catch him."

Juniper looked exhausted. "Now, that, my boy, is why I wear this fetching patch, so as not to frighten little children or sicken other rats from finishing their meals."

Vincent scratched his head. Something had been bothering him since Juniper's speech. "Can I ask you one last thing? It's about something you said earlier."

"Certainly. What is it, son?"

"When you were giving the speech tonight about Nightshade, you said you witnessed the fire of one great rat put out and brought back in two others—myself and Victor. Who did you mean just then—'one great rat'? Did you mean my father? Did you see him die?"

Juniper furrowed his brow in confusion. "Why, yes, I meant your father." Juniper thought the reference to Julius was quite clear. "But Vincent, I didn't see Julius or any of your family die. I had barely come around from my own injuries. The Coup and the flood happened simultaneously. During the takeover, Ragan and Ulrich took me Topside, out of harm's way, and the others went in search of survivors from the flood. Virden and Cole found the remains of your family. The nature of their deaths changed us all forever."

Vincent's ears wilted. "So, you're saying the Council found my family Topside *after* they drowned in the Great Flood? Victor and I had always hoped there was a chance our father and the rest of our clan had made it through the flood, lost somewhere Topside, unable to find their way home. I always knew deep down that they drowned. It's about time I accepted it—Victor too."

"'Made it through'?" said Juniper. He moved towards Vincent and put his paw on his shoulder. "You mean you didn't know how your family died? You were never told?"

"Told what?" asked Vincent.

Vincent watched Juniper's contented face contort, draining of its usual humor, his tone now deadly sober. "I don't believe this. In all this time, no one's told you? I suppose everyone in the Catacombs assumed you knew." Juniper paused for a moment, trying to think of the right words, trying to be soft. "I don't know exactly how to put this. I honestly had no idea you and your brother were unaware, no idea at all. Vincent, your family died, but not as a consequence of the Great Flood. They were murdered—eliminated. You and Victor were spared *because* of the flood. You were the two they couldn't find that night."

Vincent's insides turned to watery knots. "*Who* couldn't find us?"

"Vincent, Billycan and his majors killed your entire family. They followed you all Topside. Killdeer ordered the executions himself. Billycan convinced him the entire Nightshade Clan was too tainted, too loyal to Trilok, and the new establishment would never get the citizens' full support with your family still alive in the Catacombs. Billycan hated your father. Born with a pure heart, Julius was the exact opposite of Billycan in every way, even down to his raven fur. Simply put, Billycan got rid of a problem. Despite the deadly floodwaters, Billycan returned Topside with the sole purpose of slaughtering your mother and father, while his cohorts, now his high majors, finished off your siblings, using the flood as their cover. Your family never stood a chance. You and Victor were the two they couldn't locate, swept away by the force of the flood. A rat who survived the flood saw you. She said you swam the entire way with Victor holding on to your neck, managing to find your way back to the Catacombs. Do you remember that?"

Vincent's voice deadened. "Yes, I remember," he said. "Victor screamed and cried the whole way."

"After that, you and Victor remained unharmed because of my brother, Barcus. Billycan brought him in front of Killdeer shortly after your family's killing. Killdeer told my brother that Billycan would kill his wife and children in the same manner as your family if Barcus did not openly support Killdeer and the new Ministry. Barcus had no choice but to comply, agreeing to show no further resistance, but he agreed on one condition. He insisted that the two remaining Nightshade children remain untouched. Killdeer agreed. What harm could two scrawny boys of four and eight do? They allowed my brother to live to show their subjects that the new High Ministry could show mercy, even to a Trilok Loyalist. Killdeer would not allow Barcus to take you in or have further contact with you. Luckily, you boys had your guardian. All this time I thought you'd been sent to the army—if only I'd known.

"Sadly, Barcus and his family still lost their lives to the hands of cruel fate, taken only one year later by the second wave of the Great Flood. They had gone Topside in search of Stipend when the second wave hit Trillium. It had been very cold. My niece, Clover, about your age now, stayed behind with a case of the sniffles, asleep in the Catacombs—safe. She is Barcus's only child left. She too shares you and your brother's heartache, the heartache of a thousand children."

Vincent stared vacantly at the floor. He could no longer speak. His face grew wet with tears. Juniper inched closer. "Vincent, look at me." Vincent slowly lifted his head. "You are a rat now, not a youth. You deserve to know what your family died for and what the name Nightshade still stands for. You and I have both suffered great loss. I have but one frightened niece. You have but one young brother. We need to take back what is ours, if not for ourselves, then for them and for all the rats in the Catacombs who are too afraid to defend themselves. They are but innocents in this whole toxic affair."

After not having shed a single tear in eleven years, Vincent now sobbed into Juniper's shoulder. Then slowly he got up and wiped the tears from his face. He stood tall, his eyes bright with new resolve. The black rat knew what had to be done.

CHAPTER THREE

Hard-Core Beliefs

IT WAS MORNING. Billycan lurched anxiously in his slanted gait, pacing about Killdeer's den. The Minister was missing from his silver roost. "Where is he?" grumbled Billycan. He scowled as he pondered Killdeer's probable whereabouts, perhaps off having a bath—marinating like a sodden pork belly, immersed in flowery water—or some comparable absurdity. Billycan never indulged himself. It goaded him that Killdeer required such pampering, a grown rat that needed to be fussed over and mollycoddled—it was disgraceful.

He cursed the air. Killdeer's hedonistic urges were getting in the way of his duties. Billycan controlled the Catacombs. Killdeer merely viewed from afar, an absentee landlord. Billycan hadn't seen Killdeer pick up a weapon since the days of the Bloody Coup. The Minister had grown flabby and indolent, a far cry from the destructive force he'd been eleven years ago. In his current state Killdeer could never have conquered Trilok. Billycan found it odd, even when they'd lived Topside, scrounging for food, dwelling in the Topsiders' filthy sewers and alleys, that Killdeer had always felt entitled. Strange, in those grim circumstances.

Billycan never forgot his past. How could he forget being shot in the spine daily with painful metal needles, brusquely tossed back into his cold, plastic cage—number 111? How could he not recall the steady throbbing in his head or the dry, blue kibble forced down his throat? It tasted odd and left him feeling as if his belly were twisted in knots, but still wanting more, eternally unable to satisfy his appetite.

Billycan never had a family—he came into the world alone, raised in a cage. He knew only one rat in his youth, a diminutive stippled rat named Dorf, housed next to him in the lab. Dorf taught him to speak. He taught him a lot of things. Astonished at the pace at which he learned, Dorf fed young Billycan as much information as possible. The white rat remembered every utterance, word for word.

Dorf had been a pet at a Topsider academy, residing in the history room. A poorly paid janitor stole him and sold him to the lab. Sitting through years of history lessons, Dorf knew everything on the subject, sharing his knowledge with his albino neighbor. This is how Billycan learned the ways of war, military strategy, and combat techniques. He learned that leaders *took* what they wanted, using deadly weapons, lies, torture, even infesting enemy camps with fatal illness. Dorf's innocent teachings became for Billycan hard-core beliefs.

About six months after Dorf befriended Billycan, the spotted rat simply vanished. When Billycan came back from his daily shot of green fluid, Dorf's cage lay vacant, his tiny friend gone, his scent replaced by bleach. He heard two Topsider lab techs talking about it later that day.

The female technician, a homely woman with glasses who strongly resembled a giraffe, asked her lab associate of Dorf's whereabouts. "What happened to number 112?"

"Little bugger couldn't handle the meds. He came into the program too late, and at his size, I'm surprised he lasted as long as he did," replied the other tech, a pudgy, balding fellow. "This drug is powerful stuff. The rats keep eating and eating without any weight gain. In fact, most of them have lost weight. Their length has shot through the charts." He pointed at Billycan's cage. "Look how long that one's gotten. He's a brute, that fellow. Wear your safety gloves if you handle him. Many of them should have died of old age by now or multiple brain seizures, but they just keep going. No one expected this. I told my wife about the rats' weight loss, and can you believe she asked me to bring home a vial of the stuff for her? She wanted to lose a few pounds before her sister's wedding. She pitched a fit when I told her no. Can you imagine that?"

The male tech gazed up at the giraffe eagerly, then continued. "I told her this drug is meant for depression. Weight loss is just a side effect. Once she learned the other effects of the serum, the frenzied behavior, the fits of uncontrollable violence, she thought I saved her life. Funny how that works," he said. He grinned proudly at his long-necked colleague, who seemed entirely unmoved by his heroics. "No matter how many times they reformulate, nothing improves. The rats we've paired together have killed each other. We've been instructed to destroy the albinos next week. They seem to be the most vicious. I suppose their inbreeding would have a great deal to do with that. This drug will never get approval. At least I hope not."

The following week an animal rights group broke into the lab and freed the rats. Word had gotten out of the lab's testing and their inhumane treatment of the animals. Activists thought it obscene that these poor creatures were being tormented so that humans could get a grip on their depression.

The freed rats ran wild in Trillium's streets. Most died. Few of the escapees knew anything of the Topsiders' world and were quickly run over, poisoned, or broke their necks in traps placed all over the city by animal control.

After breaking free of his captors, Billycan began to feel much stronger. His headaches stopped and his stomach problems dwindled, although his ceaseless hunger remained a permanent side effect.

Seeing his cloudy red eyes and his muddied white fur stained with dried blood from the beasts he killed for food, most predators kept their distance from Billycan. Those who challenged him met their deaths swiftly.

Weeks after winning his freedom, he turned a corner in an alley on yet another scramble for food. Before him stood a huge rat being backed into a corner by a grimy feline. Dorf had told Billycan of the dangers of cats. Billycan sized up the cat; the bony animal stared hungrily at the large gray rat, desperate for food. Hounds were typically more of a threat than cats. Many a feline had been killed in the grasp of a Trillium rat, but feral and frenzied, this particular cat was not one to take for granted.

Suddenly, the oversized gray rat lashed forward, thrashing the cat squarely in the nose, drawing blood. Billycan reacted in kind, jabbing the tabby in the belly. With his spiny claws he pulled downward, gutting it. The cat howled in pain and dropped to the asphalt with a thump, dead.

The gray rat stood, slightly shocked, mostly impressed. He wasn't sure if Billycan had helped him or had eyed him for a kill, and going by Billycan's bizarre exterior, he wasn't quite sure if he was even a rat. He had never seen a rat the color of winter. A little alarmed at Billycan's killing prowess, Killdeer warily yet warmly addressed him. "Many thanks, my unique-looking friend. You have spared me from being that filthy feline's evening meal."

Cocking his head, Billycan stared at the rat, unsure how to reply.

"Allow me to introduce myself," said the hefty rat. "My name is Killdeer, and you, my friend, look rather hungry."

Undaunted, Killdeer slowly moved closer to the dirty white rat. "Let's go find you something to eat, eh? My associates and I have more grub than we need. We take what we want; no garbage picking for us. You don't look like the sort for picking through trash either—you're far too stately for that." Killdeer chuckled. "Let's be on our way, shall we?"

Billycan looked at the dead cat, not wanting to leave the fresh meat. His mouth salivated as the body's aroma hit his snout. "Oh, no!" said Killdeer, seeing his ravenous eyes. "You don't want that disease-ridden thing rotting in your gut. You'll end up riddled with worms. Come on, we'll fix you up with some real meat." Billycan followed Killdeer out of the alley. The dubious friendship began.

Killdeer showed Billycan how the criminal set operated Topside. Billycan took to thievery and murder as if born to it, effortlessly killing rats and other creatures, taking what he wanted without a shred of remorse. Even Killdeer was staggered by Billycan's degenerate nature, but happy for it all the same. Billycan grew exceedingly protective of Killdeer. No rat came within a yard of him without Billycan's say-so.

Billycan's fanatical devotion, shrewdness, and sheer love of the kill made him invaluable to Killdeer, who quickly made him his second-in-command. Soon their adversaries were more terrified of Billycan than of Killdeer.

Loyalty, thought Billycan. From the day they'd met, he'd been nothing but loyal to Killdeer. They were on the brink of losing everything if their subjects continued to escape, and it seemed Killdeer was not concerned in the slightest. Where was *his* loyalty? Billycan grunted, pacing around Killdeer's throne in a crooked circle as if the ritual might conjure him up.

"Collector," barked Killdeer, breaking Billycan from his thoughts. Killdeer sauntered in, looking as though he'd just woken up from a nap.

"Finally you've returned," Billycan said.

"What's got you so wound up?" asked Killdeer. "It looks as though you've left a permanent tread mark in the ground." Killdeer snickered as he regarded the warped trail circling his throne.

Billycan kept pacing. "Minister, we have *more* problems. As you are well aware, Lithgo reported the missing families from his sector. Now High Majors Foiber and Schnauss are reporting similar accounts. Hundreds of families now remain unaccounted for. I'm still waiting for the sector majors to report in, but it doesn't look promising. I'm sure once I hear from all of them, the number will grow."

Killdeer plopped down in his throne and stretched leisurely. Packed with food and wine, his only interests at the moment involved sleep and silence. "What of it, Collector?"

"As suspected, the worst is happening. These families are fleeing, but to where we do not know. Unless they've gone Topside for good, which I highly doubt, given the perils, the only answer is somewhere under the Reserve. The Topsiders' new construction is complete. The soil is freshly tilled, easy to excavate and dig out an entirely new city. Minister, we've earned our titles. How are we to keep them without a city to oversee?" Billycan halted in his tracks and looked pointedly at Killdeer. "These meager figures may mean nothing to us in the current scheme of things, but if our numbers dwindle further, our Stipend will as well. We will all feel the brunt, especially the army. We will no longer be able to provide for our troops. In that case, we will have an angry mob of greedy, hungry soldiers to deal with. Hunger will over-power their fear of us. The sector majors will not be able to handle a mutiny of that size. Billycan fears the Ministry is at serious risk."

Killdeer sank down further in his throne. He looked crossly at Billycan, creasing his thick brow like a child pouting over a mother's scolding. "Who is left from Trilok's reign? Who of his Loyalists are still alive?" he asked.

Billycan tapped his chin, thinking. "No one of any importance is left, to Billycan's knowledge. The players of note are long gone, and Nightshade and his family are dead—barring the two boys. The little cowards escaped Topside a few days back. Lithgo says the scrawny brats are nothing but mangy pests. I'm sure they'll be dead soon enough, if not already."

Billycan again began to pace. A low growl emanated from the back of his throat as he considered the remainder of the Belancort Clan. "The Trilok Loyalists are nothing more than the stuff of folklore and fable. Trilok is decaying in his grave—his avengers with him. Barcus and Juniper are dead and buried. Long back, the majors searched high and low for their little band of troublemakers, the Council," he sneered contemptuously. "They were unable to find hide nor hair of them, and presumed them dead or wasting away somewhere Topside. The only Belancorts left are that decaying rat Timeron and of course our little Clover. Timeron may have both feet in the grave, but still, there is something about him, and I do not trust her in the least. She is a shifty one. I know it."

"She's a harmless girl," said Killdeer. "You think too highly of her cunning."

Billycan chuckled. Maybe he *was* giving a mere child too much credit. "I didn't agree at first, but your strategy of naming little Clover a Chosen One has its merits. Your subjects will feel comforted to know their Minister has bonded with the daughter of a Trilok Loyalist, even a dead one, although I doubt that alone will deter them from fleeing."

Killdeer slumped sideways on his throne and scratched his backside. All this talk of subversion and dead Loyalists annoyed him, as did Billycan's perpetually nagging voice. "Double every sector's troops. Have each exit corridor manned by three armed soldiers. No one is to leave the Catacombs till the Grand Speech has been given. After I put the fear back into them, none of my subjects will dare try to flee. Have the Mistress of the Robes personally escort the Belancort girl to the speech. I want no surprises. Have Catacomb Hall cleaned and brilliantly adorned for the occasion, and make sure every soldier of the Kill Army is accounted for. If they are not manning a post, they will be in attendance at the speech. No exceptions—none."

Killdeer reached for his wine. Billycan's eyes rolled in disapproval as he watched Killdeer drain half the bottle. The Minister's daily need for the drink disgusted him.

Killdeer took another swig, finishing the contents. "Texi, get in here!" he yelled, grimacing at the empty bottle.

Billycan watched the Minister stretch languidly in his throne. Killdeer did not leap into action at whisperings of sedition as Billycan had hoped. This troubled him. Billycan's misgivings about the Minister's abilities were mounting.

The High Collector had continued to support the Minister in spite of his numerous flaws. But Billycan could not allow the Minister's idleness to turn the Catacombs into a graveyard of abandoned corridors. Ultimately Billycan would have to make a decision.

He heard Texi's feet pattering down the corridor. Her chipper disposition and cheerful smile irked him no end. He took his leave.

A sturdy young guard had been placed outside Clover's door. Everyone knew of her new title as Chosen One, and Billycan refused to see her slip from under his watch. The embarrassment to the Ministry would be epic. The guard, Suttor, stood at rigid attention. He looked similar to Cole, Juniper's spotted councilman, but his black and white spots were wider, more of a bovine pattern. His face was divided by the two hues, each eye surrounded by the contrasting color.

Suttor approached his duties with the tenacity of a lion. His parents had died five years before while searching for Stipend, killed by poisoned bait left in the cellar of a Topsider's house. He and his little brothers were immediately rounded up and sent to the Kill Army, where he embraced the army culture with as much dedication as a foundling rat could muster. He gratefully swallowed the propaganda Major Lithgo churned out to the orphaned recruits. Suttor had no choice. His only other option was to go Topside and brave the humans. His brothers, still so little, could never have survived.

So there he stood at his post. The detail bored him, but Suttor performed his guard duties as if protecting Killdeer himself. His spine throbbed from standing so stiffly, but there he stood. Suttor fought for plum assignments, hoping to show the majors he deserved a promotion. With a higher rank, he could have a hand in his brothers' futures, protecting them. For now, he ranked as a mere senior lieutenant, giving him no control over their fates. It constantly worried him.

Mother Gallo marched up to Clover's door. "Good morning, Suttor. Kindly grant me entrance so that I may speak with Miss Clover. It's regarding the Grand Speech and her role in it."

Suttor frowned. "High Mistress of the Robes, you have not been granted proper clearance, so I cannot grant you entrance. I have a list, handed to me by none other than the High Collector and Commander of the Kill Army, and I am under strict orders not to permit anyone inside unless they are named on the register, ma'am."

Mother Gallo twitched her whiskers, slightly offended at the young rat's tone. "Lieutenant Suttor, am I not on your silly little list?"

"Well, no one has been put on the register, ma'am."

"Then why for Saints' sake did Billycan even bother to give you a list? How ridiculous is that?" she asked. Exasperated, she took a more authoritative tone. "Now, boy, you *will* let me in, or I will go to Billycan myself and tell him you forbade me entrance. I was here just yesterday getting this girl prepared for the Grand Speech, as I'd been ordered to do by none other than your esteemed Commander Billycan, and I intend to finish my duties." She'd always been quite fond of Suttor and appreciated how dedicated he was to his brothers. But given the circumstances, she would have to be firm. "Now, Suttor, your parents were dear friends of mine and the late Mr. Gallo. I would never steer you into trouble with your superiors. Orders or not, I think you know that much. If it makes you feel better, I will tell Billycan I ordered you to let me in. How do you think he'll react if this young girl isn't fully prepared for her debut on the arm of the High Minister? What will the consequences be for barring my entrance then?"

Suttor had known Mother Gallo since he could remember. She and her late husband used to visit regularly, bringing their boys along to play with him and his brothers. The Gallos always brought a tin of fresh biscuits. His mother would brew her famous pumpkin tea, and his father would crack open a fresh jug of Carro ale. Suttor knew Mother Gallo made sense. If he prevented her from doing her duties, it could mean a terrible penalty for him, possibly a demotion. He had no reason to doubt her intentions. After all, she held a position of stature within the Ministry, and the register Billycan had given him surely did not apply to someone of her distinction.

"Come, now, Suttor," said Mother Gallo. "Give me your list." She snatched the parchment from Suttor, took a feather pen off her blue sash, and signed her Ministry-issued seal to the register. "There, you see? Now you can show Billycan his silly list and he can chastise me if he takes issue. I may not be a member of the Kill Army, but my Ministry title far outranks yours, lieutenant. Billycan will not punish you. Are we understood?"

Suttor shifted clumsily. "Yes, ma'am, understood. I will show him your mark." Suttor banged on Clover's door, announcing Mother Gallo. "The High Mistress of the Robes to see you, Miss Belancort." He opened the door. "Right this way, Mistress Gallo. I promise you'll get no more trouble from me."

She smiled up at the gangly spotted rat. "Now, my boy, you know as well as I do it's Mother Gallo, not Mistress. You're a fine boy and a good brother. Your parents would be proud of you. If you ever need anything, anything at all, you know where to find me." She reached up and put a paw on his cheek. "My boys miss you. Come round with your brothers anytime. I'll make sure you get the proper permission. They would love to spend some time with you, as would I."

Suttor smiled bashfully. "Thank you, Mother Gallo. I will."

"Remember what I said: You're a good boy. Always trust your heart." She entered Clover's quarters, and Suttor shut the door behind her.

Clover sat staring at the fire, daydreaming. She'd not heard Suttor's announcement. Mother Gallo entered the room, startling her. Clover shot up like a flash, relieved to see the seamstress. Impulsively, she embraced Mother Gallo, who patted her gently.

"It's so good to see you again, dear," she said. "It seems you're in better spirits, and I'm happy for that." Mother Gallo lowered her voice to a whisper. "Now you need to listen closely." She motioned to the door, pointing at Suttor's feet, which could be seen under its gap. "He's a nice boy, but a little too enthusiastic about his job, I'm afraid, so let's keep our voices down, just in case."

They sat on Clover's bed. "I've been racking my brain nonstop," said Mother Gallo. "At first I thought I could sneak you Topside on my own, but Billycan has troops posted at every exit corridor. All the entrances in and out of the Combs have been suddenly blocked off. I don't know what could be happening, but there is indeed something brewing."

Mother Gallo's offer of help came at her own peril; Clover decided she must tell her everything. "Mother Gallo, I haven't been completely honest with you. I wanted to tell you everything, but I had to be sure I could trust you." Mother Gallo looked puzzled but remained silent. "As I told you, my parents are dead, long gone, my brothers, too. That's all true, but that family friend I told you about, the elderly rat who pretends to be my grandfather, well . . . he's not elderly at all, and he's more than just a family friend. He's my father's brother, my uncle—Juniper Belancort."

Mother Gallo gasped. Her mouth fell open. "He's alive!" she whispered. "How is it possible?" She paused for a moment, gathering her thoughts. "Clover, you're telling me your uncle, Juniper Belancort . . . he's *alive?*"

"Yes. You've heard of him?"

"Why didn't he find me?" Mother Gallo looked hurt. "All this time I believed him dead, murdered. Everyone thought Billycan had assassinated him. Dear, I knew your uncle well, very well. I mourned his death for years. It seems like ages since then—I guess it has been. Bless the Saints." She let out a deep sigh. "How things have changed for everyone. It doesn't seem right, does it? Eleven years isn't a long time in the grand scheme of things, but to me it feels like lifetimes ago."

Clover relaxed a little. "Uncle's friends saved him from Billycan," she said.

"The Council," said Mother Gallo.

"Yes, they took him Topside. They've all been surviving in an abandoned Topside warehouse—up until recently, that is. Now they've their own city. They've been excavating for two years, somewhere under Trillium's Reserve District. It's only been inhabitable the last few months or so. Uncle's a bit like a shadow these days, slipping in and out of the Catacombs as often as he can, always checking in on me, and meeting with his network of Loyalists—getting them out. He's been planning to get me out too, but timing has never been on our side, and now it looks as though it may never be."

Mother Gallo's face brightened. "Juniper's friends, the Council— Cole, Virden, and the twins—those four would follow your uncle to the ends of the earth." She clasped her paws. "Oh, Clover, your uncle is a shrewd one! One of the cleverest rats I've ever known. His traps— these ingenious contraptions—were set all over the Catacombs before the Coup. That's what put him in such danger—he was betrayed by someone he thought a faithful friend. That smart mouth of his didn't help either—always getting into hot water with that devilish tongue. Never afraid to speak his mind, that rat!"

Mother Gallo tittered like a schoolgirl. Her smile changed from a motherly beam to a grin of girlish dizziness. "Clover, there's something I want to share with you, bless my late husband's soul. Before I met my beloved Mr. Gallo—who I adored, mind you—Juniper and I were a bit more than friends. Truth be told, he'd been courting me relentlessly. My father, Papa Bostwick, a very strict rat, did not like your uncle—not at all! Like I said, he had that brazen mouth, saying whatever he liked. As I'm sure you are well aware, your uncle has some strong opinions when it comes to politics—well, when it comes to anything! My father did *not* like that. I suppose it's a classic story, the daughter giddy over someone her father despises! We were in love. Whenever there was an event in Catacomb Hall, and there were a lot in those days, we'd slip through the crowd to a secret place and talk for hours and hours. Juniper even stole a kiss or two!" Mother Gallo giggled. Clover giggled too, imagining her burly uncle as a young rat in love. "Clover, it warms my soul to know he's alive! When was he here last?"

Clover's shoulders drooped as she thought about yesterday's events. "Juniper was here just yesterday, when Billycan declared me Chosen One. Juniper pretended to be my grandfather, Timeron, all wrapped up in that filthy black shroud—the same one my grandfather always wore. Billycan almost unmasked him—only a claim of the plague kept him back. Uncle says we'd surely be dead if Billycan had discovered him."

Mother Gallo got up from the bed and straightened her sash. "Juniper's right about that. Billycan despises your uncle from the deepest depths of his rotten heart. That appalling black scar across the Collector's face—your uncle gave him that beauty. Billycan's loathing for all Loyalists runs deep, but for your uncle, especially so. The Saints were looking out for you two yesterday. Now we must get back to the task at hand. Does Juniper know that the Grand Speech has been moved to this Rest Day? Does he know you've been requested by Killdeer to escort him?"

"He has no idea," said Clover. "He thinks we have two weeks, the customary wait for a Chosen One. He has no way of knowing my dilemma. Even if by chance he arrived here tomorrow, what could he possibly do? They have me guarded round the clock."

Mother Gallo paced the room. "Dear, has he told you how one gets to his hidden city? It's far too risky to try to sneak you out, but maybe I could locate him. Knowing your uncle, he already has a plan in the works. Has he given you any information that might be helpful, anything at all?"

Clover tugged the edge of her ear, thinking of recent events. "We had plans in place to get me out weeks ago, but odd things started happening. I pretended to go Topside for Stipend, planning never to return to the Catacombs, but the last few times I ventured up to Trillium City, I noticed Kill Army sector majors trailing me. After that, Uncle told me to stay put." Clover tried to focus on what her uncle had told her. "Juniper gets Topside through an old corridor. It's teeming with earthworms. Uncle has some sort of a pact with them. The corridor closed down long before the Bloody Coup. Uncle's been using it for years as his only way in or out of the Combs. Once Uncle gets Topside, he enters through a Topsider's brownstone on Ashbury Lane. There is a single hole he made somewhere in the corner of a first-floor room, a room with a long window overlooking the street. The hole leads straight to the main entrance of the city. He says the brownstone has two gargoyles on top, the only one on the block. That's why he picked it—it's easy to recognize."

"Well, there's nothing left to think about, then. I'll find Juniper myself."

Clover grabbed Mother Gallo's paws. "Mother Gallo, just having you around makes all this almost bearable. I understand you want to help, but you have a family that needs you, and I couldn't ask you to put yourself in jeopardy."

Mother Gallo spoke firmly. "Clover, let there be no further doubts. I work for the Ministry. I must. It sets my family free of Stipend and puts food on our table, food I could not provide alone. That being said, I'm not a supporter of our esteemed Ministry. They have beaten down the rats of the Catacombs. Now you tell me about Juniper's plans—giving us the possibility that all of this can change, a singular opportunity to take back what Killdeer and his followers stole from us long ago.

"Just knowing Juniper's alive gives me new hope for our future, my children's future—your future, dear. When your uncle and I were young, we had the Catacombs at our feet. Anything was possible. Your father, Julius Nightshade and Juniper were trusted advisers to Trilok and his Ministry. When they died, it seemed everything dear to us died with them. When the key players of the Loyalist cause were silenced, it silenced us all."

Mother Gallo gazed thoughtfully at the wall carving of Duchess Nomi. "This stagnant existence is the way most rats think life will always be. Clover, I firmly believe that we weren't put on this earth merely to endure its many trials and tragedies. The Saints did not design things that way. There is much more to life. We were meant to feel the joy of new babies, the festivity of birthdays and holidays, and the uncontained wooziness of newfound love. It's all right to ask for help. We all need to do so from time to time." She smiled softly and gently tapped the tip of Clover's nose. "My dear, today is *your* time."

"Thank you, Mother Gallo," said Clover, summoning a smile.

"Don't thank me yet—there is much to be done. Do you know

anything about this secret corridor your uncle uses to get in and out—any notion where it might be?"

"I'm not really sure. Uncle said it's a secret place where he and his friends used to meet, making sure no one could hear them—for fear that there could be traitors living among them. He said they could never be too careful when it came to protecting the corridor. I think only the Council knew of its existence."

Mother Gallo suddenly put her paw to heart. "Clover, do you recall if it's anywhere near Catacomb Hall?"

"Yes," said Clover. "Uncle said it's behind some falling-down pub."

Mother Gallo's lavender skin turned a rosy pink, and her voice fluttered slightly. "The corridor behind Ellington's Tavern—I'm sure of it! Your uncle and I used to steal away to that very corridor when we were courting. It would have been quite disastrous had Papa Bostwick found out! The tunnel is directly behind the tavern, covered up with rubbish and such. You would never notice it unless you knew it existed. Thank the Saints our Juniper is the sentimental sort!"

Mother Gallo gave Clover a firm hug and headed towards the door. "Now, Clover, you must do your part," she said. "Play it safe and smart. Act as if all is well and you are the happiest girl in the Catacombs. I will be back before I am to escort you to the speech. We have little time. I must depart."

"Please be careful, Mother Gallo, and good luck."

"No need for luck. Nothing could keep me from my course!"

Mother Gallo wove hastily through the bustling crowd in Catacomb Hall, finally making her way to Ellington's Tavern. She remembered how, in her youth, she would sneak away from her father's watchful eye and go to the tavern, staying up until dawn, always on the arm of Juniper Belancort. What good times those were, laughing riotously at Juniper's and Virden's comical stories, the boisterous pair finding a reason to toast just about anything, and Ragan and Ulrich endlessly telling their ridiculous jokes to stoic Cole, until he'd finally break into wild laughter.

It was nearly lunchtime, and the tavern was starting to fill. The pub's once-evergreen stain had worn away, revealing its rotting wood frame, which tilted precariously to the left, held up only by the buildings stacked on either side of it. But there it stood, more ramshackle than ever—the secret corridor waiting patiently behind it.

Remaining unseen might be easier than Mother Gallo originally thought. Rats seemed too busy with themselves to bother with her. As she headed towards the rear of Ellington's, a chubby Kill Army soldier and his gangly companion abruptly stopped her. The portly one sprayed her with a fine mist of spittle as he tried to engage her without slurring his words from one too many glasses of ale. "Good day, madam. Care for a nip of ale with me and my boy?"

"No, sir, but thank you kindly," replied Mother Gallo. She attempted to make her exit, but the soldier placed a fleshy paw on her shoulder.

"Now, wait a minute, missus," he said, leaning on his friend. "I'm an assistant major in the Kill Army. Do you really think it's wise to turn me down? I find you fair of face, and I do like a female with curves on her—more to hang on to!" Laughing heartily, he sprayed the air again, the rancid scent of half-digested Carro ale escaping from his throat.

Mother Gallo took the end of her sash and wiped the droplets of saliva from her coat. "Do you have any idea *who* you are speaking to?

Are you aware I'm the High Mistress of the Robes, reporting directly to High Collector and Commander Billycan? Do you think he would be pleased to know that a drunken underling, who is old enough to be a sector major but obviously too incompetent to move up from a mere assistant, harassed one of his key staff members tonight? Do you think he would throw a parade in your honor, perhaps grant a promotion in rank? Now, tell me your name and what sector major you report to, soldier." Mother Gallo boiled with rage.

The assistant major's face contorted in fear. He began to stutter, pleading desperately. "Now, High Mistress, there's no need for all that! We are sorry—dreadfully sorry—to have disturbed you. We were just having a bit of fun is all. Please do accept our deepest apologies. There is no need to mention this to the High Collector. It won't happen again." The soldier stood as straight as he could in his pickled condition, while his scrawny friend tried to keep him from toppling over. Mother Gallo laughed to herself at the ridiculous sight.

She pointed to an on-duty major, monitoring the crowd. "Now, get out of my sight before I call that sector major over. I'm sure he'd love to take part in our little conversation."

Before she could say anything else, the portly rat and his long-legged companion flew out of sight, as if wings had sprouted from their backs. Though nauseating and rather pathetic, the incident gave Mother Gallo's ego a slight boost. After all these years she could still turn heads, albeit drunken ones. After that, she effortlessly slipped behind the tavern, without so much as a questioning glance from the revelers.

The corridor stood intact, waiting for its next traveler. She and Juniper had sat in that corridor for hours on end, talking about their future together. She pushed under the rusted signs and decaying planking, revealing the cobwebbed hole. The sight gave her pause.

Her world ended tonight, but new beginnings awaited the moment she stepped inside. She wasted no more time.

Mother Gallo found an old crate to give herself a leg up and groaned as she pulled herself into the musty tunnel. She sat down for a second, letting the strain on her muscles fade. "Bless the Saints. I'm just in terrible shape. What's become of me? I must weigh as much as a barrel of Carro ale!"

"I wouldn't say a full barrel, but you do feel fairly solid," said a coarse, distant voice.

Fright swept over Mother Gallo. "Who is it? Who's there?" she demanded. She frantically looked in all directions, ready to jump back inside the Catacombs.

The voice came from everywhere and nowhere. "Don't get your tail in a tizzy, madam," said the voice. "What purpose sends you to my corridor?"

Mother Gallo searched the corridor, unable to see face or form of whatever had addressed her. "Who wants to know?" she asked.

The surly voice answered in a lazy, slightly pompous manner. "If you must know, my name is Oard. I run this corridor."

"Why can't I see you, Oard? Where are you?" Still afraid, she did not move from her spot.

"Well, my dear, you can't see me because you're sitting on me."

"What?" Mother Gallo jumped to her feet, backing herself up the corridor, trying to escape. Looking down, she saw something moving under the dirt. The ground suddenly thinned out, and a tubular form took shape. The moving earth dissolved, revealing a substantial brown earthworm.

The worm spoke again. "Now, then, will you please explain to me what business you have in my corridor? We don't like visitors, madam, especially uninvited ones."

Mother Gallo had never spoken with an earthworm. Tormented by the Kill Army majors, the quaggy creatures kept themselves well hidden. "I'm a friend of Juniper Belancort's, here on vital business for him," she replied nervously.

"How do I know you're telling the truth?" asked Oard brusquely.

"Because I'm a Ministry official, and if my intentions were dishonorable this corridor would be crawling with Billycan and his majors, all interrogating your tribesmen in search of Juniper and his city."

Oard grunted. "I suppose you make sense."

"Oard, Juniper's niece is in a dire situation, and I *must* get word to him straightaway."

Oard's tone softened. "Well, why didn't you say so? Juniper mentions little Clover often. I've been hoping to make her acquaintance one of these days. He said when things die down in her sector, he will be moving her to his city." Oard pulled his whole body out from the soil and coiled himself up like a snake. He was quite large by earthworm standards.

"Yes, Clover said you and Juniper have an understanding," said Mother Gallo.

Oard had a rough, scratchy voice, as if gravel were stuck in his throat. "Indeed we do, madam. In exchange for the use of my corridor and the earthworms' help in excavation, Juniper has agreed to give our tribe our own sanctuary in the rich soil of his clandestine city. The dirt in the Catacombs has grown dead and dry. Much of our Topside food supply has been sacrificed for Trillium City parking lots and factories. Plant life is scarce, and without Juniper's help my tribe will undoubtedly expire."

"Well, Oard, I know firsthand Juniper is a rat of his word. If he promised you a new home, a new home you shall get."

"Yes, I have faith in Juniper. He and I have been comrades since the

Bloody Coup." Oard slithered closer. "Madam, how may I address you?"

"I'm Mother Gallo, an old friend of Juniper's. In fact, I only just learned he's still alive. Providence led me to his young niece."

"Speaking of his niece, you'd best get back to your mission. I'll tell my tribe you're traveling up and not to get in your way. We'll get word to the worms manning the tunnel to Juniper's city, letting them know who you are. Now, off you go, and do be careful. Topside can be a treacherous place."

Earthworms were eyeless. They made their way by feeling vibrations and changes in the earth. Oard stopped for a moment after he started to slink away; he felt a faint rumble. "I can feel thunder up top, Mother Gallo. You may be in for a cold, wet trip to your destination. Take heed," he said. He vanished back into the soil.

"Thank you, Oard. I will."

Mother Gallo walked up the corridor at a steady pace, conserving her energy as she climbed to the surface. The earthworms kept out of her way, except to inform her of weather changes Topside. From what she gathered, the thunder had stopped, and a cold, wet muddle was all that remained. She could imagine the sopping muck that would stick to her feet and the biting cold that would ravage her bones, but she'd survived all these years in the Combs, so surely she could entertain foul weather for a short while.

She finally reached Topside. A young earthworm named Cherrytin, who had kept her company for part of the way, warned her profusely about the careless Topsiders, begging her not to get trampled. She had a high, squeaky voice. "You'll come up in the grass, right next to the sidewalk. Please be on the lookout, Mother Gallo. Topside children on their bicycles and even on foot have flattened many of our family, plowing right through the grass."

"My dear Cherrytin, I promise to be careful. Thank you for your help, and please thank your tribe for me. I'll be sure to tell Juniper how cordial you all have been." Mother Gallo smiled at the blind little worm. "Bye for now, Cherrytin. I hope to see you soon," she said. She had reached the surface.

The violent storm had left the streets empty—the afternoon sun had all but disappeared behind the clouds. Mother Gallo stuck her head out Topside, with only her ears and eyes visible. The wintry muck had been a blessing in disguise. "Well, thank goodness for that," she whispered to herself. She pulled herself up through the hole and into the gloom of Trillium City. She hurried on, pushing through the biting wind, trying to get a view of the corner street sign.

"Ashbury Lane," she said. "Juniper, you've made this easy on me." She braced herself as the wind picked up.

She studied the houses across from her, particularly the rooftops. There it stood—Juniper's brownstone. The two stone gargoyles gazed down at her from above, like covert Saints taking on the form of other-worldly creatures—welcoming her in. Now if only she had a way.

She circled twice round the entire brownstone looking for a hole or crack she could push herself through, but the home was a fortress, with no gaps or fractures to be found. She would have to wait. Eventually the door would open.

So there she sat. A carved Hallowtide pumpkin roosted crookedly on the brownstone's stoop. It looked blankly out onto the empty street with its hollowed, ghoulish grin. She stared at it, wondering why the Topsiders insisted on carving them every year, only to throw them away weeks later. For now it was her only companion, so, odd as it was, she was glad for the company.

Mother Gallo waited, for how long she did not know. She'd tucked herself away in a corner of the brownstone's bricked-in porch, blocking herself from the hammering winds.

Suddenly, a nearby door slammed. She jumped to her feet and peered around the red bricks. A long, white car idled in front of the brownstone. The driver, clad in a fitted black suit, jumped out and dashed towards the back of the car, opening a door. A tall Topsider got out. He had a lean build and wavy hair, the color of sweet potatoes. The Topsider stretched on the sidewalk as the driver hurriedly brought his bag up to the front door, whizzing by Mother Gallo's head. The Topsider handed the driver some rolled-up bills. "Thanks, sir, appreciated, as always. Have a good weekend, what's left of it, anyway." The red-haired Topsider waved as the car drove off.

Trotting up the stairs, the Topsider rummaged through his overcoat pocket. As he fumbled, Mother Gallo positioned herself just under the doorsill, only inches away from his shiny wingtips. Finally retrieving his keys, he unlocked the door and pushed it open. He picked up his bag, banging it into the door, and entered the home. Mother Gallo entered, remaining hidden under the dangling suitcase.

They were in a small vestibule. With the suitcase still hanging precariously over Mother Gallo's head, the Topsider pushed the inner door open with his foot. Setting down his keys and luggage, he stole up the stairs. "Honey, Ramsey, I'm home!" he called out. Mother Gallo dashed out of the vestibule and into the house.

"Daddy!" shouted a child's voice from upstairs.

Mother Gallo immediately started her search for Juniper's hole. She quickly found the room Clover had mentioned—the only one facing the street. She could see what little light the sky had to offer pushing under the door's gap.

She eyed the width of the opening under the door. Having grown rounder in recent years, she was a bit worried, but she was no match to Juniper's bulk. If he could manage his way under, so could she. She removed her blue sash, sucked in her belly, and pushed herself through the gap. Relieved, she took a deep breath; then, restoring her sash and dusting herself off, she scrutinized the room; artist's paints and charcoals lay strewn about the floor, easels leaned here and there—an artist's studio. *One of four corners*, she thought, heading towards the window Clover spoke of.

There it was—the hole. She felt the opening's smooth edges, devoid of splinters, a near-perfect circle. "Juniper Belancort, I'd know your work anywhere," she whispered to herself. Her spine shivered, and her skin rose in tiny goose bumps. She could smell Juniper in the air.

Vincent and Victor spent their first day in Nightshade City dead asleep. Virden and Cole had set them up with cots and bedding, but they would have gladly slept on the floor without complaint after dragging themselves to bed well after the sun had risen Topside.

Vincent's sleep was deep and dreamless. The sound of his brother snoring finally woke him. He rolled on to his back and put his arms behind his head, not ready to leave his comfortable bed. He stared at his brother, still sound asleep. So young at the time of their parents' deaths, Victor had few memories of them. Vincent had sworn Juniper to secrecy regarding the death of their family. He felt his brother would not yet be able to handle the facts behind their family's murders. Juniper agreed.

Whimpering in his sleep, Victor's pink tongue dangled out of his mouth, along with a spindly thread of drool, which had connected itself to his lower jaw, vibrating wildly every time he blew out a snore. It made Vincent laugh out loud, which woke Victor.

Victor stretched his long limbs, a goofy smile on his face. He had dreamed of the sparkly little Petra, with her blond fur and glittery eyes.

The boys happily relaxed in bed, until a far-too-energetic voice called from the corridor. "Boys, are you awake?" It was Juniper. "You've slept the day away. It's late, and there's plenty of work to be done." Juniper had not been awake long himself. He opened the door and stuck his head inside, regarding both boys still in their cots. "Do I need to trudge to Lex County and drag back a rooster to wake you lazy rats up?" The boys chuckled, still too comfortable to move.

Juniper entered carrying a woven basket with a dotted blue cloth over the top and a large brown jug. The brothers sluggishly sat up. Victor let out a prolonged yawn, stretching his arms over his head.

"I see I'm not the only rat lagging today. The halls are all deserted. Rats are still recovering from last night's merriment." Juniper opened the basket, revealing honey biscuits and bitonberry corn bread. The boys eyed the food ravenously. "Ah, you're hungry, I see! Well, c'mon, then, I've got fresh goat's milk as well." He uncorked the jug, plunking it on the wooden table. He took a seat and rubbed his paws together eagerly. "Now, boys, we've got many things to do before the day is done. Lunchtime has come and gone. These pastries are from Cole's wife, Lali, who I think would be quite shocked to learn that her breakfast biscuits were being had for an early dinner—highly improper!"

The boys sat on opposite sides of Juniper, all three tearing into the biscuits like mad dogs. "All right, boys, let's eat like we mean it, then we must go to the main hall—I mean Nightshade Passage," he said, winking at Vincent.

"What's going on?" asked Vincent.

"You'll find out soon enough. First things first, just eat now," said Juniper, stuffing a generous chunk of corn bread in his mouth.

CHAPTER FOUR
The Feast of Batiste

MOTHER GALLO HAD NO IDEA how far she had traveled. The tunnel felt like it went on forever, far deeper than the Catacombs.

She had always thought that if she ever saw Juniper Belancort again, it would be as a phantom haunting her dreams—what *could* have been. She tried to be angry with him, alive all this time, never getting word to her. In her heart she knew he did it to safeguard her. She would have surely followed him Topside. She would have followed him anywhere, no matter how dangerous. Trillium's Topsiders exterminated rats by the hundreds. It amazed her that Juniper had survived all this time.

A few years after the Coup, she met Mr. Gallo and the pair wed and had a family. Life was hard in the Combs, but they had each other to lean on. She wondered what the last eleven years had been like for Juniper. Had he been lonely? He *did* have freedom Topside. In that way he was lucky. Freedom to choose means a great deal when you don't have it.

The corridor started flattening out and widening. She heard voices overlapping, but was unable to make out their words. Her heart beat in time with her footsteps as she raced down the corridor. The dim light grew brighter with every stride. She stopped and caught her breath, listening to the now-audible conversations ahead of her—some sort of debate.

"The earthworms have agreed to the plan. We've set it in motion, and it's already working," said a male voice.

"Yes, it's the only way of getting into the Combs for now," agreed a female, loudly.

Another rat barked back at them harshly. "Killdeer and Billycan have all the entrances on lockdown. No one can go in or out without proper authority. All we have are the earthworm holes and the old corridor behind Ellington's. There *has* to be another way! Things are moving too slowly. Until the earthworms dig more tunnels, we are at a standstill!"

"Now, everyone, we all need to calm down," said a reassuring voice, coming from farther into the room. "The earthworms are excavating as fast as they can, much faster than we ever anticipated. They listen for the signal in the chosen Catacomb quarters and dig directly to it, burrowing a hole through the floor of each room and straight back to us. They have yet to miss a mark. If we push them too hard, they'll become anxious and end up digging into the wrong quarters, putting everyone at risk. That will be *our* fault, not theirs. Now, the melody that Virden chose is ideal. The worms identify its tempo quickly, following it all the way from Nightshade to their *precise* location in the Combs. My friends, Loyalists of Trilok, just as it took time and perseverance for Killdeer and Billycan to steal what belonged to us, it will demand the same time and perseverance for us to take it back. The only difference is that time is on *our* side now." The rats began to speak amongst themselves, discussing the pros and cons of their stratagem.

Mother Gallo quivered. "Juniper!" she whispered. She waited in the shadows of the tunnel, not sure how to make herself known. The crowd of rats faced away from her. She could see only tails, backs, and shoulders. Juniper stood on a platform, well above the others, the only rat facing in her direction, just as captivating as he'd been all those years ago. It was little wonder why he was leader.

She exited the shadows and walked into the light. No one noticed her. Juniper carried on with the discussion, answering questions and listening to proposals. The meeting was an open forum. "Any other thoughts?" Juniper asked the assembly. Mother Gallo seized the opportunity.

"Juniper!" she called out, almost choking on the name. "I'm afraid time is *not* on your side." All heads turned towards her. "Minister Killdeer has moved up the Grand Speech. He knows something is afoot in the Combs. He has planned the speech for midnight—tonight—Rest Day. Killdeer is presenting your niece Clover to the Catacombs. She is to stand at his side. Afterwards, she is to carry out her Chosen One duties. You *must* get her out of the Combs tonight." The sight of Juniper pressed on her chest like a brick. She couldn't breathe. She couldn't move. Try as she might to hold back tears, her eyes grew wet, burning as she and Juniper locked eyes.

Everyone stared at her in silence. Juniper's confident expression dissolved. His mouth and ears dropped. His proud tail fell limply to the ground. He stood frozen on the platform. Looking towards the back of the room, he strained to see her. The assembled rats parted like cornstalks bending in the wind, all trying to catch a glimpse of the strange female rat.

"Madelina," whispered Juniper. "Maddy . . . is that you?" Juniper walked to the edge of the platform, grabbing Victor's shoulder for support as he bounded to the ground. He walked slowly to the back of the room. The fur on his neck bristled. He stopped just a step away from her, afraid to move any closer. "Madelina Bostwick, is it truly you?"

"Yes, Juniper—it's Maddy—it's me." She timidly reached out and touched his arm, feeling his wiry coat. She never thought she'd touch his disheveled mahogany fur again. She studied his face, muddled with scars, the patch over his eye. She winced, imagining the suffering he must have endured.

As if waking from the dead, Juniper's face burst into an exuberant smile, his eyes lit up with joy. "Maddy, my Maddy!" he shouted. He grabbed her shoulders, his heart racing as he felt her soft coat. "It's you! It really *is* you!" He threw his generous arms around her and hugged her tightly. Mother Gallo squealed in surprise as he plucked her off her feet.

Vincent and Victor observed the exchange. "Who *is* she?" asked Victor.

Cole, who was standing in between them, replied. "That's the love of old Juniper's life."

"Bostwick Hall," remembered Vincent. "I asked Juniper who Bostwick was, and he said a rat the Saints had other plans for."

"Yes, you're right. Maddy Bostwick, Juniper's Maddy. Juniper has several regrets in this life, as do we all, but his biggest regret was leaving his girl behind, letting her think him dead all this time. Those two were sweethearts up until the Coup. When Killdeer announced him dead and no one questioned otherwise, Juniper made the tough decision to let her be, to let her get on with her life. He knew it was safer for her that way. The *only* time I ever saw Juniper shed a tear was on Maddy's wedding day. She is his one true love."

Vincent thought about his father's theory on the subject of love. Juniper's world must be beginning and ending all in the same breath, just like his father had told him.

Juniper spoke rapidly, as if she might vanish into thin air if he stopped. "This is so hard to fathom, but it's really you! Maddy, how did you find me? So, you've met my niece, Clover—beauty, isn't she? What did you say about her? The moment I saw you, my ears stopped listening!" Juniper still held her firmly, fearful of letting her go. She gently pulled free, gathering herself and smoothing her tousled coat.

"Juniper," she said, "you must listen to me now. Clover's future depends upon it. She is in dire trouble and needs you desperately. Killdeer is giving his Grand Speech in Catacomb Hall *tonight* at midnight. For some reason he's moved up the date, deciding to present Clover to all of the Catacombs—to stand at his side—and to carry out her Chosen One duties immediately following the proceedings. The poor dear is petrified. She has no way out of her quarters. There is a Kill Army guard at her door at all times. No one is allowed in without direct authorization from Billycan. Juniper, something has to be done and done *now*."

"I should have known they'd pull something like this," said Juniper. "Maddy, how did you come to know all this? You must have risked your life getting this information from the Ministry." Mother Gallo's entire face fell. Her ears sagged downward in shame. "Madelina, what is it?"

"Juniper, the Ministry is my employer." She wrung her paws nervously. "I'm afraid . . . I'm afraid I work for them. I'm High Mistress of the Robes." Juniper listened, his face emotionless. "I despise the job, but by doing it, I've kept my children out of the Kill Army ranks and provided them with full bellies. After Mr. Gallo died, I didn't have a choice. If we had fled Topside, my family most certainly would not have survived."

Juniper remained silent for a moment, contemplating. He folded his arms, one paw covering his mouth, tapping his lips with his claws. His smile crept back. "Maddy, you have always been far too hard on yourself. Don't ever be ashamed of the choices you've made. You put your children first—your clan. There's no disgrace in that. You kept them safe—that's what a mother's supposed to do. Here you are after all this time trying to save what's left of *my* clan. You are an amazing rat, always have been." Mother Gallo grinned bashfully, her skin once again turning a ruddy pink.

"Maddy, I think you know the Council, all a little older now, but still the same lads you knew back in the Combs. We'll all catch up in due time." He smacked his paws together. "Well, now, we need to rally and get in front of this while we still have time," he said, glancing at the hourglass on the platform. "We must make haste. Virden, Ulrich, get word to Oard as fast as you can, within the hour if possible. Ragan, find out what you can from your informants: Why the sudden jump in Catacomb security? What, if anything, do they know about us? Cole, start going over the maps you and Virden drew up with Oard. We can start outlining a plan." He looked seriously at Vincent and Victor. "Boys, now is the time. I told you you'd prove yourselves useful sooner rather than later. Well, *sooner* is upon us. My niece is depending on me, and so I'm depending on you. We have only hours till midnight."

Mother Gallo stared intently at Juniper, transfixed. Never had he shone brighter than now, when all the stars aligned against him. Nothing could weaken his resolve, not with the last remnant of his clan on the line. He would not be the sole surviving Belancort.

* * *

Clover tossed restlessly, the speech only hours away. She lay in her parents' bed thinking about Mother Gallo. Where was she at that very moment? She should have insisted she stay in the Combs.

Clover left her bed and walked softly to the door. She listened for the guard but heard nothing. She decided she must force herself to eat again. She retrieved her razor blade and some cured meat and berries provided for her by the Ministry. She thought it was the least they could do, since they had imposed her house arrest.

Clover jumped, almost cutting herself with the blade. She heard a sudden commotion just outside her door, something that sounded like stumbling and then loud voices coming from farther down the corridor. She listened intently, trying to identify the rats. Billycan—nothing could muffle that serrated tone, erupting like acid from the back of his throat. The other voice belonged to the guard, Suttor. The last voice she did not recognize, at least not at first.

Suttor had bolted off his stool, nearly falling face-first into the dirt when he heard Billycan calling down the corridor. Billycan scowled at Suttor as he clumsily picked himself up off the ground.

"Well, boy, are we disturbing your nap?" asked Billycan.

"No—High Collector—sir—awake and on duty," Suttor replied uneasily.

"I wonder. . . . of no matter, Lieutenant Suttor. We are here to see Miss Clover, not you. Do announce us and open the door."

Suttor's eyes lingered over to the hulking figure next to Billycan. It was Killdeer. Suttor had never seen him up close. He was a mountain, tall like Billycan, but wide in every direction. Suttor felt sick. He tried to stop himself from stammering. "Yes, sir—right away, sir—right now." He spat nervously as he spoke, a childhood habit that came back when he panicked.

Billycan sneered. "Why, High Minister, I think you've impressed the lieutenant. He never slobbers like such a fool around me."

Killdeer laughed. He was in good humor and found the soldier's spluttering and tripping over himself in fear rather comical. "Calm yourself, boy," said Killdeer. He leaned against the corridor wall and lazily scraped a speck of old meat from under his claw. "Hurry, now, soldier, and tend to your duties." He nodded towards the door.

"Oh, yes! Yes, sir—High Minister—sir," said Suttor, trying to control his spittle. He knocked solidly on the door, ready to announce the High Minister, when Clover opened the door herself. She looked up at Killdeer with a coy smile. She had dressed in the sash and jewels Mother Gallo had left for her. Killdeer's eyes shone hungrily at the sight.

Clover had taken Mother Gallo's advice to heart: Be smart and play the part. Act as if she were the happiest girl in the Catacombs. Clover swallowed hard, summoning up her most demure voice. "Why, High Minister, I wasn't expecting you. What an honor. I was just trying on the lovely attire you have so graciously bestowed on me. I want to make sure I look perfect for you." She curtsied and bowed her head.

Billycan looked on skeptically. What was she up to? He cracked his jaw, thinking. He would find her out, he thought, all in due time.

Suttor felt deflated. He hadn't gotten to give the announcement at Clover's door. He tried to make up for it, clearing his throat importantly and declaring, "Presenting Miss Clover of Clan Belancort to High Minister Killdeer." He felt sufficiently redeemed, saluting Killdeer and Billycan.

"Thank you, Lieutenant Suttor." Killdeer's eyes did not waver from Clover. She shifted uncomfortably under his gaze. "That will be all for now, soldier. Run along with Billycan to the kitchen and get yourself some dinner." Killdeer waved his paw in Suttor's direction, shooing him away.

Suttor looked at him in stupefaction. Killdeer had addressed him by name! This was something to talk about. His brothers and the other soldiers would be gripped by his every word. This detail wasn't so boring after all. The High Minister knew his name!

Billycan felt uneasy about leaving Killdeer alone with the girl, unable to tell how much Oshi the immense rat had taken in, but the Collector was starving, and for now his hunger outweighed his worries of a scandal. "Now, boy, off to the kitchens. Billycan is famished. That crone of a cook better not have closed the kitchen early. Off we go. Our High Minister would like some privacy with Miss Belancort." Suttor did not respond. He stood starstruck, mesmerized by Killdeer. Billycan slapped Suttor viciously on the back of his head.

Suttor's ears rang from the blow. "I'm sorry, High Collector," he said.

"If you don't take your leave, you'll be more than sorry, Lieutenant Suttor." Suttor marched swiftly to the kitchen. Billycan trailed behind, thinking he might go mad if food did not pass his lips soon. His frustration with Killdeer did not help his surly mood. He would have some pigeon, custard, and bitonberry toast, then go straight back to Clover's to collect the Minister. In his inebriated state, it was not wise to let Killdeer stay too long. For now, he seemed easy to control, made pleasant and malleable by the drink. That could change—rapidly, depending on the quantity Killdeer had consumed. He had insisted on seeing Clover, assuring Billycan his manners would remain those of a respected Minister. Despite Billycan's recently wavering opinion of the High Minister, he wasn't about to challenge him outright—at least not yet.

* * *

Clover stood in the corridor with Killdeer. She watched helplessly as Suttor and Billycan's figures became smaller and smaller, eventually fading into the dark. Never did she imagine there would be a time when she wished for the return of Billycan.

Killdeer cleared his throat. He had an oily grin on his face. Clover forced herself not to draw back in distaste, remembering that she must act the part.

"Won't you come in, High Minister?" she asked softly. "You'll have to excuse my quarters. I'm afraid I don't have much to offer a rat such as you."

Killdeer snickered as he ducked under the doorway. "I'm sure you have *plenty* to offer me, my dear." Clover pretended not to hear the unseemly comment.

"Please, High Minister, sit anywhere you like. It's a bit chilly in the Combs today. Why don't I light the fire pit and make us something to eat?"

"That would be heavenly. Some dinner would do me wonders." Clover's stools were too small for Killdeer, so he sat on the floor across the fire pit from her. "Now, my dear, I think it's only fitting that you address me as Killdeer. After all, High Minister is a little too formal, given our situation, don't you think?"

Clover lit the dry kindling with a match. "Yes—Killdeer. If I may inquire, to what do I owe this visit?" she asked, desperately trying to keep him talking.

His tone was almost fatherly. "I thought it only appropriate that we get to know each other before my Grand Speech. I want you to be at ease standing by my side. Billycan says you're brighter than most, so I thought I should find out for myself. If you are as smart as you are pleasant to regard, I would be a fool not to investigate his claim, wouldn't I?" Killdeer stretched his body to its full length and leaned on an elbow. Clover didn't answer his question and continued to fuss over the fire. She could feel Killdeer's black eyes staring at her, pulsating against the flames, beating through her skin.

He reached for his silver medallion. It had warmed from the heat of the fire. He flipped it between his claws. Clover couldn't help but focus on it. "You like my silver medallion, do you?" He picked up the pendant, holding it with his claws, and tapped on the front of it. "You know who this is, don't you?"

"Why, yes, that's High Duchess Nomi," she replied.

"Yes, the High Duchess. Her reign was a long, long time ago. From what I've heard, she was rather astute for a female, not to mention lovely." He leaned in closer. "Have you ever thought about what it would be like to be the High Duchess of the Ministry?"

"Well—no, sir. My days revolve around collecting Stipend, chores, and taking care of my grandfather. I don't have time to think foolish thoughts of royal stations."

Killdeer pulled around the fire pit. Clover shrank back as he moved close. Grinning, he traced a circle on her shoulder with a black claw. She could make out the grooves in his incisors as his snout neared her face. He spoke in a deep whisper. "What if I told you you would never have to worry about any of those horrible chores again? No more toil, no more Stipend, no more worries over your guardian's well-being. What if I told you the High Ministry wanted a new High Duchess, that I wanted a new High Duchess—someone like *you*?"

For a moment, Clover questioned his sanity. What could he be speaking of? "Like me?" she asked, aghast at the idea. "I don't understand. Are you offering—are you asking me—" She couldn't form the words. "Minister, the whole idea of me—as a duchess—it's absurd!" He drew closer, slinking around the pit like a lion skillfully stalking its prey.

"You're smart. You're beautiful. What's absurd about that?" he purred.

"Minister, you don't even know me," she said, edging away from him.

"I'll get to know you. That's what this is all about, my dear, getting to know you. That's why I'm here." He lunged forward, startling her. She scrambled backwards towards the door, banging her back against it with a thud. Killdeer pounced. He loomed over her like a malicious storm cloud. His chest heaved. "Don't play modest, my sweet. That time has passed."

Clover pressed her eyes shut as he pushed closer, powerless against his size. Suddenly she felt something tugging on her neck, jerking her out by the scruff—out from under Killdeer. Her whole body lifted off the ground as she was yanked into the empty corridor.

Killdeer hit the floor hard, slamming his muzzle into the dirt. He looked up from the ground. There stood Billycan, his face resembling a barracuda's. He held Clover tightly by the scruff of her neck as she dangled off the ground. Killdeer leaped to his feet, humiliated. He did not speak.

Billycan glowered at him. "Billycan thinks Miss Clover needs to get some sleep, Minister," he said, clenching his jaw as he spoke. "She looks quite tired, and we want her to be fresh and rested for your Grand Speech. Now, run along, Clover dear. A nap will do you good."

He dropped Clover on her feet. She raced back into her quarters like a frightened rabbit. Billycan slammed the door behind her. His nostrils flared. He pointed a long, jagged digit at Killdeer, poking him hard in the chest. "What were you thinking?" he screamed. "Your subjects distrust you already. Such folly has brought down many an empire!"

Ignoring Billycan, Killdeer brushed the dirt from his coat and lumbered back towards his den. Billycan shadowed him. "A new High Duchess," he mumbled. "Billycan thinks not."

Clover leaned against the door, listening. They had departed. She slid to the ground as her heart slowed to a normal beat. She took off the jewelry, throwing it across the room. She pulled the pink sash over her head and set it on her lap. She turned the frock inside out, pulling out the razor blade she had hidden in the folds, which she was about to wield when Billycan came to her aid.

Since he could not protect her at all times, Juniper had trained his niece to slit a throat, but she was not eager to take a life, not even Killdeer's. A moment later and he would have been dead, bleeding out on the dirt floor of her quarters. She had Billycan to thank for saving her from that. How odd.

Ragan's Loyalist informant from inside the Combs said something was afoot, but he could get nothing from the sector majors, who were ordered to keep their mouths shut. All he could tell Ragan was that Catacomb security had doubled in all sectors and the Combs were on lockdown until further notice. No rat was allowed in or out without direct authorization from Billycan.

Virden and Ulrich returned to Nightshade Passage after tracking down Oard. Oard told them if someone could get to Clover's quarters in time and pound out the signal, they could dig a corridor from Nightshade City directly underneath. Virden calculated the time of the dig. He surmised that the rats and the earthworms could get the job done shortly before the Grand Speech, giving Clover just enough time for safe passage to Nightshade. The worms would stay after the rats departed, swiftly backfilling the hole—leaving the Ministry yet again clueless as to how its subjects were escaping.

Someone had to get to Clover as soon as possible. The vibrations had to start within the next few hours, or there would not be enough time. Juniper turned to Mother Gallo, his expression one of desperation. "Maddy, I need your help. I need you to go back to the Combs. If you can get to Clover's quarters and make the signal for Oard and his tribe, we may have a fighting chance. With your Ministry position, I fear you're the only one who can reenter the Combs safely. Will you do this for me?"

"Juniper, this is why I have come. I am here to help and do whatever you require."

"I thank you, Maddy. When we break through, you *must* go down the tunnel with us. You can live in Nightshade, never having to work for the Ministry again."

"I have three little boys at home. What shall I do with them?"

"You must all come to Nightshade," Juniper declared. He wanted Mother Gallo with him. He couldn't lose her a second time. His life was filled with regrets, but if he could rectify this one, perhaps his biggest regret of all, he could get part of his past back, part of the life he had before the Coup—before Billycan.

"I gladly accept your offer." She smiled. "We would be honored to come to Nightshade when the time is right."

"Maddy, Nightshade would be honored to have you." He gave a gentlemanly bow of his head. "Speaking of Nightshade. . . ." He looked over at the boys. "Vincent, Victor, come spare a few moments for Miss Bostwick." The boys had been sitting at the table with Cole, who'd been explaining a map of the Catacombs to them. He showed them how Nightshade's new corridors were silently intertwining with the Catacombs'. The brothers came over and stood next to Juniper, one on each side.

Mother Gallo needed to correct Juniper out of respect for her dead husband. "It's Gallo now, Juniper, not Bostwick. Everyone calls me Mother Gallo. I know it's a little old-fashioned, but it does me just fine."

"I think it suits you well," said Juniper. "May I still call you Maddy?"

"Yes, of course you may." She giggled.

"Well, boys, it's my pleasure to introduce Mother Gallo." He put a shaggy arm around each boy. "Mother Gallo, this is Vincent Nightshade and Victor, his younger brother, the only two survivors of the Nightshade Clan, the sons of Julius, to be exact, and recent escapees of the Catacombs."

"As I live and breathe," she exclaimed in astonishment, "I can't believe my eyes. All this time, and I had no idea you two were in the Combs. I knew you had gone missing during the flood. I heard you two were never found. If only I had known. I could have helped you."

"It's all right," said Vincent. "We purposefully kept to ourselves, trying to go unnoticed, avoiding trouble—and the majors."

"Smart, like your father," said Mother Gallo. "Just look at you." She grabbed Vincent's chin with her paw, turning his head from side to side, as if examining a fresh piece of produce. "Why, you're the spitting image of him. And look at those emerald eyes. You'll have all the girls flocking to you with those sparklers!" Vincent grinned shyly. "I knew your father well. He loved you children very much. And you, Victor, you have that same spark that Julius did. Your father always had that buzz about him that drew others to him. Use it wisely, my boy. It's a powerful gift." The boys smiled, pleased to know they each shared something of Julius.

"All right, then, everyone pay attention!" said Juniper. The Council and the others gathered round their leader. "Virden, I need you to teach Mother Gallo the vibration to signal the earthworms. She must be on her way back to the Combs without delay. Ulrich and Ragan,

Vincent and Victor, I want you four to lead the dig to Clover's quarters. We can get a good start before the worms arrive. Start in the corridor leading up to the Combs. Cole, show them on the map where they need to start digging and which direction to follow. The last thing we need is a tunnel to collapse, killing the lot of us. Cole and I will solidify the details of the maneuver. Everyone, we must hurry. I *won't* be the last of my clan. This *cannot* be the ending."

Everyone separated as instructed and got to their tasks. Juniper stood over the maps and blueprints Cole had laid out, scratching around the empty socket of his eye. His mounting anxiety caused him to perspire, irritating the scars under the patch. He always worked best under strain, but never had that strain been so dear to his heart.

Not looking up from the table, Cole spoke in a steady voice as they studied the maps. "Juniper, don't you worry," he said quietly. "You won't be the last of the Belancort Clan. There will be *no* ending tonight."

Virden worked with Mother Gallo on the signal for the earthworms. "Now, Maddy," he said, "you remember that ghoulish old tune from our childhood, 'The Feast of Batiste'?"

"Oh, dear," said Mother Gallo. "That ghastly rhyme, how could I forget? Why on earth did you choose something so morbid?"

Virden laughed. "I chose it merely because it's lively, clever, and simple to recall, although it did scare the tar out of me as a boy. My father told me if I didn't keep up with my studies, Batiste would get me! Needless to say, I learned my ABCs on the double—best in my class. I could never forget that grisly jingle."

"Nor could I," said Mother Gallo. "The ghostly rat named Batiste, who haunts the Catacombs, playing deadly tricks on its residents— positively chilling." She remembered the gruesome song well.

Batiste was killed on Hallowtide Night, while searching Topside
for sweet delight.
Batiste was killed at quarter past three, while searching for food
in the Battery.
Now he is lonely, now he is dead, now he pennies-and-pranks
for your tail and your head!

Virden gave Mother Gallo a heavy wooden mallet to pound out the song with. It seemed to pierce the soil the deepest, and the earthworms heard it sooner than other tools they'd tried. "Don't worry about hitting the dry ground of the Combs," he told her. "The worms will hear the sound, but rats cannot. The ground will absorb it, sending the signal directly to Oard's tribe."

The time for the dig to commence had arrived. The two sets of brothers, Vincent and Victor, Ragan and Ulrich, were ready to lead the dig. The excavation would start in Nightshade Passage's unfinished corridor, which led up to the Catacombs. They would begin digging through the east wall of the incomplete tunnel. Going by Virden's maps and word from Oard's tribesmen, Cole showed the foursome where to best initiate the dig to avoid a deadly cave-in.

Vincent dove in first, swiftly burrowing through Nightshade's soft, healthy soil. Victor followed his brother's lead, pulling out mounds of dirt, gouging into the earth with his claws. Using their hind legs, Ragan and Ulrich started kicking the upturned soil down the length of the corridor at breakneck speed. More rats were positioned at the entrance, lined up with several wheelbarrows, ready to remove the earth from the corridor.

For now the digging was effortless, the soil in Nightshade fresh and pliable. Much of the upturned earth could be pressed into the walls, helping to shape the newly formed corridor. The dirt of the

Catacombs was dry and powdery, useless for rebuilding. Most of it would need to be removed, a time-consuming process. More teams of rats would soon join them to help in the effort. It would be a long, dirty dig.

As the excavation progressed, Ragan and Ulrich's slate-blue coats became solidly blackened with dirt, making it hard to tell the team of four apart, barring Vincent's green eyes and Ulrich's stubby tail.

Virden brought Mother Gallo back to Juniper for further instruction. "Well, Juniper, I think our pupil knows what she's doing," Virden told him.

"She always was a sharp one," said Juniper.

Virden, much larger than Mother Gallo, bent down and took her paw in his, patting it gently. "Maddy, I'm sure the Saints will guide you safely back to the Combs and then back to us."

"Of course they will," she said. "How else am I to take part in one of your memorable Oshi toasts?"

"It's so good to have you back," he said with a smile. With a quick bow of his head, Virden left her and Juniper alone.

She looked over the room with everyone working feverishly. "Juniper, you have a good group here. You should be proud of all this, your Council, your city—it's quite an accomplishment."

"I'm afraid we're not finished yet. You're right, though, I've been blessed in my friendships. There's not a bad apple in the bunch." Juniper exhaled heavily. He smiled briefly, trying to hide his dread. "Now, Maddy, may I suggest an escort back to Ashbury Lane? I think it would be best."

She adjusted her sash as she prepared for her departure. "I'm not as worried about my well-being as I am of getting out of that house. It's built like a stronghold, a far cry from the ramshackle apartments in the Battery District."

"Don't worry too much about that. This Topside family seems to go in and out at all hours, always with one errand or another." Juniper looked at the hourglass again. "You shouldn't have much trouble, but I would feel better if someone escorted you, at least until you arrive at the earthworms' corridor. I would go myself, but I can't risk the time away from the dig. I'll send Cole or Virden with you."

"I can handle myself Topside, and I doubt you can spare either of them. I'm not that silly girl you remember. You don't need to worry about me. I'll be fine."

"You'll always be that silly girl to me," he said tenderly.

"Juniper, I'm a mother and a godmother. I can take care of myself—always have."

He chuckled as he inspected her sash adorned with needles and scissors. "All right, then, Maddy, you win. Off you go! Here is my satchel." He gently put it over her head.

She examined the ragged leather bag, a gift she had made for him. "I can't believe you kept this. It's practically falling to pieces—are you still so sentimental about this old thing?"

"You gave it to me. I'll wear it till it turns to dust! You can put that cumbersome mallet inside, and please take something to eat. I don't want you wasting away on me." He smiled at her. "Please be careful. I need to see you again."

She took his paw, squeezing it tight. "Now, Juniper, you'll see me and that girl of yours soon—not to worry."

She grabbed a few chunks of cheese and put them in the satchel. The bag felt comforting across her frame, easily molding to her form. Its weathered exterior and fusty scent matched its owner, as if Juniper were traveling with her the whole way. She turned to go. Juniper abruptly grabbed her, and pulling her close, he embraced her firmly.

She smelled his fur, burying her head in his shoulder. Neither uttered a word.

She pulled away and headed up the corridor back into the house on Ashbury Lane. Juniper watched as she faded into the dark.

Mother Gallo galloped most of the way Topside, reentering the brownstone through Juniper's hole, and back into the art studio. Catching her breath, she scaled up the arm of a wing chair and looked out the window onto the lane. It couldn't be too late in the evening, as cars were whizzing down the residential street, so she surmised she had made good time.

She scurried over to the door, the same one she'd squeezed under earlier. Noises came from the other side, thunderous crashes and booms, intermixed with shouting. Her heart raced for a moment before she realized that the clamor came from a television. She laughed. She had forgotten about Topsiders and their televisions.

She peered under the door. She couldn't see any Topsiders in the darkened hallway. As she scanned what she could see of the family room, she quickly spotted a tuft of red hair hanging off the couch, nearly touching the floor. She strained to see more, fearing it might be a tabby or even a red collie, but to her relief the hair belonged to a small Topsider. She could see its freckled forehead and its blue eyes, staring at the television—upside down. She remembered the Topside man from last night and his wave of ruby hair. *Must be his child*, she thought.

The child's head sank closer to the floor. He watched cartoons, hanging upside down on the couch, his face getting ruddier with each passing second.

A male voice yelled from the second floor. "Ramsey," it said cheerfully, "time to go. Come upstairs and wash your hands and face." The boy didn't move. "C'mon, Ramsey, get off the couch, lazy bones. We're going to Marbagold's to buy some gifts for Saints' Day. They're open late tonight for all the last-minute shoppers. If we hurry, we might have time to stop by the toy department!" Hearing the last part, the boy, Ramsey, leaped off the couch and dashed up the stairs.

Mother Gallo listened carefully. She heard muffled voices and footsteps, the floorboards creaking above her. She poked her head under the door. It looked and sounded as though all the Topsiders were upstairs. She swiftly took off her sash and Juniper's bag and once again squeezed under the door's gap. She re-dressed and dashed to the house's main entrance.

Hiding behind a white pillar nearest the front door, she saw the boy bounding down the stairs and diving back onto the couch to watch some more television.

Again, the father shouted down the stairs, this time a little irritated. "Ramsey, I told you, no more TV! Turn it off and get your boots on. Your mother put them in the vestibule. If you don't do what you're told, you can forget about the toy department!" Ramsey made a sour face in the direction of the stairs and begrudgingly shut off the television.

He sluggishly walked towards the front door. Wasting no time, Mother Gallo seized the opportunity to take her leave. The boy grabbed the doorknob leading out to the vestibule and pulled hard. The door creaked open, and the child tiptoed into the small foyer to grab his shoes. As he bent down for his boots, Mother Gallo darted in behind him. She ducked under the doorsill and out of sight. The boy snatched his shoes and hopped back into the main house.

A female voice called down this time. "Ramsey, can you get my umbrella? They say more rain."

Mother Gallo heard the boy's feet drumming against the marble floor, racing back in her direction. He popped back into the drafty foyer, grabbed his mother's umbrella off the floor, and quickly whirled around. Still only in his socks, he slipped on the tile floor, falling on his belly, now eye level with the doorsill—eye level with Mother Gallo.

Their eyes locked. The boy gawked at the plump gray rat. His carroty hair, a mess of curls, matched his ginger freckles. His blue eyes stayed glued to her. He held his breath, as if exhaling might set off an attack.

Mother Gallo stayed calm. *He's just a little one,* she told herself, putting aside the fact that he outweighed her at least tenfold. She thought of her own little boys at home in the Catacombs. How different could little boys be? She smiled at him, not sure if a Topsider could pick up on a rat's smile, but she smiled just the same. She held out the edges of her blue sash and curtsied.

Ramsey's eyes widened. He stared in awe, then whispered to himself, "An underground rat—it must be! The Trillium legend is true. Dad was wrong!"

Ramsey had recently watched what was, to him, a gripping documentary about the alleged super rats that lived deep under Trillium in a web of secret tunnels. The creepy host interviewed several eccentric-looking Topsiders. All claimed the myth of the Trillium rats to be no myth at all. Ramsey was especially taken by a chisel-chinned archaeologist who dressed as if on safari, looking more like an action hero than a man who dug in the dirt. He swore the rats were real—a booming metropolis of vermin with humanlike intellect, directly under Trillium citizens' feet. Ramsey's father said it was just a ridiculous urban legend and that the so-called witnesses were nothing more than a bunch of crackpots and charlatans. Ramsey couldn't wait to tell his father how wrong he was.

Ramsey sat up on his knees and cautiously studied Mother Gallo, scrutinizing every inch of her. Mother Gallo edged towards the main door; long, narrow windows bordered each side. She rapped on a window and pointed to the outside.

"The window, what about the window?" asked Ramsey. Mother Gallo tapped on the window again, pointing animatedly out to the street. "Outside, is that what you're pointing to?" Mother Gallo jumped up and down. "You want to go out there?" She nodded. Ramsey scratched his head with a slight look of disappointment. "Will you come back if I let you out?"

Mother Gallo nodded yes, and then she reached into Juniper's satchel. She pulled out a tiny piece of cheese and held it out to the boy. He gingerly took it from her small paw. "Cheese!" he said elatedly. "I knew rats loved cheese! Thank you."

She tapped on the door, clicking it lightly with a claw. "Oh," he said, "the door! Let me help you with that!"

He turned the dead bolt and cracked open the door. The cold night air rushed in through the small opening, stealing Mother Gallo's breath for a moment. With no time to waste, she waved to the boy and darted down the stairs and across the street, pushing against the blustery gust. She heard the boy run into his house, yelling up the stairs, "Mom, Dad—you'll never believe me—never!" His voice faded as Mother Gallo crossed the street.

A blue moth followed her to the entrance of the Combs. It spun around her head, trying to get her to pay it some attention. With the sudden cold, she was surprised to see it still alive, let alone so energetic. She shooed it away. Moths were sweet, dumb creatures, but she didn't have time for pleasant exchanges. The deadline was looming.

Oard and his earthworm tribe had arrived to finish the job. Ragan and Ulrich doggedly moved the earth out of the corridor and directed the others, while Vincent and Victor kept digging, the vitality of youth on their side. All four were caked with a thick coating of dirt.

Ulrich trudged down the corridor with a full wheelbarrow. Oard suddenly poked his head through the wall. "Hello, there," he said in his raspy tone. Ulrich jumped in fright, knocking over the wheelbarrow and falling face first into the tilled earth.

"Oard," shouted Ulrich, "don't do that! I nearly leaped out of my skin!" He got up and shook the dirt from his head.

"Sorry about that, old boy. Are you all right?"

Ulrich laughed in spite of himself. "Yes, bright-eyed and bushy-tailed, what's left of it, anyway! We're all just a bit on edge and getting sore."

"Well, the entire tribe is here now, ready to take over. So everyone can breathe easier for a while. From what I sensed on the way over, you've done quite a bit of excavation, much more than we expected. This should save us a good deal of time."

"You have Vincent and Victor to thank for that," said Ulrich. "I've never seen two rats dig like that."

"Vincent and Victor—who might they be?" asked Oard.

"Oh, I suppose you haven't heard. Those two lads are the last known members of Clan Nightshade—sons of Julius. They're the reason that I'm not flat on my back right now."

"The sons of Julius," said Oard, "how extraordinary. Point me in their direction. I would like to meet them."

"Go up a ways. Trust me, you'll hear them, still digging away. Those boys must be about to break. I'm sure they'll be happy for your tribe's help."

Oard sped through the soil.

* * *

The brothers ignored their throbbing arms and backs and wiped away the itchy dirt that assaulted their ears and nostrils. Victor paused for a moment. A tiny pebble had lodged under his claw, making its digit swell. He leaned against the wall of the corridor, trying to pick it out. Oard popped his head out of the wall, nearly knocking into Victor, who flew backward in surprise, slamming himself against the opposing wall.

Oard was straightforward as always. "Did I startle you? I'm sorry. Apparently, I have a habit of doing that. Which one are you, Vincent or Victor?" Victor stared curiously at the earthworm. He'd never seen one before, and such a meaty one at that.

"I'm Victor," he replied guardedly. "Who are you?"

"Victor, I am Oard, tribal leader of the earthworms. I knew your late father. I'm glad to hear your voice. It reminds me of his. We all miss him very much."

"I wish I could remember him the way everyone else seems to," said Victor.

"It must be difficult for you, but if anyone can tell you stories about your father, it's Juniper. By the way, I'm curious as to how you found him," said Oard.

"Dumb luck," said Victor. "We found the entrance to the city by mistake. We thought maybe it was an abandoned hole, somewhere we could live."

"Interesting," said Oard. "It seems our most pivotal moments happen by mere coincidence—some would call that fate. You'll have to excuse me, Victor—I ramble off-point. There is much to be done. We can get philosophical on the subject another day. Time is of the essence for Juniper's niece. Now, where is that brother of yours, Vincent, is it? I'd like to meet him—always smart to know your team."

"Vincent," shouted Victor up the corridor, "can you come here for a moment?"

"In a minute," answered Vincent. "The earth is getting a bit harder up here." He grunted as he jerked out a considerable clump of soil.

Vincent marched down the corridor. "What is it?" he asked, out of breath. Victor stayed silent, looking at his brother mischievously. Vincent quickly noticed something moving from the wall. He slowly turned and saw Oard's coppery head sticking out. He jolted, turning to his brother in alarm.

Victor broke out in a toothy grin, snickering. "Vincent," said Victor, trying hard to hold his laughter in, "this is Oard. He is the leader of the earthworms and is going to be heading up the rest of the dig."

"Oh, yes—Oard," said Vincent, glaring at his chuckling brother. "Juniper told us all about you."

"He knew Father," said Victor.

"Vincent, it's a pleasure to meet you." Oard's voice echoed through the corridor. "Your father was special, an exceptional rat. He did a lot for you rats, and for my tribe as well."

Vincent wiped the sweat from his eyes. He quickly changed the subject. "Thank you, Oard, but we must get back to digging."

"Not right now, you won't," said Oard firmly. "I want you boys to get some rest, have something to eat. My tribe can take over. We'll send word when we need you. That's an order." He paused before fading back into the wall. "By the way, boys, Nightshade is a fine name for our new city—the best of the lot."

The earthworm corridor was silent, as Mother Gallo made her way back to the Catacombs. On her way Topside, she had heard Oard's tribe talking and moving through the soil. Now she heard nothing. "They must be to Juniper by now," she said to herself.

"I'm not," said a faint voice.

Mother Gallo recognized the squeaky pitch. "Cherrytin, is that you?"

"Yes," she answered in a crestfallen sigh. "They wouldn't allow me to go."

"I'm sure it's for the best, dear. They were probably just worried about you. It's a long trip, and I'm sure Oard and the rest of your family didn't want you to get lost or hurt. Are any of your brothers and sisters here with you?"

"A few, but they are mad at me," replied Cherrytin.

"Mad—at you? Why would they be mad at you?"

"They said if I were bigger they would have gotten to help, but instead they're stuck here with me." Mother Gallo swore she heard Cherrytin sniffle. She didn't think earthworms *could* sniffle, but who knew for sure?

"Well, Cherrytin, sometimes brothers and sisters don't understand how hard it is being the smallest. For now, don't you worry about it. You'll grow," she said reassuringly. "Now, Cherrytin, I've got to hurry back to Catacomb Hall. Would you like to accompany me? I would love to have someone to talk to, especially you. We can talk about anything you like."

Cherrytin's demeanor shifted. "Can we talk about our new home?"

"Why, of course we can. I'll tell you all about Nightshade City."

"Nightshade City," Cherrytin repeated. "I like that name! Everyone will call me Cherrytin of Nightshade."

Mother Gallo laughed. "C'mon then, Cherrytin of Nightshade, we've a long way to go."

The earthworms were making short time of the dig, plowing through the earth at a healthy speed. Teams of rats carried full wheelbarrows of dirt out of the corridor, while Virden, Cole, and a crew of big-shouldered fellows packed as much soil as they could into the newly-formed tunnel, strengthening its walls.

Oard directed his tribe, his gruff voice bouncing off the corridor walls. "Forge through the soil!" he shouted. "Forget your training, no time for exactness, no need for symmetry. Momentum is the key. Our velocity cannot wane! Drill through, worms—drill through!"

Vincent and Victor joined Ulrich and Ragan at a table, all four taking their mandated rest, as the others worked the tunnel. Both sets of brothers were encrusted with dirt and were as hungry as they were filthy. Thankfully, Cole's wife, Lali, had baked a slew of egg custards for the occasion.

"How does Lali find the time to do all this?" asked Vincent, cramming his mouth with an oversized spoonful of custard. "Never in my life have I seen so much pastry."

"Well, she sleeps only a few hours a night," said Ragan. "She hasn't always been that way. You see . . . her and Cole, they will never be blessed with family—mind you, not for lack of trying. That's the reason she never sleeps. She is brokenhearted over the matter. Cole always wanted little ones, children he could raise properly, in a real family, something he never had after his parents passed on. When Cole dwells on the topic, he turns dark and gloomy—won't talk to anyone."

Ulrich nodded in Lali's direction. "Our Lali is quite the opposite. She rushes about, doing a hundred chores in a day. She turns her sorrow outward—into this," he said, holding up his ramekin of custard.

Mother Gallo had reached the Catacombs. "Cherrytin, it looks as though you've seen me through. I can't thank you enough for your company. Now, listen closely. I need you to track down one of your siblings to send to Nightshade. I need to let Juniper know I've arrived safely and am on my way to Clover's quarters. Do you think you can do that for me?"

"Yes, Mother Gallo," Cherrytin replied. "I'll find Quip, my oldest brother. He's the fastest of us."

"Off you go. Ask Quip to go as fast as he can! Cherrytin, I must leave you now."

"Good-bye, Mother Gallo. Be careful," said Cherrytin.

Mother Gallo dropped from the hole into the alley behind Ellington's and crept around the tavern. Catacomb Hall was quiet, apart from a group of laborers decorating for the Grand Speech, now just a few hours away.

The laborers were hanging rich fabric swags in Ministry colors, crimson and navy, intertwined with shiny silver garland. Killdeer's mark was sewn in the center of each drapery. *How ironic,* she thought, staring up at them. She had done the stitching herself.

After leaving the hall, Mother Gallo raced through the maze of corridors, finally making her way to Clover's sector, all the while singing the earthworms' song to herself in a whisper. " 'Batiste was killed on Hallowtide Night, while searching Topside for sweet—' "

Turning a corner, she smacked right into Billycan, banging her nose into his rock-hard torso. She winced in pain. "Collector, you scared me half to death," she said, clutching her nose. "Your chest is like cast iron."

Billycan had no misgivings when it came to the High Mistress of the Robes. She did as ordered and did it well. "High Mistress, let me check that for you," he said. He took her muzzle in the tips of his claws. Pointing her jaw upwards, he examined her nose, poking it with a yellowed nail. His eyes churned, folding into different shades of red, as he inspected her injury. His face was so close, she could feel his dank breath intermingling with hers, assaulting her senses.

He released her. "You'll be fine, High Mistress. Maybe a lingering twinge, no more than that."

"I suppose I need to slow down," she said, trying to act at ease. "It's just that I've been in such a harried state today. I've been rushing all over, making sure all is perfect for the Grand Speech. I suppose I haven't been paying much attention to where I'm going. Right now, I'm on my way to the see the Belancort girl to double-check her garments before I escort her to the speech. You know how the young ones are, careless when it comes to their appearance."

"Ah, yes, our little Chosen One. The Minister visited his new beloved just a few hours back, as a matter of fact. Miss Clover has already modeled her attire for him. He was impressed with your choices, those emeralds especially."

Billycan's statement disturbed her. She knew too well of Killdeer and his *visits*. She kept her poise. "How wonderful for her. I'm sure it thrilled her to no end."

A subtle smirk branched across the Collector's face. "Yes, something like that," he said with a satisfied air. He motioned down Clover's corridor with a spidery digit. "Run along, Mistress. Billycan does not want to keep you from your duties."

About to turn the corner, he abruptly doubled back. "Wait," he commanded. He eyed Juniper's satchel, cocking his head as he scrutinized it. "Where did you get that?"

"Oh, this horrid old thing?" she answered nonchalantly. "It belongs to Clover's grandfather, that sickly old one, Timeron. I'm afraid things look grim for him, and Clover fears he won't be coming back from the healer alive. The dear asked me if I could fix his satchel for her. The strap had broken a while back, and she begged me to mend it. She would like to wear it in his memory. It's all she has left of him. How could I refuse?"

Billycan lifted the bag to his snout as it hung from Mother Gallo's neck. He inhaled. "The scent eludes me," he said crossly. "Billycan has smelled this exact odor before, and not from the old one, Timeron. It's someone else entirely. I have the niggling feeling someone is mocking me." His chin stiffened, cracking with a hollow pop.

"Who would dare mock you—the little girl, the old one? No one would chance provocation from a Ministry official, especially you, High Collector." She gently took the bag from him. "These items tend to change owners many times over. You know how it works in Catacomb Hall. Clover's grandfather might have traded it with some fellow or purchased it from a peddler. Maybe you *did* know the rat who once owned this satchel. Scents are tricky things. They overlap and mingle, changing over time."

"Perhaps you make sense," he said, peering at the bag once more. "I have no doubt I will soon remember. Off with you, then. Your girl is waiting." He wiggled a claw at her. "Mistress, do mind where you're going and stop your singing. The Minister would be most upset to learn that his seamstress suffered injury on account of Batiste." He sauntered around a corner and out of sight.

Mother Gallo leaned against the corridor wall for support, feeling she might faint dead away from the encounter.

Suttor stood aslant at Clover's door, so tired that he dared not crouch on his heels or sit on his stool. He would surely nod off, a serious offense if spotted. Unable to stand much longer, his spine throbbed. While he was supposed to be resting, he stayed up with his brothers and the other soldiers instead, telling one and all about his auspicious meeting with Killdeer. Now in pain, he twisted and squirmed uncomfortably, trying in vain to realign his vertebrae. His once-easy task had become torturous.

Mother Gallo came rushing down the corridor. Suttor moaned in agony under his breath as he compelled himself to uncurl, reclaiming proper military stance. "Good evening, High Mistress," he said hoarsely.

She mustered up a merry smile. "Now, Suttor, what did I tell you about addressing me? Please, let's stop with these silly formalities."

"Sorry, Mother Gallo," he replied dimly. He swayed a little, still trying to stand straight.

"That's all right, lad. How are you today? You're looking worn, rather peaked around the eyes." Mother Gallo retrieved a piece of cheese from Juniper's bag. She placed it in Suttor's paw. "Eat this, please. I know it's no substitution for rest, but it's better than nothing at all."

"Thank you, Mother Gallo. I could really use something to eat." He dropped back against the wall for a moment. "I have not had any sleep."

"That's certainly plain to see. Billycan had you here all this time, with no other soldier to relieve you?"

"The High Minister came round dinnertime, and he and the Collector sent me on my way. My fatigue is of my own doing. I was told to sleep, but couldn't do so after meeting the Minister—too excited, I suppose. Mother Gallo, Minister Killdeer spoke to *me*. He said my name."

"Suttor, you do realize Killdeer is just a rat, just like everyone else? In the grand scheme of life, he's no more valuable than you or I."

"It sure doesn't feel that way," he said with a yawn, opening Clover's door for her.

"I know, boy. It never does."

Clover huddled in her parents' bed, buried under her mother's coverlet. Mother Gallo would have thought the room empty if she hadn't spotted the tip of Clover's creamy tail peeking out from under the covers.

She leaned over Clover, speaking in a whisper. "Clover, are you all right?" She sat on the edge of the bed and gently lifted the blanket off Clover's face. Clover sat up and hugged her, unable to speak just yet. "Dear, it's all right now. It's all right. We have a way out. Everything is going to be fine. I promise." Mother Gallo adjusted the fur on Clover's head, smoothing it out as her mother had done for her. "What happened here?"

Clover wiped her eyes. "Thankfully nothing—Billycan came to my aid, if you can believe it. He pulled me away from the Minister just in time. Of all the rats—at first I thought the Saints had come to rescue me, but it was him, of all the rats, who helped me."

"Billycan or not, we'd best thank our lucky stars. Billycan will do anything to avoid a scandal. The Ministry's reputation is far too fragile. Now, listen closely. I found Juniper. He is doing everything within his power to get you out. The rats and the earthworms are tunneling through. Time is precious, so listen well. As we speak, a corridor is being dug right to your quarters—right up through the ground. Once they've broken through, you'll be on your way to your new home."

Mother Gallo pulled out the mallet from Juniper's satchel. "A Council member, Virden, has taught me a tune I'm to pound on the ground with this mallet. It's from an old children's song—'The Feast of Batiste.' It's a nasty little jingle from the old ones' era, but it's witty and quick, easy for the worms to pick up through the soil. You and I will pound out the beat. Now take this." She handed Clover Juniper's leather satchel. "Put the few things you can't live without inside it. I'm afraid everything else must stay put. I'll start the signal, which you'll need to learn, so listen closely as you pack your things. My arms will only last so long."

Mother Gallo sang softly as she began to beat the earth with the mallet. Clover listened to the morbidly clever words. She placed the few small mementos she had left of her parents and brothers in Juniper's bag. She wondered if there was any truth to the grisly tale of Batiste.

The dig had been at a standstill. Oard surmised they had gone as far as they could without wasting precious time and energy digging in an unknown direction. Juniper worked in the tunnel with Oard, waiting for word. No longer able to hide his dread, he paced the unfinished corridor, cursing under his breath.

"I should have gone with her myself," groaned Juniper. "I should have sent someone with her. She could be trapped in that house, or worse. I knew it was a bad decision to send her alone. They are *both* lost to me now. It's too late! I know it to be true."

Oard could hear Juniper panting, his rat heart racing. The earthworm spoke bluntly. "Juniper, if I could shake you by your shoulders, I would. Calm yourself—you must! All will be well. Mother Gallo is perfectly competent. She found a way out. I'm sure of it. You need to get hold of your emotions or you're no good to any of us."

Juniper growled and sat down in the corridor. Frustrated, he put his paws on his knees, exhaling long and hard. He closed his eyes and prayed.

Oard felt rapid movement in the wall as one of his tribesmen raced toward them through the soil. "Someone's coming, hopefully with word."

Noc, Oard's second-in-command, poked his head through the dirt. "Oard, Quip has reported Mother Gallo to be back in the Combs. She is with the girl. We have picked up her signal farther ahead. We need to keep digging east until we can decipher the exact coordinates."

"Juniper, call out to your teams," shouted Oard. "Let's get this dig back under way!"

The worms and rats moved quickly through the dry earth, grinding through the chalky dirt of the Catacombs with renewed vitality. Rats had broken claws and sprained limbs, swollen eyes and nostrils inflamed with dust, but still no one showed signs of slowing down.

Clover pummeled the ground with such resolve that Mother Gallo was afraid she might injure herself.

Mother Gallo rubbed her arms and paws, aching from the many jarring blows with the mallet. She peered vigilantly under the door's gap. All she could see were Suttor's black and white feet. If they were discovered after the Nightshade rats had broken through, one and all would surely be killed. Nightshade City would easily be found, straight down the tunnel, and all hope would be lost.

Without warning, an earthworm's head popped up through the floor, so near to Clover that she almost flattened it with the mallet. Startled, she stopped hammering and scrambled backward, letting out a short yelp. The earthworm shook his head like a wet canine, showering Mother Gallo and Clover with small clumps of earth.

The worm spoke politely, his tone refined: "I'm dreadfully sorry if I frightened you. Did I strike you with dirt? It gets in my mouth. It makes it difficult to speak properly, so please do excuse me. Miss Clover, is it?"

"Yes, I'm Clover."

"Very good. I am Noc, Oard's second-in-command. I bring word from Juniper. We should be through to you in under an hour's time." He turned. "Mother Gallo, I presume you are here as well?"

"Yes, Noc, a pleasure to meet you," she said.

"Thank you, Mother Gallo. Now, ladies, I would love nothing more than to stay and chat, but regrettably we all need to get back to our duties. Now that we've found your coordinates, you two need no longer strike the ground. Clover, please have yourself ready for departure. Good-bye for now." His russet head dissolved back into the ground, and his voice faded down the tunnel. "I'll be back before long."

As they waited, Mother Gallo prepared herself for questioning. She would be the last one to see Clover in the Combs. She would need to account for her actions and whereabouts. Billycan would undoubtedly interrogate her. How would she explain things? The most logical choice was to tell Billycan she left Clover ready for the Grand Speech and the girl escaped before she came back to escort her at midnight. She then realized she hadn't taken Suttor into account. He would be the scapegoat, blamed for the Chosen One's exodus, or even worse, found to be a guilty party, involved in a plot to help her escape. Without a doubt, execution would be his punishment. She racked her brain for a solution.

They heard a sudden thud outside Clover's door, and then dead silence. Mother Gallo put a claw to her lips. Clover stood motionless. Mother Gallo listened at the door. She heard nothing. She crouched down and looked through the gap. Suttor lay unconscious, sprawled out on the floor, his limp body pressing against the door.

Mother Gallo opened the door. "Clover, we must get him inside—quickly, child! You grab one arm, I the other."

Suttor had collapsed, no longer able to fight his fatigue. He'd cut his head on the stool, and a lump was forming there as well. Blood trickled down the side of his face. They dragged the rat into Clover's quarters and shut the door. Clover grabbed her mother's coverlet and balled it under Suttor's head.

"You won't be needing this anymore," said Mother Gallo. She took the sash she had given Clover to wear for the Grand Speech and blotted Suttor's swelling wound. The pink fabric quickly turned a murky crimson.

"Here," said Clover. She retrieved the remainder of her waterchip root, unwrapping it from a piece of burlap.

Mother Gallo waved it under Suttor's nose. Its pungent, vinegary smell served as a remedy used to revive the faint or wounded. Suttor slowly came to and opened his bleary eyes. He sneezed at the strong scent, which caused his head to pound. He sat up and felt a tender bump.

"My head," he said throatily. "Where am I?"

"Suttor, it's Mother Gallo. You're in Clover's quarters. We found you bleeding outside the door. Do you remember anything?"

Suttor began to focus. Seeing Clover and Mother Gallo staring at him, he quickly sat up as straight as he could, clearly pretending he wasn't in pain.

"Suttor, relax, dear—no need for that military nonsense," said Mother Gallo. "We know it must hurt. Now, try and remember what happened."

Suttor, far too drained to feign strength, gladly leaned back on the coverlet. "I was standing in front of the door, wondering how I was going to sit through the Grand Speech without falling asleep. That's all I remember. Now I'm here."

Mother Gallo patted his leg. "Suttor, I think you fell asleep on your feet. Sit here and rest for a moment. If Billycan comes looking for you, I'll tell him I needed your assistance, which is why you are in here now. You're simply overtired, dear. Nothing bad will come of this. I'll see to that."

Clover had given him the remainder of her Ministry-provided rations. "Here, eat this while you rest," she said.

"Thank you," he said softly, a bit humiliated over the incident. What she must think of him, he thought. He began to eat. It felt good to be off his feet, even for a few moments.

"How does your head feel?" asked Mother Gallo.

"It feels a little sore. Once I get some sleep, I'm sure I'll be as good as new." He slowly rose to his feet. "I should be getting back to my post. You two have been of great help, thank you, but I'm sure I've wasted enough of your valuable time."

Suttor bowed to Mother Gallo. As he bent down, the blood rushed to his head. He staggered, then fell to the ground. Mother Gallo tried rousing him again, but the waterchip proved useless. He was immobile.

They felt a disturbance below their feet. The ground started to rumble. Clover's fire pit sank into the earth, disappearing altogether. Suttor lay near the door, undisturbed by the noise. Two burly, dark paws appeared from where the fire pit had been, hastily ripping down more chunks of hardened dirt.

Juniper pulled himself up through the opening and spotted his niece. "There's my girl!" he said, relieved. He whisked Clover up off her feet, hugging her tightly as he balanced her on his arm.

"Uncle, you're filthy," she giggled.

"I suppose I am," he said, laughing quietly. He stepped towards Mother Gallo, Clover still sitting on his arm. "Thank you, Maddy. Thank you for this." He nodded towards Clover.

"I think this one was worth the trouble," she said, squeezing Clover's foot. Clover smiled happily for what seemed like the first time since Mother Gallo had met her.

Juniper set Clover on her feet and peered at Suttor, out cold on the floor. "Who's this poor fellow?"

"This is Suttor," said Mother Gallo. "I knew his late parents.

He's a Kill Army soldier, but a good boy just trying to raise his two brothers. His youngest brother is still a baby, the same age as my son Hob. Suttor was posted to guard Clover's door, but he fell in the corridor, hitting his head. We revived him once already, but now he's down for the count."

Juniper examined him. "That's a sizable cut he's got, but his breathing is strong, as is his heartbeat. I think he's more asleep than unconscious."

"Our plan has put him in harm's way, and I don't know how to keep him safe," said Mother Gallo. "If we leave him here, I'm afraid he will meet a terrible end. He will be blamed for this. Suttor is ambitious, that I know, but only for the sake of his brothers. He's just another misplaced boy, trying to make sense of his circumstances."

Juniper scratched his chin and regarded the fallen rat. He glanced at his niece. It was clear what had to be done. "No one will be harmed this evening. Tonight, our population grows by two."

CHAPTER FIVE
Alive!

THE GRAND STAGE was set up at the end of Catacomb Hall in front of the horseshoe of establishments, including Ellington's Tavern.

Billycan meticulously examined the hall, making sure the laborers had done as instructed for the approaching Grand Speech. He had soldiers posted throughout the hall to ensure that none of the workforce were lackluster in their duties.

The laborers had been working since early morning and were just finishing up with the decoration. They chatted amongst themselves as they worked, discussing rumors of a big announcement. Billycan strolled from group to group, inspecting their handiwork and eavesdropping on their conversations.

"Well, you heard the rumor, didn't ya?" said a lanky, undernourished rat to his much smaller, equally scrawny associate.

"No, what's the gossip?" said the other, not looking up from his work.

"Rumor from the troops is Killdeer is announcing a new High Duchess."

"You don't say. A new High Duchess? Well, I'll be! So, who is this mystery girl? Who is to be our new esteemed duchess? Don't leave me standing here, holding my tail!"

"That's the kicker," said the taller rat. He smiled with a pinched grin of crumbling teeth. "You won't believe who it is!"

"Well, out with it, then," said the other.

"You wouldn't believe it if I told you!" The short rat looked crossly at his friend, who finally gave in. "All right, all right, I'll tell you. It's ol' Barcus's daughter, Clover. She's to be the new High Duchess. The Minister is announcing it tonight!"

"You mean the daughter of Barcus *Belancort*—the niece of Juniper?"

"One and the same," said the tall rat with a fiendish giggle.

"Well, what do ya know? I wonder what those dead buggers might think of all this?"

The tall one scratched his head. "What about the rest of the Belancort clan? They must be dumbfounded by the pending nuptials!"

The small rat finished tacking up his end of the swag. "Who's to say? No one's heard hide nor hair of the Belancorts in years. Not since Julius Nightshade got his, anyway."

"Barcus, Juniper, and Julius Nightshade—all three must be rolling over in their graves. A Belancort, daughter of a Loyalist, betrothed to Killdeer! What a tasty scandal!"

The short one lowered his voice. "Now, listen here, I don't deem it to be true, but I heard another juicy tidbit. This one concerns Juniper himself."

Drool dribbled from the tall one's mouth. "Now what'd ya hear about ol' Juniper?"

"I was at Ellington's last night, and some tipsy old ones were insisting that the ghost of Juniper Belancort has taken to lurking in the corridors of the Combs, seeking revenge against the Ministry. The ol' codger floats around in a grubby black shroud—looks like the grim reaper himself, they say, giving Batiste a run for his money."

The tall rat shuddered. "If I were the High Minister, I'd watch my back, I would. He's gone quite soft in the belly. He wouldn't be able to outrun Juniper. No one outruns the undead, especially when the undead has a bone to pick!"

"Well, Juniper's lucky he can't die twice, for it'll take him another lifetime to find a bone on our roly-poly High Minister!"

The two rats laughed wildly, spraying spittle on one another. The pair separated and went about finishing their duties, each with a grimace of ghoulish glee.

Billycan seethed, his entire body clenched in anger. He thought Killdeer's words to Clover were merely a drunken ploy, a meaningless ruse to lure her into submission. Could Killdeer have meant what he said: Clover Belancort—daughter of a dirty Loyalist—was to be the High Duchess to the Ministry? Did that tartish schemer have that tight a grasp on Killdeer?

The grandfather! The girl couldn't pull off such a stunt alone, weaseling her way into the Minister's heart! Yes, Timeron had to be involved, feeding her words to persuade Killdeer—treacherous Loyalist filth. Billycan's suspicions were not unfounded! He knew there was something afoot all along!

Billycan flashed back to his first meeting with Clover and how she had steered him away from her ailing grandfather. That scent—it wasn't death he smelled. It was something—*someone* else!

His mind raced back eleven years to his bloody confrontation with Juniper. He remembered his skin tingling with pleasure as Juniper moaned in agony, his eye splattered in the dirt. How he effortlessly tore at Juniper, ripping his flesh down to the muscle. Billycan's eyes flashed with sickening satisfaction as he recalled his white coat soaked in Juniper's blood and the smell of hot viscera as he tore into Juniper's torso. The attack would have been seamless if he hadn't gotten tangled in the strap of that cursed satchel, allowing Juniper to slice his snout from stem to stern. That infernal satchel—Juniper wore the tattered bag as if it were a uniform.

"The satchel!" he shouted. The laborers stopped working and stared at the High Collector. He stomped back and forth. He grabbed his head, pulling wildly at his ears, humiliated at his own stupidity. How could he have been so foolish? That stale sack, it did not belong to the grandfather—it belonged to Juniper! There was no shrouded ghost in the Catacombs. It had been Juniper all along. Timeron *was* Juniper! Juniper was *alive!*

How could he not remember that pungent scent? Of all the rats to forget! He had left him for dead. He *was* dead! How could Juniper—anyone—live through that assault? Juniper's blood coated the walls of the corridor. How could he possibly have survived?

Billycan went back to that night, into details he didn't care to think about, hadn't thought about for eleven years. Before he fled the scene, before Ragan and Ulrich had come running, Juniper had grabbed hold of his neck. Through all his suffering, the violet rat managed to fight back one final time, squeezing resolutely around Billycan's throat, constricting it like a slowly closing vise, Juniper's black nails piercing his colorless flesh. Billycan remembered Juniper's fiery eyes starting to bulge while he himself gasped for breath and tore at Juniper's paws, slicing them to shreds. It was the first and only time Billycan had been afraid—afraid he would die. Had his fear blocked his memory? Had his oxygen-starved brain destroyed his recollection of that scent, the scent of the one—the only one—who could have killed him?

Everything made sense now. It was Juniper who had been stealing the Catacombs' subjects. Juniper was the instigator behind all the upheaval in the Combs. He and his guileful, rotten little niece!

"The Jezebel liar! The traitor shrew!" Billycan roared, his wrathful shrieks growing louder with every word. "Toxic little viper—tricky, tricky girl!"

Billycan leaped on the stage, kicking its wood podium, punting it like a pumpkin, smashing it to dust. He tore down the garland and swag lining the back wall, leaving deep claw marks in his wake. The soldiers standing guard and the gaping laborers looked on, their eyes fixed on Billycan in silent shock.

"Clean this mess up!" he hollered. The laborers were paralyzed with fright, unable to move. "Quit staring, you toothless imbeciles, and get back to work!" White foam seeped from Billycan's snarling mouth. "Back to work—*now!*" He bounded off the stage and lurched towards the nearest rat, his spiny claws protracted. The panicked laborer jumped out of his path and scurried onto the stage, picking up the torn garland as fast as he could. Everyone started back to work, lest they end up a cold corpse.

Billycan flared his teeth, deadly yellow blades dripping with saliva. "No one leaves this place," he shouted at the guards, "no one!" He stormed out of Catacomb Hall, tearing down a tapestry as he left, back to the Kill Army barracks to gather more of his troops.

Behind him, the laborers stood befuddled but thankful to be alive. Even the soldiers were shaken; one of them looked as though he might be sick.

* * *

Juniper muffled his voice and called down the tunnel. "Vincent," he said, "come up here, son. I need your help." Juniper crouched down on the edge of the hole and put a paw out to Vincent, pulling him up. Vincent looked around the room. His eyes briefly halted on Clover. He couldn't help but stare at her for a moment. He glanced quickly and looked away. It was clear why Killdeer had chosen her.

He saw the black and white rat, still passed out on the floor, his body seemingly lifeless. Vincent knelt over the rat and briefly studied his face.

"It seems we'll have an additional traveler tonight," said Juniper. "Vincent, this is Suttor. One of the unfortunates gobbled up by the Kill Army."

"I know him! I know Suttor," whispered Vincent excitedly. "We were friends when we were children. We used to play together. What happened to him? Is he all right?"

"Apparently the boy bumped his head and knocked himself out cold. He'll be held responsible for Clover's desertion. They'll make an example out of him. He must come with us. It's the only way to shield him from Billycan."

"He's got two brothers he looks after. What about them?"

"I'm aware," said Juniper. He tiredly rubbed his brow, already thinking of how to get Suttor's brothers to Nightshade. "We'll get them out; I'll see to that, but for now, Suttor must be our priority."

"What about Billycan?" asked Vincent. "What if he comes after Suttor's brothers?"

"Don't worry about him," said Juniper. "We'll make it look like Suttor was an innocent victim. Billycan will think we kidnapped him. His brothers will be left unharmed."

Oard thrust his head through the wall. "Listen to me, everyone! We are in trouble. Noc has reported numerous footsteps not far from our location and getting closer. He says they're thundering down the corridors in military step, on their way to this sector. Juniper, I'm afraid we've been found out. We have to get out of here now!"

"No need to be quiet now, I suppose," said Juniper at full volume. He looked down the hole and shouted down to the Council. "All right, then, first things first. Cole, Virden, stand underneath the hole while Vincent and I lower Suttor down to you."

Juniper grabbed Suttor under his arms and Vincent grabbed his legs. They lowered the limp rat down to Cole and Virden. "Careful, now," said Juniper. "He's got a nasty wound on his head." Cole and Virden cautiously put him in a wheelbarrow on a soft bed of powdery dirt.

"Clover, it's your turn now," said Juniper. "Vincent, you hop back in and help Clover down." Vincent jumped in the tunnel. Juniper threw down his satchel to Vincent, who tossed it over his shoulder and held his paws up to Clover. She knelt down on the edge of the opening, and Vincent gingerly lifted her down. As he set her on her feet, they briefly made eye contact. Vincent's chest suddenly tightened and he felt quite woozy for a moment—exhaustion, he thought. Clover's eyes reminded him of his mother's lemon preserves.

Mother Gallo trembled in panic. "Juniper, how do I contend with Billycan?"

Oard interrupted. "Juniper, the army is close on our heels. They should be here any moment. We must go *now!*" he pleaded.

Juniper grabbed Mother Gallo's shoulders. "Maddy, this will sound odd, but please just listen and do as I say. Lie down on the ground, facedown. Do it now!" Mother Gallo did as Juniper asked. He grabbed Clover's blood-stained sash and tied Mother Gallo's wrists and ankles behind her. "I'm sorry to do this to you, Maddy.

You need to look above suspicion, and there is no other way to protect you from Billycan. You'll be alone. No one can prove false anything you say. You tell him me and my men were here. You tell him *we* took Clover."

Mother Gallo understood. "Make them tighter! Billycan will check the knots—hurry!"

Oard grew frantic. "Juniper, time is wasting. You must be off! We still need to backfill the hole."

Juniper quickly tightened the knots. They felt authentic. "All right, Maddy, I'm going to cover your mouth. I have to." He took a rag and knotted it tightly around the back of her head.

He grabbed a piece of parchment and Clover's quill pen. He scribbled something on it and tucked it under the knot on her wrists. "You tell Billycan a gang of large rats barged in here and took Clover and Suttor. Say you didn't recognize any of them but one. You tell him the rat looked like Juniper Belancort. You will come out of this unscathed and unsuspected." Juniper groaned in frustration. "Maddy, I'm sorry, but I'm doing this for your own preservation. Lift up your head." He gave her a kiss on the cheek so that she wouldn't know what was coming. He opened his paw and cracked her hard on the side of the head, knocking her senseless. She lay unconscious on the ground. "I'm sorry, Maddy. At least you're safe for now."

"Juniper, apologize later. Get out of here!" said Oard.

Juniper jumped into the tunnel. The worms made fast work of the hole. The Nightshade rats kicked back the dirt under the gaping hole as the worms propelled the excess earth back in from the ground above. After the hole was filled, the earthworms twirled and rolled their vine-like bodies against the floor of the quarters, smoothing away any trace of disturbance to the ground.

"They're here!" called Noc. The earthworms evaporated into the walls of Clover's quarters just as Billycan and his soldiers approached the door.

Suttor was nowhere to be seen. Billycan cursed and spat as he and the pack of soldiers reached Clover's door. "Where is that softheaded lieutenant?" he screeched. He kicked the door in, ripping it off its hinges. The door flew across Clover's quarters, smashing against the back wall.

He all but tripped over Mother Gallo. "High Mistress?" he said, nearly stepping on her. She lay flat on her belly, prostrate on the ground. Her head was stretched out in front of him. "Lieutenant Carn, help me with her."

Carn grabbed a stool, and he and Billycan hoisted Mother Gallo onto it. Still unconscious, her head fell on her chest. Billycan sniffed the air. "Waterchip—over there," he said, pointing a knobby digit. "Bring me the vile root." Lieutenant Carn quickly grabbed the root and gave it to Billycan, who dangled it under Mother Gallo's nose. Billycan spoke to Mother Gallo as he tried to revive her. "C'mon, my pet, let's wake up, shall we? Billycan has many questions for you, questions only you can answer."

Lieutenant Carn untied her while Billycan balanced her on the stool. The rolled parchment fell to the ground. Carn picked it up and handed it to Billycan. "Sir," he said, handing him the note.

Billycan read the document. His nostrils flared as his whole body quaked with anger. Crumpling the paper in his fist, he let out a baleful wail, a grunting, guttural howl from deep within his chest. He sprang to his feet and began tearing Clover's quarters apart.

Lieutenant Carn caught Mother Gallo before she fell, and

he carried her out of the room before Billycan could take out his rage on her.

The pack of soldiers stood in the doorway and watched as Billycan shattered everything in his path. He saw the carving of Duchess Nomi on the wall and furiously clawed away at it until blood dripped from under his nails. He threw Clover's parents' bed across the room, smashing it into kindling. Snatching up matches, he lit the dry wood ablaze. The fire quickly engulfed the room. Billycan looked around without direction; his pupils glazed over, shifting color, in league with the flames.

Lieutenant Carn stepped in and reached for him. "Commander—please—you must come out now! Sir, the flames will eat you alive!" Billycan did not respond. "Commander, please listen to me! You must get out of here!" Carn boldly grabbed Billycan by his shoulders, shaking him, trying to bring him back to reality. The flames licked at Carn's ankles and tail. "Commander, wake up!" he yelled in one final attempt to rouse him. Carn fled the room and watched in horror as the flames climbed the walls.

Billycan finally snapped to. His eyes darkened, returning to the world of the living. He ignored the inferno he had created and exited the room, now strangely calm. He turned to Carn and looked at him blankly, his voice a monotone. "Put that fire out."

He aimlessly drifted down the corridor, leaving the scene. Carn quickly directed a dozen bewildered soldiers, who scrambled about the sector, banging on doors and shouting for help, yelling for water. Rats ran from all directions to aid the soldiers, passing Billycan with buckets and jugs overflowing with water, milk, whatever they could find to help put out the rising flames. Billycan didn't seem to notice. He just kept walking. Turning a corner, he disappeared from view. The contents of the note played over and over in his head.

Your Chosen One sends her regrets.
The Minister is not to her liking. Your
lieutenant has been taken captive,
courtesy of Nightshade City.
                                    —J. Belancort

Juniper pushed Suttor in the wheelbarrow himself. He didn't want the Nightshade rats to do any further work, unless it involved bringing a mug of ale to their lips. Suttor must have been comfortable in his bed of dirt, as he began to snore—loudly. Everyone held in their laughs, not wanting to wake him.

The earthworms had gone home. They had proven themselves more valuable than Juniper ever thought possible. There would surely be no Nightshade without them.

Vincent and Clover lagged behind the others. They were deep in discussion about their fathers, two best friends with children who'd never met, at least not that they remembered. Juniper glanced back at the pair. He liked the way they looked next to each other, and it was nice to see them both smiling for a change.

The Grand Speech never took place. Disgraced and embarrassed, Killdeer lurked about his compound all night and early into the morning, pickling himself with Oshi. Billycan left the Minister alone, as he was more useless than usual in his current state.

Billycan sat in an uncomfortable wooden chair in the center of his barren den. He compressed his paws into tight, bony fists, peeling open his self-inflicted wounds from the night before. The blood dripped from beneath his claws in small droplets, ticking his snow-white fur with scarlet dots. Billycan watched as the beads of blood dribbled between his paws, one by one by one.

Mother Gallo's sons had gathered around her. Lieutenant Carn had assured them that their mother would be fine, but the boys stood watch through the night, much concerned for her well-being. Mother Gallo had not stirred once. She finally shifted a bit. The boys sat up in eagerness, glad to see her move about. She slowly turned over on her back and stretched her arms and neck. She opened her puffy morning eyes and yawned. As she focused, she realized her three sons were staring closely at her.

She jolted up, alarmed. "Boys, what on earth is the matter? Why are you looking at me so?"

Her youngest son, Hob, answered. "You hurt your head, Mother. Don't you remember?"

"I hurt my head?" She looked around the room for a second, gathering her wits. "My head—I remember now."

Like their mother, Tuk, Gage, and Hob were gray, but to varying degrees. Little Hob, the baby of the family, had an identical hue to his mother, soft ash gray. Tuk, the oldest, was a dark bluish charcoal, almost black, while Gage was mottled, his coat speckled with lead and silver.

"Mother," said Tuk, handing her a mug of bitonberry juice, "you do understand you were attacked last night, don't you? Someone hit you over the head, and that Chosen One, Clover—she's missing; Suttor too. You don't think Suttor did it?" Tuk and Gage had known Suttor and his brothers years before they had been claimed by the army, but they could only guess how a few years in the hands of the majors could change them.

Mother Gallo took a drink of juice. Until Juniper could devise a clear-cut escape plan for her and her children, she thought it best to keep the truth from the boys. It was only a matter of time before Billycan would come calling. The mere mention of Billycan unsettled her boys enough as it was. Billycan could easily read faces, especially those of scared little ones. He knew it if a young one tried to hide something. Her boys were not experienced liars and would never forgive themselves if they unintentionally gave their mother away.

"Now, Tuk," she began, "Suttor is the same boy you knew before his parents died. He would never hurt anyone, especially me or an innocent girl. We were all ambushed. They tied up poor Suttor and stormed into Clover's quarters, hitting both Suttor and me over the head. I don't know why they chose to take him. I'm just lucky they left me in one piece."

Mother Gallo sent her boys out. She explained to them that Billycan would be coming to talk to her about last night and she needed quiet time so she could concentrate on the details. Her boys were more than happy to oblige. They'd heard about the Collector's bizarre behavior and the fire he had set. The boys had no desire to meet the creepy white rat with the monstrous reputation.

Mother Gallo was reaching for her toast when she heard the telltale scraping against her door. "Already?" she mumbled to herself. "No rest for the weary—or the wicked—I suppose."

Billycan called from the other side of the door, his voice feigning concern. "Mistress Gallo," he purred, "are you awake? Billycan does need to speak with you, urgently, I'm afraid."

"Yes, Collector, do come in." Mother Gallo rested in a chair, her feet up on a stool.

Billycan slinked in, followed by two sector majors, who waited just inside the front door. Mother Gallo was glad to see three faces instead of one. It was not as though the majors were friendly, but she felt slightly more comfortable with extra bodies in the room.

"Well, High Mistress, Billycan is pleased to see you're awake and hopefully recovering from last night's traumatic events."

"A little weary, but healing. I'm more shaken up than anything else. What an appalling night," she said. "That poor girl, and young Lieutenant Suttor, both abducted—dreadful business."

"So, you *do* remember. Billycan worried that knock on the head might have destroyed your memory of the incident. Well, then, I need some information, if you would be so kind," he said. He pulled up a stool near Mother Gallo, far closer than she would have liked.

"Well, Collector, Clover and I were going over the schedule of the Grand Speech when we heard a loud noise at the door and what sounded like someone falling to the ground. I looked under the door to see what the sound was, and there lay Suttor, flat on his back. I opened the door to assist him, when four large rats bounded in. All four were tall in stature, like you, but with plain brown coats—all but one."

Billycan stiffened on the edge of the stool. "And what did this fourth rat look like, Mistress Gallo?"

"Rather large, like the others, larger, in fact, and his coat was coarse and unshorn, almost canine. Strange, really," said Mother Gallo.

"What's strange?"

"The color of the rat's coat was like ripe plums, deep and purple, and it instantly reminded me of someone, though I can't seem to drum up the rat's name." She tapped her chin. "Oh, wait, Collector. Here's something useful. This rat had some kind of patch over his eye."

Billycan cringed, clicking his jaw back and forth; he popped his knuckles, trying to control himself.

"He had a loud, commanding voice and seemed to be the leader of the pack. He did all the talking, while the three browns simply followed his orders."

Billycan's nostrils flared, his temper brewing. He cocked his head from side to side, stretching his neck. "And where was little Clover in all of this hubbub?"

"The poor dear just stood there, frozen in fear. I don't know if she really knew what was happening. That's when I was hit over the head, and I guess I collapsed. Shortly after that, I heard the purplish rat yell something—some kind of declaration. In fact, I think I heard him mention *your* name. Regrettably, that's all I can tell you—it's the last thing I remember."

Billycan squirmed in his seat and said snappishly, "Do you recall anything else—anything at all? It's very important to the Ministry that you tell us everything you possibly can, even the most negligible detail—everything."

"Now that you mention it, I do recall something rather odd," she said, as if slowly searching her brain for the information.

Billycan rolled his eyes. "Out with it, Mistress. Time is wasting!"

Mother Gallo paused, acting oblivious to his frustration. "Well . . . do you recall our meeting in the corridor yesterday? I had that tattered satchel with me, the one belonging to Clover's grandfather?"

Billycan exhaled in exasperation. "Yes, yes, get to the point."

"Well, the wine-colored rat took it. He took the satchel off the table and threw it over his shoulder as if it were his. I found it quite peculiar. Why would he want that filthy old leather bag?"

Billycan had all the confirmation he needed. This was neither a hoax nor a rebel prank—Juniper lived. Now that he had his niece hidden away, Juniper had nothing to lose but his life. That made him even more dangerous. *How he must be gloating,* thought Billycan, *building up a ragtag army of his Loyalist friends and turncoat Catacomb subjects!*

The words on the note were seared into Billycan's memory. He would find Juniper's little city. He gazed at Mother Gallo fixedly. "Have you ever heard mention of Nightshade City? Does that name mean anything to you at all? Think hard, now, Mistress."

"Nightshade City—you mean as in Julius Nightshade? He's been dead and buried for years now. Clover had mentioned that her father had been close with Julius, along with her uncle. She paused a moment. "Billycan, you know the uncle. He's the one all the soldiers chatter about ... you know ... you had that legendary clash with him—Juniper, that's it! Juniper Belancort! Why, the rat from last night looked just like him!"

Billycan jumped to his feet, ignoring her revelation. "Mistress, the High Ministry thanks you for your report. As a Ministry official, you are well aware that last night's events and all talk relating to it are strictly confidential. Am I clear?"

"As a church bell," replied Mother Gallo.

Giving a formal bow, Billycan walked out the door, his sector majors following. He tramped down the corridor back to Killdeer's compound, his white skin flushing an angry red. "Go retrieve the High Majors and have them wait for me in the War Room," he told his majors. "It's time for Killdeer to wake up."

Still caked with dirt from the dig, Nightshade's citizens waited patiently, saying prayers to the Saints for everyone's safe return. Cole emerged first from the tunnel. Everyone gasped. He quickly put a claw to his lips, signaling the greeters to stay hushed. He motioned down the tunnel. Juniper came out next, pushing Suttor, still asleep and snoring on the wheelbarrow. The rest of the travelers filed in behind him.

Juniper pulled Vincent over and motioned to Victor, who had stayed behind. Juniper whispered something to them; both nodded in agreement. Victor took the wheelbarrow from Juniper, and he and Vincent faded down a corridor with Suttor in tow.

Juniper cleared his throat. He walked with Clover to the center of the rotunda. The rats gathered around them. "Our mission—a success!" The rats of Nightshade unleashed in congratulatory thunder. "Nightshade citizens, I've been waiting to bring my niece here when the time was right. Well, thanks to the Ministry, the time for our impromptu rescue was forced upon us, so in a way, I'm grateful to our portly High Minister. Without his Chosen One decree, my niece would still be in the Catacombs, living in fear. This gave us the push, the inspiration—the *desperation*—we needed to move forward and get her out. We worked as a city, and we won as a city!" The rats stomped their feet in unity.

"All I can say to each and every one of you is—thank you. You have reunited me with the one family member I have left in the world and brought her to safety." He put his arm around Clover. "Everyone, without further delay, this is Clover Belancort, my niece and the daughter of our long-departed ally, my dear brother, Barcus Belancort. Now, everyone, grab yourselves a mug of good cheer!"

The rats celebrated—briefly. It was well into the morning hours, and everyone was exhausted. Juniper couldn't stop thinking about Mother Gallo and her boys. He had to get them out, not to mention Suttor's brothers. But now he needed rest.

Juniper's quarters were cluttered and disheveled, a male's mess of this and that, unsuitable for his young niece, or any respectable female, for that matter. Cole and Lali gladly took her in. She could stay with them until other preparations could be made or at least until Juniper could get his chaotic quarters in order. Clover did not mind the arrangement. She was thankful for Lali's company.

Juniper was alone, too tired to think straight, too tired to concentrate on anything. His jumbled thoughts drifted to the night of Billycan's assault. He wondered what the white rat was doing at that very moment.

Billycan stared flintily at Killdeer. The Minister slept on the floor, sprawled on his back, reminiscent of a Topsider's holiday goose. His chest was stained with crimson blotches of Oshi. A sickening odor emanated from his mouth—a stench of turned wine and fetid meat.

Billycan looked at him, disgusted. He held himself back from carving out the Minister's heart. He could effortlessly kill Killdeer right now and declare himself High Minister. Then he would find Juniper, rip out the one-eyed rat's heart, and butcher his little niece—destroying the Belancort bloodline forever.

Billycan violently kicked Killdeer in the side. He did not move. Bitter bile climbed in Billycan's throat. He snarled, "Wake up, Killdeer!" Killdeer lay as stiff as a cadaver gone into rigor. Billycan's entire body shook. He got as close as he could to the foul smell. He screamed in Killdeer's face. "Killdeer—wake up!"

Killdeer sprang into a sitting position. He looked around, disoriented: "What—what on earth is wrong?" Killdeer shouted back at him.

Billycan seethed with contempt. He positioned his teeth to attack. Killdeer catapulted to his feet, still bewildered. The Collector came towards him, set to maul him. Killdeer held his paws in front of him, trying to keep Billycan at a distance.

Killdeer spoke calmly. "Billycan, what's got you in such an uproar? What has happened? Tell me, old friend. Talk to me." He had never been the focus of one of Billycan's eruptions before, but he knew to take it seriously.

Billycan held himself back, certain he would murder the Minister if he did not let his anger abate. In Killdeer's current shape, it would be an effortless kill. Billycan did not want to do it—not yet, not until he was absolutely sure it was necessary. Killdeer had taught him how to function in the world—how to survive—how to win. For that, Billycan would grant him one final chance.

Billycan threw himself down into a chair across from Killdeer's throne, exhausted and frustrated. Killdeer, still puzzled at Billycan's outburst, climbed into his throne and waited silently for the white rat to speak.

Billycan spoke coolly. "Killdeer, do you remember the Bloody Coup?"

Killdeer thought Billycan might be losing his grasp on reality—the whole business with Juniper. He thought it best to keep things cordial. "How could I forget one of the most gratifying days of my life? We planned our attack perfectly. With you at my side, there was no way we could lose."

Billycan leaned back and stared at the ceiling. "Don't you fancy that glory any longer? Don't you wish to relish that sensation yet again?" Killdeer looked at him strangely, not following his questions.

Billycan turned his eyes to Killdeer, his gaze glacial, his voice plain. "It seems to be the opinion of the Catacombs that you've lost all respect for your title. Our subjects grumble of your noticeable lack of interest. It appears to most that you are more interested in females and Oshi than in your duties to the Combs. As you learned last night,

Juniper is very much alive. With him and his Loyalist cohorts now back in the picture, you may lose your throne, possibly your life. As for your dignity, that's already lost."

Killdeer stayed slumped in his usual lackluster position. He looked down at Billycan from his lofty throne, his expression aloof, his tone superior. "Do you have any idea who you are speaking to? We may be close associates, but I'm the leader of the Catacombs, the High Minister, not you. Have you forgotten that, Collector?" Killdeer picked up his tail, admiring its lustrous skin. "Have you forgotten what I'm capable of? Has your rank made you think you are worth more to the High Ministry than the army you command?" Killdeer raised an eyebrow as he spotted a flake of dead skin on his tail. He carelessly flicked it off and stretched in his throne, as if Billycan were no longer in the room.

Billycan abruptly vaulted from his chair. He grabbed onto the lip of Killdeer's goblet throne, thrusting himself up. His claws shot out from his skinny digits. He shoved them under Killdeer's chin, poking his fleshy folds as he lurched over the Minister, his mouth twisting into a menacing leer.

Billycan sneered as Killdeer recoiled. "Your question—do I think I'm worth more than I am? I *know* what I'm worth. I have single-handedly built the Kill Army. I have controlled the Ministry, while you sit idly by." He pushed his claws in harder, on the verge of drawing Killdeer's blood. "The real question is, how much are *you* worth? You sprawl lazily in your throne day after wasteful day. You fill your bloated belly with food and wine. You prey on the frightened females with your Chosen One decrees. You leave the running of this so-called Ministry to me and my majors—and let me assure you, Minister, they are *my* majors. They are loyal to *me*.

"You are a laughingstock to the Kill Army—comic relief. Only the young ones look up to you now. They don't know the real you. They have yet to see their Minister stumble into Catacomb Hall, drunk and unintelligible. They have yet to watch you harass the females and torment the old ones, throwing your soft frame around as if it were a weapon. You are obese and foul—a disgrace to the throne—a disgrace to rats." Billycan wiped away the frothy white foam that had started to seep from the corners of his mouth. "And as for your first question, do I *know* who I'm talking to? Unequivocally, yes—I do. I know exactly the worthless lump that sits before me. I can forecast his drunkenness, his lechery, his gluttony. I can smell his putrid liability from miles away. You are the burden anchored around my neck."

Billycan shoved his snout against Killdeer's and pressed his claws in deeper, forcing a thin trail of blood down Killdeer's neck. "Mark my words, Killdeer, if you do not make a change for the better, starting right now, you will be eliminated from the equation. You merely serve as packaging for the entity that is the High Ministry. You are my marionette. Do not think yourself anything more than that—do not *dare* think it."

Billycan's claws retracted. He released Killdeer. "There is a meeting in the War Room in three hours. If you are not in attendance and are not acting the role of a High Minister, I will hunt you down and deal with you myself." Billycan reached over Killdeer and grabbed the bottle of Oshi he kept stashed in his throne, then viciously smashed it on the dirt floor, spattering his white feet with red droplets. "I have been tolerant of you, Killdeer. I felt I owed you for all you did for me years ago, but those years are long since gone, and I have reached the end of my tether. Do not attempt to push back. That would be a deadly mistake. The majors back me. At my command, they will *end* you. Redeem yourself or die."

Billycan leaped to the ground and exited the room. Texi scurried down the corridor from the opposite direction. Billycan spoke to her as he passed, not bothering to stop or look at her. "Get your brother some breakfast—now! No sweets, no lard, and *absolutely* no wine or ale. If I find out you brought him any of those things, I will slaughter you and every last one of your imbecilic sisters."

Texi halted in the corridor, watching as Billycan's white coat disappeared into the dark. What had her brother done now?

Vincent and Victor gently turned the wheelbarrow through the doorway and brought the still-sleeping Suttor into their quarters. Vincent wasn't certain what he would say to his old friend, but he wasn't too worried. He had heard the horror stories about the Kill Army changing otherwise fine rats into callous assassins, but he just couldn't see his childhood playmate mutating into a coldhearted killer. Growing up, Suttor was always good. He never got into trouble and was devoted and caring to his two little brothers.

That brought up another problem—his brothers. Vincent knew Suttor would be near frantic once he realized they were so far out of his reach. Vincent had all the faith in the world that Juniper would get them out somehow, but for now he had no words to ease Suttor's mind. Vincent needed to get the hard conversation over with, and he figured there was no time like the present. Suttor had been asleep for hours.

"Suttor," Vincent said. He softly pushed on the sleeping rat's shoulder. "Suttor, wake up. It's Vincent Nightshade." Suttor started to move. "You bumped your head, but you're all right. You just needed some rest. Suttor, do you hear me?"

Suttor slowly opened his eyes and stretched his lanky arms, splotched with black and white. He had a partial smile on his face, and he smacked his lips together as his fuzzy eyes adjusted.

Vincent stood over him cautiously, hoping he wouldn't

startle him. "Suttor, don't be alarmed. It's Vincent—Vincent Nightshade—and my little brother, Victor. You remember us, don't you?" Suttor idly rolled over on his belly and pushed up on his elbows. He slowly focused on Vincent's face, and, recognizing him, his lethargy instantly faded.

Suttor sat up with a jerk and looked down at his bed of dirt on top of the wheelbarrow. "Vincent Nightshade!" he blurted in amazement. "What are *you* doing here? I heard you escaped this ghastly place. Why on earth would you come back?"

Vincent grinned. "Here, let me help you down," he said. He took one of Suttor's arms, Victor the other, and they helped him out of the wheelbarrow.

Suttor stood upright, wobbling on his feet. "It's been a long time, Nightshade! Where have you been?" Suttor looked at Victor, taller than both he and Vincent. "And Victor, you're huge! Last time I saw you, I could pick you up with one arm!"

"Hello, Suttor," said Victor. "Sorry to say I don't remember you too well. I don't remember much of anything from those days."

"No worries," said Suttor cheerfully. "You could barely talk back then. Now that you're both back in the Combs, we can get to know each other all over again, just like old times! How did I end up in your quarters? Does anyone know I'm here? I could be in serious trouble with the Ministry. I was supposed to be guarding the Chosen One. Did Mistress Gallo bring me here?"

"Well, I suppose, yes, Mother Gallo did bring me here," said Vincent, helping Suttor over to the table where Lali had left a basket of biscuits. "The Ministry knows you're here, and everything is fine."

Suttor eyed the biscuits. "Would you mind if I—"

"Oh, go right ahead," said Vincent. "Have as many as you like."

Suttor bit into a thick butter biscuit. It tasted like nothing he'd ever had before. "This biscuit—it's amazing," he said with a full mouth. "Who made it?"

"A female named Lali. She seems to keep everyone fed around here."

"Well, give her my compliments. I'm surprised I've never heard of her. I've been around your sector enough times. What clan does Lali hail from? The name does not ring familiar."

"I'm actually not sure what her clan name is. We only just met her ourselves."

"She should talk to the Ministry about a station. High Cook Long-tooth could take a few lessons from her. The cook's pastry is as dry and tasteless as she is!" he said with a snicker. "So, how did you two get back in without being punished? I hate to sound morbid, but after your stunt, I'm surprised to see you alive. Major Lithgo wanted your heads!"

Vincent glanced at Victor. He wasn't sure where to start.

Victor shrugged his shoulders. "Just tell him the truth," he said.

"Tell me what?"

"Well, that's the thing, Suttor," said Vincent delicately. "Victor and I never did go back to the Catacombs. Lithgo *would* have killed us. We can never go back."

Suttor smiled as he gnawed his biscuit. "Ah, still the clever one, I see," he said, thinking Vincent was teasing him, "always telling a good yarn!"

Vincent crinkled his forehead, thinking of another approach. "Suttor, do you know anything about Clover Belancort, the Chosen One you were guarding?"

"Not really. She's a Chosen One—what else do I need to know?" asked Suttor, taking another bite of biscuit.

"Suttor, Clover is the daughter of Barcus Belancort and the niece of Juniper Belancort, both important members of the Loyalists who fought against Killdeer during the Bloody Coup."

Suttor seemed more interested in eating than listening to Vincent's history lesson. "Well, I knew all that, but that was years ago. Besides, they're dead. So what does it matter now?"

Vincent flashed Suttor a deadly serious look, forcing eye contact. "Suttor, listen to me carefully. There is much you don't know about Clover's uncle—Juniper."

"Well, I know he was a vocal Trilok Loyalist, getting himself killed by Billycan because of it. I hear tales about it in the barracks all the time. That fight is legendary. Billycan ripped Juniper to shreds. What else could I possibly need to know?"

"What you've heard, it's not true. Suttor, the rat lives. Juniper is very much alive."

Suttor looked confused. "How do you know this? Where is your proof?" he demanded. "Even if it is true, what does it have to do with anything and why did you say you can never go back to the Combs? We are in the Catacombs right now! This joke has gone too far!"

"Suttor, this is *no* joke! You passed out a second time in Clover's quarters, moments before we dug through her floor to rescue her—taking her out of the Catacombs for good. Juniper saved your life. Billycan and a dozen troops were seconds away. If we had left you there, you would have been blamed for everything. Guilty or not, they would have punished you for it, just to prove to their subjects they had caught the perpetrator. The Ministry does not take kindly to treason. They would have strung you up in Catacomb Hall for all to see. You know it to be true!"

Suttor threw his biscuit to the floor and jumped up from the table. "I'm *not* in the Catacombs?" He bounded to the door and ran out into the hall. The colors and decorations made him halt in his tracks. There were no sector guards to be seen. The corridors were fully lit—welcoming. He was surely *not* in the Combs. He staggered back into the room and stood in front of Vincent—mystified. "So . . . where am I?"

Suttor looked about to crumple. Vincent helped him back to his chair. "Suttor, do you remember my father?"

Suttor nodded weakly. "Of course I do. Everyone remembers Julius Nightshade—the Citizen Minister. Your father is a legend. My parents loved him. Everyone did." Suttor looked around the room. "Where are we, anyway?"

Vincent smiled. "We are in my father's city."

Billycan entered the War Room, a narrow, egg-shaped hall. Maps and blueprints were tacked over every inch of wall, meticulously detailing everything Topside of Trillium City all the way to the internal workings of the Kill Army kitchens. No area that involved the Catacombs or the area above it was left undocumented.

All Kill Army majors were present and awaiting Commander Billycan. They bolted from their chairs as Billycan entered, standing at full attention. High Majors Lithgo, Schnauss, and Foiber stood at the front of the room, facing the crowd of majors, standing just behind Billycan. The three high majors, next in command to Billycan, had all been members of Killdeer's original Topside faction, all banished to the surface by Minister Trilok, charged with malevolent harm to citizens, thievery, skullduggery, and murder.

Major Lithgo was a heavy brown rat with an oversized belly. He had a pleasant, open face and an outwardly jovial nature, making him extremely successful in securing new recruits. He used his welcoming features and notable manipulation techniques to lure young rats into the Kill Army, preventing Topside escapes. He would give the youths a tender hug, a pat of fatherly love on the head, convincing them that he looked out for their best interests. In actuality, he slowly squeezed the will from them, killing their fragile spirits.

Major Schnauss was nearly ancient. He was built similarly to Billycan, tall and bony, but even more emaciated, reminiscent of a mummified corpse. He was the color of oil with dashes of ivory sprinkled throughout, his skin a dry cinder. He had two graying snaggleteeth that hung over his lower lip, pressing it back, as if in a perpetual snarl. His grizzled nose and upper lip turned skyward, making him look as though he smelled something foul. Adding to Schnauss's repellency, one eye glowed a gauzy blue, the other—a dead eye of ghostly whitewash, which bobbled aimlessly around its socket like a sickly fish.

A hairless rat, Major Foiber was short and fleshy, with skin the texture of dried corn and bulbous eyes like two rotting pumpkins. Creased and desiccated, his casing draped in folds around his belly, haunches, and chest as if several sizes too large. Foiber was eternally cursed with red, scaly rashes, concentrated around his joints and neck, irritating the foul-tempered rat no end.

Foiber and Schnauss, masters of torture, worked in concert, interrogating the soldiers when deemed necessary. Whenever a major called a soldier's devotion into question, the pair exposed the truth, at least their version of it. They could smell fear on the young ones and sense deceit, and they had a talent for making even the older boys cry. The boys would squirm and lather at just a glimpse of Schnauss's wandering eye or a whiff of Foiber's infected skin.

The Ministry believed that Lieutenant Suttor had been kidnapped by Juniper and his cohorts. They knew only one thing about Juniper's alleged city: It had to be somewhere under the Reserve. The freshly tilled earth made it the perfect place to build. Any other area of polluted

Trillium was as lifeless as the Catacombs. Of late, several corridors had fallen in on themselves; the Catacombs were crumbling, taking scores of rats with them.

Billycan's faith in the Ministry and its army renewed as he inspected his majors. The lot stood strong and firm, imperial and intimidating. Cleaned and pressed, his navy and crimson sash held fast against his inflexible chest, his billy club dangling at his side. He walked front and center, standing before the large throng of majors, his paws clasped behind his back.

"At ease, majors, at ease; take your seats. Billycan is glad to see you all here together. I don't know what you may know of the past day's events." Billycan began to pace. "The Kill Army has controlled the Catacombs for some time now. Several of you have been here since the beginning and took part in the victorious battle we waged on the old regime—and have the scars to prove it," he said, tapping his disfigured muzzle. "All of you have been promoted through the ranks because you showed the Kill Army and your Ministry that you have what it takes to be leaders. You have the drive, the tenacity to keep the Catacombs in our power, because you know that without that power . . . we are *nothing*."

Billycan cleared his throat. "Now, once again, we have a battle to wage. A new city has emerged, and it threatens our very existence. Last night, a band of rats from this covert city kidnapped one of our young lieutenants—Lieutenant Suttor—along with the Chosen One, Clover Belancort." The room rumbled softly with muffled talk. There had been murmurings of deserters and traitors, but nothing of kidnappings, let alone a new colony of rats.

"Silence!" roared Billycan. "The Chosen One—little Miss Belancort—is not the angelic creature she has feigned to be. Clover Belancort, the scheming little harpy, led us to believe she lived under the care of a guardian, her sickly grandfather, Timeron. But this shrouded, yellow-bellied rat is by no means ailing and is certainly no grandfather at all! He is the leader of this new city, he was—he is—Juniper Belancort. Juniper—lives."

The room went completely silent. Up until that very moment, the majors had all believed that Billycan had killed Juniper during the Bloody Coup. They could only imagine their commander's rage—his humiliation—upon discovering that the Trilok Loyalist was alive and had been plotting a takeover all this time.

Billycan searched the stone faces in the room. His majors avoided eye contact at all costs, lest they bear the brunt of his ferocious tongue-lashing or the head of his billy club. "I know what you all must be thinking. Billycan thinks it himself. Your respected Kill Army Commander, your High Collector—a failure. Oh, yes, it's true. I made the regretful mistake of leaving a job unfinished. Had I stayed to make sure the job was done, the Loyalists surely would have killed me. A choice had to be made, and now I alone must live with that choice. Juniper, the conspirator, has programmed his rabble-rousing fabrications into the minds of our dim subjects. He is luring families out of the Combs with dreams of a better life."

Billycan's eyes rippled with wrath, his pupils disappeared, overcome by his expanding irises, now a lightened hue of indignant vermilion. Utilizing all available air in his concave chest, he bayed mightily. "He is a liar!" No one moved. The sector majors seated in front felt a mist of his spittle on their snouts and heard Billycan's jagged knuckles crack behind his twisted back. "Juniper has once again tricked his way into the hearts of our simple subjects. He has established a city. A city whose mere name is an affront to the High Ministry—Nightshade City," he hissed. Whispers buzzed through the room. "Yes, it's true! Juniper has smugly named his little city in memory of that sanctimonious Trilok Loyalist, Julius Nightshade!

"Julius Nightshade," he sniped mockingly, "friend to Trilok, the Citizen Minister, the weasel who tried to spur the Catacomb rats to rally against us, to keep us from what should have been ours all along! His parasitic legacy still spreads through our subjects like a lethal pestilence."

A cavernous voice thundered from the back of the War Room. "Julius Nightshade," the voice roared, "a scoundrel, a greased snake slithering amongst us, an ugly blemish on our noble heritage!" Everyone quickly turned round to the back of the packed room. Killdeer strutted down the aisle between the seated majors. Groomed to perfection, he swaggered past the majors without a hint of the alcoholic haze he had been in hours before. He wore his Kill Army-issued sash, the navy and crimson gabardine strapped across his chest, his polished silver medallion shimmering in the torchlight.

Billycan was stunned by the transformation. Killdeer slowly strode to the front of the room and approached him. They stared at each other, both a bit leery. Killdeer turned. "Majors, it has been brought to my attention that there has been talk of late—unflattering talk in reference to me, suggesting that maybe I'm not quite the leader I used to be." The majors looked uncomfortable, all guilty of having condemned the High Minister. "Well, let me assure you, the talk was warranted— all of it! No one likes to admit their shortcomings, especially one in a position of such power, but admit them I must, at least if I'm to lead you properly once more. Your Commander, Billycan, has told me in no uncertain terms that I have been a hideous, wine-soaked stain on the High Ministry, the Kill Army, and our beloved Catacombs."

He looked Billycan squarely in the face. "But all that is going to change, starting now. We have a battle to wage. We have demons to slay, demons long thought dead. I would like to tell you that Belancort and his Nightshade City will mean nothing to us, that they are insignificant, irrelevant—that we will crush them effortlessly, but

Commander Billycan has taught me over the years never to underestimate our enemies. We will fight with everything we've got. Lives will be lost, but not our *way* of life. The Ministry and army will remain intact! Not only will we keep the Catacombs, but we will take over Nightshade and claim it as our own!" Killdeer raised his arm in concert with his voice, resounding through the War Room. "We will triumph! Juniper Belancort will die! His corpse will at last rot in the underworld, where it rightly belongs!" The majors jumped to their feet, shrieking and yowling, screaming out the shrill war cry of their ancestors. Killdeer could rally the troops like no other.

The High Minister approached Billycan amidst the clamor. He grabbed the white rat, embracing him firmly, slapping his back. He whispered in his ear. "You were right, old friend. I am guilty of all that you charged. We have a battle to win. We will once again crush and conquer. We will prevail!"

Billycan's body shook with unfettered admiration. He grated his teeth, clenching his barbed jaw—electrified by the Minister's resurgence. He grabbed hold of Killdeer's shoulders. He stepped back and looked at him, amazed. It seemed his long-lost brother had miraculously returned from the dead.

CHAPTER SIX
More Flies with Honey

SUTTOR WAS AWAKE. He lay on his cot, staring at the ceiling, worried about his brothers. As much as he had embraced the Kill Army, he knew it was no place for him. It had been a necessity, a way to insure the safety of his brothers. He *was* thankful and relieved to be out.

He knew word about his alleged abduction had almost certainly spread in the Kill Army barracks. He could only imagine what his little brothers might think, hearing grisly rumors about his fate. He was sure they would fear the worst.

Vincent awoke. He turned over on his cot and noticed Suttor. "How long have you been awake?" he asked sleepily.

Suttor gazed at the grooves in the ceiling. "Long enough to work myself into a dither. Mind you, I'm glad to be out, but I must get my brothers. I can't leave them there alone—wondering if I'm dead or alive. Kar barely fits his Kill Army dress sash. It hangs on him like a bedsheet. He should be playing with toys, not marching in formation.

And Duncan, he can't make it in the army without me. He's always daydreaming. I can't even let him trim his own whiskers, for fear he'll cut himself."

Vincent rubbed the crust of sleep from his eyes. "We can figure this out. First, let's get some food. I'm sure Lali has put out a spread. You need food in your belly. It will help you think. After that, we'll go find Juniper and work things out. He's a brilliant rat, as smart as my father, I'd say. If anyone can help you, he can—and he will. He told me last night he would. He would never go back on his word—never."

Suttor sat up. "Can we go right now? I really don't think I can wait any longer," he said, wringing his paws.

Vincent eyed his waking brother, who moaned lazily as he stretched. "Of course we can. Victor, are you coming?"

Victor yawned and spoke at the same time. "Yes. I'm hoping Lali has a few more of those egg custards."

The boys made their way to Bostwick Hall. It was busy, almost hectic. With city building and the planning of the Combs invasion, the hall was used as a meeting place and provisional mess hall. The Council had built a makeshift kitchen lining the back wall. Juniper believed that at times like this, the one thing a rat should not have to worry about was its belly. There were designated groups that searched Topside for food, the Hunter Rats. Having lived aboveground for so long, Juniper and the Council knew where the best edibles were to be found and the best time to retrieve them. Food was plentiful.

Rats were eating, talking, going over strategies, spread out at tables, or standing in clusters throughout the hall. Suttor scanned the faces. Rats were laughing, smiling, telling stories. It reminded him of life before his parents' death.

Lali ran around the kitchen as usual. A group of Hunter Rats had brought back some chocolate they found Topside, most likely Hallowtide remnants. Lali was scurrying behind the kitchen line, speedily frying up chocolate griddle cakes, when she spotted the Nightshades and Suttor. "Boys, come here," she called with good cheer. The boys ambled over, and Lali handed each of them a cake. "Vincent, Juniper told me you're an admirer of my corn bread, but I have something new for you to try. Go on, now, give it a taste."

Vincent took a big bite. It had been so long since he'd had anything with chocolate. Even the Topsiders' hoarded that particular sweet. "Lali, this is good," said Vincent, packing the rest of the cake in his mouth, "really good."

"Well, I did have some help," said Lali, nodding over her shoulder with a little grin. Clover was working just behind Lali, chopping up bits of chocolate and coating them in sugar.

Vincent swallowed the rest of the cake with a hard gulp and quickly wiped the crumbs from his face. He wished he'd seen Clover before he stuffed the whole thing in his mouth. He waved shyly to her, still choking down the griddle cake. "Good afternoon," he finally got out.

"Good afternoon," said Clover. "It's a fine one, isn't it?" She brushed the chocolate and sugar from her paws and joined Lali by the griddle.

"Certainly is," replied Vincent, still pulling cake from his whiskers. "So, how are you feeling today?"

"I feel wonderful," said Clover. "Nightshade truly is a whole new world."

"Well, you look wonderful," said Vincent. His face suddenly felt hot as he realized how that may have sounded. "I mean you look, well, you know—healthy. Not that you don't look *wonderful*, because you *do* look wonderful—but I . . ." Vincent gave up before he sank himself deeper. Victor nudged him in the shoulder, thinking it quite funny to see his brother so tongue-tied.

Clover smiled kindly. "You look wonderful too," she said. Vincent's neck hairs stood on end.

Lali winked at Vincent. Cupping her paw around Clover's ear, she whispered something to her. Clover giggled and swatted Lali on the shoulder. "Lali, you're terrible," she said, her cheeks turning rosy. Vincent pretended not to notice, but he knew—hoped—that whatever was said was about him. Suttor waited slightly behind the Nightshades, looking despondent.

Lali tried to pull him into the conversation. "Suttor, how are *you* feeling today? Better, I hope."

Suttor tried but could not muster up a smile, even a phony one. "Yes, better—thank you."

Lali pointed to the center table. "Juniper's over there," she said to Vincent. "Take Suttor to him. He and the Council are already thinking up a plan to get those boys out."

Lali smiled at Suttor tenderly. She leaned over the wooden counter between her and the boys and spoke softly. "Suttor, family means everything round here. Juniper knows the importance of it better than anyone. He almost lost his," she said, nodding towards Clover. "He would never allow you to suffer that fate."

Juniper and the Council were eating rapidly at the main table, filling their mouths with spiced fish, meat, and pastry. Juniper concentrated on his brimming plate of food and not much else. Vincent tapped him lightly on the shoulder. "Boys!" said Juniper, looking up from his meal. "Finally awake, I see."

Spotting Suttor standing off to the side, Juniper got up from the table. "Suttor," he said, taking his paw and shaking it firmly. "I'm glad to see you're all right. That was a nasty blow you took."

"Yes, I'm fine," Suttor replied softly.

"Well, we saved some seats for you three," said Juniper, motioning across the table. "Come join us. We've a lot to talk about."

Lali trotted up behind the boys, setting heaping plates of food in front of them. "Eat up," she said. She set a particularly full plate in front of Suttor.

Suttor stared at the food, piled high. Far from hungry, he felt rather green at the sight of heaping sausages and sardines.

Juniper watched Suttor thoughtfully. "Now, Suttor, I've spoken to Oard, the earthworms' tribal leader, and he's getting word to our friend Mother Gallo. Can you tell me a little bit about your brothers? From what I gather, they were mere babies when you entered the army. We need to know what they look like now." Juniper took a huge bite of beef and gravy, talking through his mouthful. "Now, it's two brothers, yes?"

"Yes, Duncan and Kar," said Suttor.

"Good, that's a start. Mother Gallo will be seeking them out. Her status in the High Ministry allows her full access to the Kill Army. We are once again enlisting her much-needed help, but this time we plan on returning the favor. Now, Suttor, what can you tell me about them?"

Suttor sat for a moment. "Uh, well, there's little Kar. He's very small. He has black fur, except all four paws are solid white, and he has a big white splotch taking over most of his face, like someone spilled cream on him. Duncan is about Victor's age, a little younger. He's a little on the chubby side—well, more than a little, I'm afraid—with carrot-colored fur. Between his girth and his hue, he'll be a hard one to miss." Virden scribbled down the information as Suttor spoke.

Juniper inwardly chuckled at Suttor's descriptions. "Thank the

Saints your clan runs thick with unusual markings. This will simplify our search. Anything else we should know about them or their day-to-day comings and goings?"

"Just that they do everything together—they're still so young, they're both in training, no active duty. Mealtimes are at seven, twelve, and six sharp. That would be the best time to get word to them."

"Virden, do you have all that?" asked Juniper.

"Yes," said Virden. "This should be more than enough. I'll track down Oard. He said he'd stay close to Nightshade." Virden got up to leave. He patted Suttor on the back. "Don't worry, lad. We'll find them."

Suttor reconsidered his plate of food. He began to feel a little hungry after all.

After dinner, Mother Gallo and her boys sat in a circle around the smoldering fire pit. She had roasted some walnuts and sausage, received from High Cook Longtooth. Longtooth was, by and large, foulmouthed, cranky, and unpleasant. But for whatever reason, she had taken a shine to Mother Gallo, always giving her the best and freshest food available that day. With three growing boys to feed, Mother Gallo tolerated the tetchy cook; her generosity was well worth the price.

Mother Gallo looked seriously at her boys. "Boys, before we go to bed, we need to talk. Now, you all know of the Chosen One, Clover Belancort. Well, she has an uncle, a very heroic uncle, who once fought Billycan before he and Killdeer took hold of the Ministry. His name is Juniper Belancort."

"The rat that Billycan killed?" asked Tuk. "The one they tell the stories about?"

"Yes, but Billycan did *not* kill him. Juniper is quite alive," said

Mother Gallo. "As it turns out, Billycan didn't finish the job, and Juniper is as lively as you and I. He's built a new city—Nightshade City—buried deep under Trillium, deeper than the Combs."

"How do you know this?" Tuk interrupted.

"Well—I've been there. I've been to Nightshade," she replied.

"You have? When? What's it like?" asked Hob.

"Yes, what's it like? Is it as big as the Catacombs?" asked Gage, moving in closer.

Tuk stared skeptically at his mother, unconvinced. "She's joking. Aren't you, mother? You're playing a trick on us!"

Mother Gallo's voice turned stern. "No, Tuk, I certainly am *not*. I helped Juniper get his little niece, Clover, over to Nightshade and away from Killdeer." The boys gasped. They leaned into the circle, their heads almost touching. "Now, listen. Nightshade City is a different sort of place. It's not run by a Ministry. It's run by its citizens. Everyone has a say in what goes on there, and no one pays Stipend—ever."

Gage was aghast. "No one pays Stipend? How do they feed their army?"

"There is no army," said Mother Gallo. "If there's trouble, the citizens fight together. They all take care of each other, like one enormous family." The boys gawked at the thought.

Tuk suddenly looked alarmed. "Mother, what if Billycan finds out you helped Juniper? What will he do to you? He will hurt you or—"

Mother Gallo cut him off. "We won't be here to find out. We are leaving the Combs. We are moving to Nightshade, all of us. I will no longer have to work for the Ministry, and you boys can grow up in a safe, wonderful place. The kind of place I grew up in."

Tuk spoke very softly, as if the Kill Army were on the other side of the door. "Mother, how can we escape? The Kill Army is everywhere."

She studied her boys' three round faces, all staring nervously at her. "Juniper made me a promise. He doesn't break promises, and neither do I. I promise we'll get out safely."

Hob felt something pushing under his legs, inching him up in the air. "Mama!" he yelled. He jumped across the fire pit, nearly scorching his tail, and leaped into her arms.

Noc's shiny head popped up through the dirt floor. "Mother Gallo and family, I presume?"

Hob shook uncontrollably. "Oh, Hob, darling," said Mother Gallo, hugging him as he trembled. "This is Noc. He's an earthworm. Noc and his fellow tribesmen are helping us to build Nightshade City." Hob stared at the foreign creature. "He's a friend, dear. He would never hurt you." Hob loosened the rigid grip he had on his mother's neck. Leaning forward, he teetered precariously in the crook of her arm and inspected the worm.

Noc spoke gently to the boy. "I would never hurt you; certainly not. Your mother is a friend, so that makes all of you friends too. Mother Gallo, I gather it's safe to speak?"

"Yes, Noc, your timing is ideal. The boys and I were just talking about Nightshade."

Noc addressed the boys as if they were grown. "Now, boys, it seems Nightshade City is once again going to have to call on your mother for help, but this time we may need *your* help as well. Do you think you might be able to assist us in our efforts?"

The boys all nodded their heads in silence, unaware that worms were sightless. "They said yes, Noc," said Mother Gallo. "They are not used to having visitors, especially those who aren't rats. I hope you understand."

"Oh, yes, indeed I do," said Noc. "We think rats are as strange as you think us. You rats have an odd aroma and all that itchy hair—

horrible stuff!" The boys giggled. "Mother Gallo, we need to request an additional favor."

"What can I do?"

"Well, our friend Suttor, who is doing much better, by the way, is desperate to have his brothers join him. With your Ministry ties, we were hoping you could track down their location within the Kill Army and find a way to get them back to your quarters."

"Noc, of course I'll fetch the boys. I know just what to do."

"Wonderful," said Noc. "Now we can move your family and Suttor's to Nightshade together. All we need is for you to find a way to get Suttor's brothers back to your quarters. We worms can do a bit of reverse engineering and dig a corridor from here, meeting Juniper and his rats, and then dig straight down to Nightshade—so everyone can leave together."

"So soon! How exciting!" said Mother Gallo. "Boys, do you understand? We are leaving the Catacombs. Noc, I think I can have Suttor's brothers here by morning, shortly after breakfast."

"But how can *we* help?" said Tuk, who was at the age when helping was most important.

"Well, my young friend," said Noc, "what I need you to do is of the utmost importance, paramount to our mission's success. Suttor's brothers are going to be rather nervous, maybe even afraid. I need you to reassure them that everything is going to be just fine. Can you boys do that?"

Tuk spoke most assertively. "We can, Noc. I promise."

"Well, then, I hold you to your promise," said Noc. "Mother Gallo, before I take my leave, I've been instructed by Oard to give you the boys' descriptions."

"Not to worry, Noc. I remember them well, Duncan and Kar. With their features, they are a hard pair to forget."

"All the better, then. We are going to start the dig in the early morning hours, so get your rest, the lot of you. I'll be back soon to help guide you out."

"Noc," she said suddenly, "how did you know where to find me? I didn't pound out the signal."

"Juniper plans well in advance. He asked Oard to have me stay behind after Clover's rescue and follow the soldiers who took you to your quarters that night—a silent escort, if you will—making sure you were all right *and* learning the location of your home. Well, I'm off to Nightshade. I will be back soon with Oard and as many tribesmen as it takes to get the job done. Boys, it was a pleasure to meet you." Noc spindled gracefully back into the earth.

Hob looked down the hole as the worm vanished into the dirt. "Bye, Noc," he whispered.

"Good-bye, Hob," Noc's voice echoed back, already sounding awfully far away.

Morning came quickly to the Gallo household. In order to gain access to Suttor's brothers, Mother Gallo would have to clear it with Killdeer and Billycan. She was uneasy. It was one thing when Billycan questioned her in her own home, but to go to Killdeer's compound, to enter his den and lie to his face—well . . . "Eat up now," she told her sons. "You'll be of no good to anyone without a proper breakfast. Now, boys, I must go."

Mother Gallo unpinned her blue sash from the clothesline. "Now, do not answer the door for anyone, and for Saints' sake keep your voices down." She threw her sash over her head and arranged it neatly. "Tuk, you are in charge. Now, that doesn't mean you can bully your brothers. This is not the time for that sort of nonsense. Lives are at stake. Do you understand me?" The boys nodded as she headed towards the door.

"All right, then, you know what to do. I'll be back soon, hopefully with Suttor's brothers. Say a prayer for me—in fact, pray to the Saints very hard. Be good to each other and do everything the earthworms ask. I love you, my little ones." She slipped into the corridor.

Tuk locked the door behind her. "Hob, Gage, please finish your breakfast. Mother is worried. She is not letting on, but this is danger-ous. If we don't work together, things could go horribly wrong, and it will be *our* fault." Hob and Gage nodded seriously and gulped down the remains of their breakfast.

As if timed perfectly, Noc poked his head through the dirt wall, directly over the table. "Well, boys, good morning to you!" Tuk nearly scaled the wall in fright. Gage and Hob giggled. "I deduce your mother has left to gather Suttor's brothers?"

"Yes, sir," said Tuk, scowling at his brothers and wiggling his claw at them, just as he'd seen his mother do.

"Young Tuk, man of the house. We've a lot of work to do. For now, I need your help getting things prepared for the dig. The rats are already digging from Nightshade. The rest of our tribesmen will be here momentarily to start the excavation. Boys, your mission is to help move the tilled ground out of the way. We have no place to store the dirt, and we won't until the tunnel is open, so pick a good-sized part of the room and we'll start moving earth there."

Tuk directed his brothers. "Gage, let's start over there. Leave every-thing where it is. It doesn't matter if it gets dirty. It will all have to stay behind. Hob, you find anything small you think Mother might want to take with us and put whatever you find in one of her baskets—gently."

Mother Gallo stood in the corridor outside Killdeer's den. Trem-bling, she exhaled a shaky breath and knocked on the massive doors of the compound.

She heard small feet racing from within. They stopped abruptly. A door opened partway, and Texi poked her head out.

"Mistress Gallo," she said cheerfully. "How are you today?" She slipped out into the corridor, speaking again before Mother Gallo had a chance to answer. "I'm glad it's you and not another major. They've been coming in and going out at all hours—very pushy bunch."

Mother Gallo acted surprised. "You don't say? Well, the Minister must be awfully busy, then."

"Yes, it's been rather hectic around here. Killdeer and Billycan are in an uproar over the Chosen One's disappearance. I heard them saying she's been taken to *another* city." She whispered, "A *secret* city—they don't know where it is, but they are having the majors scour the Combs for information on its whereabouts. My brother said he is 'waging a *war*.'"

Mother Gallo acted aghast. "My goodness, Texi, did you say war? That sounds awfully serious. I won't take more than a few moments of their valuable time, then, but I do need to speak with the Collector or the Minister—either one will suffice. It's a Ministry matter, dear."

"You're in luck. They just finished a long meeting in the War Room with the majors. It lasted all night. They're both having breakfast in Killdeer's den. Follow me."

Mother Gallo followed behind Texi. Senior lieutenants and sector majors zipped in and out of rooms within the deep workings of Killdeer's compound.

High Major Lithgo plodded past them as they turned the corner towards Killdeer's den. "Mistress Gallo," he said, nodding courteously at her. Mother Gallo nodded back in acknowledgement, hoping her smile covered her panic.

"Here we are," said Texi as they arrived outside Killdeer's throne room. She took Mother Gallo's paw and squeezed it. "I heard about the blow you took to the head. I'm glad you're all right."

"That's sweet of you, dear. Yes, I'm just fine. Perhaps we can talk a little later."

"Maybe," said Texi, "but I am very busy today. Billycan ordered me to get rid of any Oshi or Carro ale I find in the compound. I'm to toss it all away—must have gone sour, I suppose. Bye, now." Texi skittered down the corridor.

Killdeer's sudden sobriety concerned Mother Gallo. It was clear that the Ministry was planning something big.

Mother Gallo entered the den. Killdeer and Billycan were seated at a table, both devouring fatty chicken legs. Killdeer set down a newly stripped bone and licked his claws as he addressed her. "Mistress Gallo," he said, sucking the grease from a claw. "Good to see you up and about. We were all quite distressed to hear of your ordeal."

Mother Gallo curtsied. Billycan looked up from his fowl and nodded his head in recognition of her presence. As he was still very much involved with his chicken, conversation was not essential. "Gentlemen, I'm so glad to have a short moment of your time," she said. "I know you're in a hurry to catch the culprits from the kidnappings and—"

Killdeer interrupted. "I'm just delighted to know you're all right. Why, we would be inconsolable if our enchanting High Mistress was snatched from us. Now, how may we be of service, dear Mistress?" He leaned back on his chair and stretched out his packed belly.

"Minister, I thank you for your concern. I've come for a favor, a mission of goodwill. I'm hoping you will allow me to take Lieutenant Suttor's brothers back to my quarters for the day. Spending some time with my family might just take their minds off Suttor, at least for a while. Suttor's brothers are far too young for active duty, and I can only imagine what the poor dears must be going through after hearing the dreadful news of Suttor's kidnapping."

Killdeer turned to Billycan. "Well, Collector, what do you think? Should we allow Mother Gallo this good deed?" Billycan shrugged indifferently and ripped into another chicken leg, stringy meat dangling from between his stained incisors.

Mother Gallo was well known and respected, and Killdeer hoped word of his generosity would spread. "Mistress Gallo, thank you for thinking of these forlorn boys. It is not in the boys' best interests to be left to their own devices at a time like this. Go retrieve them with my blessing. If you hurry, you may still be able to catch them in the mess hall at breakfast. Be sure to have them back to their barracks in time for head count. I wouldn't want the sector majors pushing down your door, terrifying you and your boys."

"Thank you, Minister," said Mother Gallo, clasping her paws together. "This is a wonderful favor you grant me. I will have the boys back by curfew, I promise."

"Very well, then, off you go. Do give those brave boys my deepest sympathies," he cooed unctuously. "And feel free to let others know I was all too happy to grant you this favor." He smiled a slippery grin, his teeth glossy from the greasy bird.

"Thank you, Minister, I certainly will," she said. "Thank you, Collector."

Killdeer nodded to her. Billycan waved her off, still focusing on the chicken leg, making sure every speck of flesh had been stripped from it.

Mother Gallo quickly left Killdeer's compound and made haste to the Kill Army mess hall, but not before stopping at her High Ministry workshop. There was something in the jewelry chest she needed.

The Kill Army mess hall overflowed with soldiers at this time of day. She would need help locating the boys in the massive hall, and she knew just who to ask. *More flies with honey*, she thought, as she bustled down the narrow corridor.

High Cook Longtooth sloshed the remainder of her mushy pig hash into a dented metal pan and placed the breakfast leftovers in a large pantry off the main army kitchen. The High Cook was not a cleanliness fanatic—not by far. The troops were lucky for their strong constitutions. Rats, unlike Topsiders, could endure the multitude of bacteria growing on their food. It seemed to make their systems stronger. They could safely digest everything from sawdust to concrete.

The troops were all still eating as the cook called for final serving. She hoped to close up early so she could go home and soak her tired, dirty feet. She lifted her oily apron and scratched a leg. Cook Longtooth had sinewy gray hair that tended to fall out in strange clumps, leaving dry, itchy patches that made her even more cantankerous. Her eyes were opaque, invaded by cataracts. She was missing many teeth, and the few she had left were brown, stained from years of working in the thick smoke that emanated from the kitchens. There were several large holes above the kitchen leading Topside, relieving the smoke, but the taint still lingered in her skin and teeth, adding to her unsightly appearance. Her nasty temper certainly didn't help soften her revolting looks.

Mother Gallo entered the swarming mess hall, coming upon the throng of young rats, all talking loudly, loading their mouths with lumps of food. She inspected as many rats as she could on her way back towards the kitchens. She looked for splashes of orange and the contrast of black and white, but she could not find Suttor's brothers.

She spotted Cook Longtooth, scuffling about, sticking utensils here and there. The cook was born with an abnormally long front tooth that hung over her lower lip, ending well past her stubbly chin. The cook made the best of her oddity, using her snaggletooth as a crude can opener, which came in quite handy.

Mother Gallo put on her brightest smile. She had a cheerfully wrapped parcel under her arm, done up in colors of plum and silver. "Cook Longtooth," she said. "It's Mother Gallo, come to say hello, if you have the time."

Longtooth twisted around, her teeth splintering into a fractured grin. "Mistress Gallo," she said in her craggy, broken tone, "to what do I owe a visit from the High Mistress?" Mother Gallo took the wrapped parcel and presented it to the old cook. Longtooth's voice crackled. "Well, what's this, Mistress?" She scratched her head. "It's not my birthday—is it?"

"Cook Longtooth, please call me Maddy. You've always been so kind to me. I feel I need to reciprocate your generosity. Please take this gift as a gesture of my appreciation. I insist. The Ministry insists." She put Longtooth's decrepit paw on top of the package.

Longtooth grimaced shyly. "I don't remember the last time I got a present. It seems ages, perhaps when I was a girl." As detestable as Longtooth could be, Mother Gallo couldn't help but feel for her.

Mother Gallo smiled. "Now, this is just a little something special I came across in my workshop, and I thought if anyone deserved it, it was you. We girls have to stick together, especially surrounded by all this Kill Army bravado and bluster."

"I suppose we do," Longtooth said with a sigh. She used a ragged claw to sever the silver string, letting it fall to the ground. She tore open the colored paper, revealing something shiny, a silver beaded necklace and matching bracelet. "Oh, Mistress, you shouldn't have! It's lovely—just lovely!" Her ashen skin prickled in delight.

Mother Gallo lowered her voice. "Now, Longtooth, these silver beads belonged to Nomi, our beloved High Duchess from days long gone. You know what a strong female Nomi was, and I know she would be proud for you to have these."

"Oh, Mistress, how can I ever repay you?" Longtooth wiped away tears with a corner of her soiled apron.

"Longtooth, we are friends, you and I. I'm repaying your kindness. You owe me nothing."

Out of character for the old cook, she hugged Mother Gallo, squeezing her with all the might her raggedy arms could muster. "May the Saints bless your soul. There must be something I can do for you."

"Well, as a matter of fact—there is."

As it turned out, Longtooth did know Suttor's brothers. Their atypical markings made them hard to ignore. She cackled as she told Mother Gallo that Kar looked as though he'd been smacked in the face with a bucket of whitewash. She did, however, have a soft spot for Duncan; the chubby orange rat had quite a fondness for her creamed corn with bacon. "I like that young fellow. He's a tubby thing—likes my food, he does."

Longtooth pointed to where the boys usually sat, then hustled back to the kitchen, clutching her new treasure in her bony digits.

Mother Gallo spotted the boys. They looked the same as they did the last time she saw them—five years bigger, but the same. She knew little Kar would not remember her, but Duncan was old enough.

She approached the table. The boys were picking at their meals, shifting food around on their plates. "Boys," she said, leaning towards the table, "do you remember me?" The boys looked up from their plates. Kar looked at her with a blank expression. Duncan stared at her for a moment. His pumpkin face brightened slightly.

"I know you," said Duncan. "You're Tuk's mother—Mother Gallo. You make those cherry tartlets."

"Yes, Duncan, that's right. Do you remember my boys, Gage and Hob?"

"Yes, ma'am, Gage used to play hide-and-seek with me. He *always* found me, though," said Duncan, crinkling his forehead. "I never knew how he did it." Mother Gallo chuckled to herself. Clearly Duncan had no idea that his size and tangerine hue made him rather easy to spot.

Mother Gallo leaned in closer. "Now, boys, I have news of Suttor—good news." The boys' mouths dropped. Their ears perked.

Duncan slid over on the bench as fast as he could move his pudgy frame. "Come sit, Mother Gallo. What news do you have of our brother?"

"Boys, Suttor is alive and well," she whispered. "He has asked that you come with me and meet him in a new city, far away from the Combo and the army. Killdeer and Billycan have agreed to grant you leave for the day, to spend time with me and my boys. As I speak, friends of your brother are digging an escape route. Now, then, if you want to stay here in the Kill Army, I'll tell your brother myself. You *do* have a choice. You do not have to come."

Little Kar looked up at Mother Gallo. He seemed a bit overwhelmed, curling in closer to Duncan. "You mean we can leave this place?" he asked in a quivery voice.

"Yes, darling," said Mother Gallo, "you can leave forever. We are building a home for you boys, a wonderful home." Kar sniffled, wiping away stray tears. "Now, boys, you have to leave all your things behind in the barracks, or it will look suspicious. We must leave right now, agreed?" Both boys nodded. "All right, then. Follow me—no dawdling."

She got up from the table. The boys trailed behind her. Mother Gallo cleared their departure with a sector major, and they walked out of the Kill Army mess hall, smiling silently.

Noc could hear the boys rushing about, dashing to and fro as they moved buckets of tilled earth from the hole to the corner of the room. "That's it, boys! You're doing a fine job," he said.

The rickety door to the Gallo household creaked open. Tuk and his brothers froze in their tracks. They had tried to stay quiet, but perhaps their constant scurrying had been heard. The boys exhaled with relief as Mother Gallo stuck her head in.

"Bless the Saints," she said, stunned at the mountain of earth in her once-pristine home. "Come in, boys, quickly, now." Suttor's brothers followed quietly behind her. They looked round the room, bewildered.

Tuk nudged Gage. The two approached Duncan. "Duncan," said Tuk, in his most grown-up voice. "It's good to see you. We have a lot to catch up on."

"Yes," agreed Gage. "We can all talk on the way to Nightshade."

"You mean—you're going down the tunnel with us?" asked Duncan.

"Of course," said Tuk, "we are going to the new city, too. We'll all be back together, and you and Kar will see Suttor tonight!"

Mother Gallo took Kar over to Hob, explaining how they had played together as babies. "So you see," she told them, "you are friends already. You just don't remember."

Oard suddenly poked his head through the ground, surprising the boys. He spoke in his croaky voice, but his tone was subdued. "Hello, boys, I am Oard. Juniper and the others are about to break through, so you can stop your digging. Your hard work has given us a brilliant start. Worms, get into position. We need to be ready to backfill!" Oard zipped back into the earth like a brown wisp of smoke.

Hob led Kar over to his mother's bed, where he had set the bulk of his toys, and gave Kar a wooden rat to keep. Suddenly, the bed started to shake and the center of the floor started to rumble. There was one final tremor, and the ground gave way, dropping into the fresh tunnel below. Juniper and the others pulled down more earth, widening the hole as best they could.

Juniper popped his head and trunk through the hole, his coat matted with dirt and pebbles. He shook his head vigorously, flinging dried earth everywhere. He looked round the room. The boys all gawked at the oversized rat.

He chuckled heartily, grinning. "Now, who is who? I see five surprised faces with five open mouths. Who are their owners?"

"I see you're back for more trouble, Mr. Belancort," said Mother Gallo. She smiled prettily at Juniper, a smile her boys had never seen before.

"Maddy, you are a sight for my weary eyes," said Juniper. He pulled himself up into the room and dusted himself off. "Now, who are these fine fellows before me?"

"Juniper, this is my son Tuk, the oldest. Next comes Gage; he's mine too. And this fellow with the lovely orange fur is Duncan, one of Suttor's brothers."

"Boys," said Juniper, nodding his head. He bent down, eyeing Hob and Kar. "And who are these strapping young rats?"

"These two little ones are Hob and Kar. Hob is my youngest, and Kar is Suttor's baby brother."

Kar clutched the wooden figurine Hob had given him. "Well, hello, there," said Juniper. "Are you boys ready to go to your new home?" They both nodded. "Well, we'd best get going, then, eh? We've a long way to travel, so we must depart—"

The door suddenly rattled. Someone was pounding on it. "High Mistress Gallo," called the voice from the corridor. "It's Lieutenant Carn, Aide to the High Collector. I need to speak with you right away."

The boys glanced at one another nervously. Juniper put a claw to his lips. Everyone stood very still. Terrified, Kar dropped his wooden figurine to the floor.

"Mistress Gallo," called Carn again. "Please come to the door directly. I can hear you inside."

Holding a paw to her heart, Mother Gallo replied, "I'm coming, Lieutenant Carn."

Juniper silently directed the boys away from the door and then nodded to Mother Gallo. She grabbed the handle of the door, pulling it open only a crack.

"How can I help you, Lieutenant Carn?" she asked in an official tone.

"Mistress Gallo, I was sent by Billycan. He'd like me to transcribe the details you gave him in regards to the Chosen One's disappearance." Carn looked over her head and noticed that her quarters were in disarray, completely covered in dirt. Overpowering her, Lieutenant Carn flung open the door. He stared in amazement, taking in the scene. It was clear that she was escaping with the boys. His eyes abruptly halted on Juniper. "You!" he hissed. "So, it's true!"

"Now, lad," said Juniper calmly. "Let's not do anything hasty—"

Carn looked down each end of the corridor. A patrol of sector majors was rounding the corner. "Quickly!" he said to Juniper. "Sector majors are on their way. Get everyone down the hole and out of here now! You *will* be discovered!"

For once, Juniper was speechless. He knew Carn's face, but how?

"Now, go!" said Carn, trying not to shout.

It was late. The travelers had walked a good distance and were just steps away from Nightshade Passage. Juniper carried Kar, while Cole held Hob. Despite the bumpy trudge down to Nightshade, both little boys had fallen asleep on their shoulders.

Vincent, Victor, and Suttor had been waiting restlessly in the passage. Suttor was still dizzy and weak from his fall, and Juniper had thought it best for Vincent and Victor to stay with him. Suttor had protested, but Juniper told him an injured rat would only be a liability. Suttor reluctantly agreed, so there he sat in a miserable state—waiting.

At last, Ulrich and Ragan entered the passage. Suttor jumped to his feet.

"What of my brothers?" he asked, trying to push past the twins.

Ragan put his paws on Suttor's shoulders. Suttor did not look well, his skin felt hot to the touch, and his eyes drooped. "Calm down, lad. They're just a few steps behind us. The boys are fine, son, just fine. You have some tired but happy brothers ready to greet you." Suttor's whole body relaxed. Ragan kept tight hold of Suttor's shoulders, worried he might fall to the ground. "They're none the worse for wear, Suttor—none the worse."

Juniper called out from inside the corridor. "Suttor, my boy!" He emerged from the corridor with a sleeping Kar attached to him like a pet monkey. "Kar, it's time to wake up, now," he whispered. Kar lifted his heavy head and rubbed his eyes.

Suttor rushed over to Juniper. Without a word, Kar reached out his arms to his older brother. Suttor took hold of him, squeezing him tight. "Kar, are you all right?" Kar nodded blearily. Duncan wandered in, looking up at the rotunda in wonder. "Duncan!" shouted Suttor. The three bothers embraced in a tangle of black, orange, and white.

"Juniper," said Suttor, "thank you, thank everyone."

"You're quite welcome," said Juniper. "Lad, do you know a Lieutenant Carn?"

"I know *of* him," said Suttor. "He's Billycan's aide—keeps mostly to himself."

"Do you know his clan name?"

"All I know is Lieutenant Carn has been Billycan's aide for as long as I can remember. Why do you ask?"

"He helped us tonight," said Juniper. "He could have handed us to Billycan, but he let us go. This lieutenant—Carn—he clearly knew who I was. I feel like I knew him too. I don't know why he allowed us to get away."

Billycan sat in the War Room with Killdeer and the majors. Texi had just cleared their late dinner away, and they were getting back to work. As much as he hated to admit it, Billycan knew Juniper was clever, probably more so than his own high majors. Juniper was well aware that there was no point in creating a new city if you couldn't keep the inhabitants alive. The city had to be under the Reserve. The question was—where?

Billycan stared at the map. It was old, so old; it still said "Brimstone" across the top, the Reserve's former name. "This map is useless," he growled in frustration. "We know the general area where these traitors are hiding themselves, but that is all. We have to determine how our rats are being smuggled out. Someone must have left a trail. We will find it and kill Nightshade's turncoat residents—filthy Loyalists. The Combs are slowly crumbling. We'll claim Nightshade City as our territory—the *new* Catacombs."

"Agreed," said Killdeer," but how are my subjects fleeing? We've had all the deserted quarters inspected, we've sent our best trackers to scour the Combs, and no evidence of escape has been reported. It's as if the missing families have evaporated into dust."

There was an urgent knocking at the door. "Enter," barked Billycan, hoping for some fresh information. Carn entered the room. "Lieutenant Carn, as you can see, we are busy. Whatever you have to say better be important."

Carn took a moment, catching his breath. "Sir, I just came from Major Lithgo's sector," he huffed.

Billycan's temper was well past its tipping point. "Yes, yes, spit it out, Lieutenant Carn."

"Sir, Training Lieutenants Duncan and Kar are missing."

"Missing? What do you mean, 'missing'?" asked Billycan, clearly annoyed. "Why do you pester me with this? Go find them!"

"They missed head count, sir. We've searched the entire barracks and training ground. They simply aren't here. They were checked out earlier by the High Mistress of the Robes, and she never returned them to their unit. I don't know if you're aware, but they are Lieutenant Suttor's brothers."

Billycan scratched his chin, not yet alarmed. "The High Minister gave Mistress Gallo permission to have the boys for the day. Could it be possible they are simply late? Perhaps our High Mistress lost track of the hour."

Lieutenant Carn's body tensed. He gulped stiffly, as if trying to swallow a rock. Billycan had a tendency to release his rage on the messenger. "Commander, curfew came and went hours ago. As ordered, I'd gone to Mistress Gallo's earlier to take down the details of the Chosen One's kidnapping. She was not there. I thought nothing of it until the boys had been reported missing from the barracks and I was informed that *she* had checked them out. I went back to her quarters straightaway and knocked several times on the door—in fact, pounded. I thought it best to come to you before beating it down, given her station within the High Ministry."

Billycan was unaware of the late hour. They had worked well into the night, losing track of time. He paused for a moment, thinking about Mistress Gallo's movements of late. Suddenly, everything connected. Billycan abruptly slammed his fists on the table, realizing once again he had been swindled. "How could I have missed it? *She* is the culprit! She is the biggest turncoat of them all—deceitful, double-dealing traitor hag!"

Killdeer stood up. "Billycan, are you suggesting our High Mistress is a conspirator?"

Billycan snarled wildly, wailing at Killdeer and the majors. "Yes, it's her! She met with Clover. She had that filthy sack—Juniper's sack! Too many coincidences—her *innocent* involvement with Clover's desertion and the lieutenant's kidnapping, and now—she's taken the boy's brothers! The lethal little harpy!" he roared, slamming his billy club on the map of the Reserve. "I'll rip her serpent tongue from her mouth! We have found our link to Nightshade City. It's been Gallo all along! She will pay with her hide! Majors Schnauss and Foiber, come with me to Gallo's quarters. Lithgo, go find the soldiers who know these brothers and question them. Lieutenant Carn, go to the barracks and meticulously inspect the boys' belongings for clues. Report back any findings in an hour's time. We *will* find a trail!" Carn and the majors saluted Killdeer and exited, following Billycan, who'd already stormed feverishly out of the War Room.

Killdeer sat alone, not sure what to do with himself. He decided he would examine each and every one of the Catacomb maps. That segment of his mind, the part once so brilliant at planning and strategizing, had been dormant for years. Perhaps, he thought, this would allow for a fresh perspective, something the others may have missed. Killdeer needed to win back the full respect of Billycan. His life depended on it.

Billycan kicked in the Gallos' door. He, Schnauss, and Foiber entered the abandoned residence. Not much in the way of belongings seemed to be missing. Nothing was suspicious other than things appearing disorganized from what Billycan remembered of his last visit, as if items had been pushed around.

Schnauss examined the room with his one good eye. His voice cracked and gurgled as he spoke. "Commander, either Gallo's housekeeping skills are sorely lacking or mischief is afoot." He ran a decaying digit over Mother Gallo's rocking chair. The room's contents were covered in a fine layer of dirt. He rubbed the powder on his palm and looked up. "Her ceiling and walls are intact. There is nothing falling from above, so how did this coating get over everything in sight?"

Foiber studied the floor. The earthworms had swept the floor impeccably, leaving no trace of the dig. "What I don't understand is this floor," he said, feeling the ground with the sole of his foot. "The floor is strangely smooth, not dusty like everything else in this room. It's immaculate." He looked at Billycan. "Does this seem logical to you, Commander? A house full of rowdy boys, with not so much as a claw mark marring the floor?"

Billycan circled the room. "I noticed the same dust spread about the Belancort girl's quarters, the night of her escape. At first, Billycan thought it was caused by the scuffle. Though now, I wonder. What could cause such a dusting?"

Foiber scratched his scaly haunches. "In my days of serving the Kill Army, I've led many a dig, especially back when we were expanding the Combs. The part I could never tolerate was the veneer of dry dirt that coated everything in sight. It irritated my skin to no end—always being caked with parched, prickly earth. The dusting in this room is the same, Commander. I think Juniper and his rats are digging into the Combs. The question is, how are they cleaning up the mess so quickly? There are traitors within the Combs. How else could they go undetected? Security has never been tighter, checkpoints never so strict."

Billycan grunted, pounding the rock-hard floor with his food. The earthworms had packed it solid. "We were at Clover's door minutes after her escape, and the floor was wholly intact. No rats could accomplish that so quickly and still have time to flee. The moles would never assist our kind, not even Juniper. They're too lumbering and far too lazy. The skittish shrews would not dare venture this deep into our world."

Billycan picked up one of Hob's toys, squeezing it harder and harder as he spoke. "Question everyone in Gallo's sector. If anyone seems even the least bit deceptive, take them to holding for a proper interrogation. Someone has to know something."

Schnauss grimaced, causing his front teeth to smash his lower lip. "Gallo will be caught," he said. "You will have the distinct honor of butchering Gallo and her rotten sons in Catacomb Hall, giving our subjects an eyeful as a warning to others hoping to escape. You can leave her alive while she watches her precious boys bleed out before her traitorous eyes. Revenge is yours for the taking."

The two high majors plodded out of the room. Billycan stood alone in the Gallo quarters. Still clutching the boy's toy, he looked down at it contemptuously. It was a wood carving of Trilok. He crushed it to splinters.

It was morning. Juniper and the Council had arrived in Bostwick Hall early for some peace and quiet. Their numbers now strong enough to go into battle, they needed to strategize.

Juniper thought the strange happenings over the last few days were signs from the Saints, signs that it was time to move forward—the discovery of the Nightshade brothers, Clover as a Chosen One, his reunion with Mother Gallo, and now the mysterious Lieutenant Carn, who allowed them to escape. It all seemed to point to something bigger. It was time to liberate the Catacombs.

The Nightshade rats had filled in the escape corridors they had used only a quarter of the way, corridors that led to multiple residents throughout the Combs. This way they could excavate quickly, launching surprise attacks in small groups on the Kill Army—guerrilla warfare, of sorts. They would invade from all sides of the Combs.

Suttor and his brothers would be of great help to Nightshade. They had full knowledge of the Kill Army comings and goings, numbers, etc. Juniper felt that if he could separate the troops from the majors, he could convince them to defect. The youths were programmed, led to believe the Kill Army to be the best thing that life had in store for them and that they should feel privileged to serve. Juniper wondered how easily a young rat could change back from soldier to boy. Only time would tell. Suttor and his brothers gave him hope.

The orphan girls were another matter entirely. Clover had told her uncle the stories she'd heard: their horrible living conditions, crammed into little rooms with odds and ends for food, many times with nothing at all. Longtooth tried to slip them what she could but was constantly watched by the sector majors, making it almost impossible. With so little to survive on, many had died. The ones that survived kept to themselves, silent and subservient, the best way to steer clear of the backside of a major's paw. The number of boys to girls in the Catacombs was alarmingly unbalanced. Juniper's heart ached for them, so forgotten. If Clover had ever been found out—he could not finish the thought.

Vincent, Victor, and Suttor entered Bostwick Hall. They'd left the younger boys in bed, still worn from their trip. Suttor looked healthier.

"Boys," said Juniper, "come and sit. Suttor, I was just thinking about you."

"You were?" Suttor asked, taking a seat with Vincent and Victor at the table.

"Well, lad, I could use your help."

"My help? What can I do?"

Juniper pushed over a plate of biscuits to the boys. "We need your knowledge of the majors' typical comings and goings, everything from where they take their meetings to what time they change shifts, even when they relieve themselves!" he said with a chuckle. "My boy, every bit of information you can give us might be of great help, even if it seems inconsequential. The smallest detail could facilitate our victory."

"I don't think anything I know will help, but I'll tell you everything I can," said Suttor, ripping into a biscuit. "I owe you that and more."

"Suttor, you don't owe anyone anything, least of all me. This is your home now. This is everyone's home," he said. He looked round the room, slowly filling with hungry rats ready for breakfast. "We need to get one and all out of the Combs. That's what all this is for—a new way of life." The Council nodded in agreement. "Now, let's get started. Virden, are you ready?"

"Yes, ready as always," said Virden. He pulled his feather from behind his ear and dipped it in ink, standing by to take notes.

Suttor sat with the Council for a large part of the morning, providing a wealth of information. He explained when the soldiers woke up, when they slept, when they ate, when and where they trained, when they were given leave—anything he could think of. He explained about the War Room, located in Killdeer's compound. It was right next to the High Minister's den. With some risky exploration, Oard and his tribe might be able to find it. Suttor said that's where all sorts of maps, blueprints, and historical documents were stored. He said Lieutenant Carn had pointed out the room to him once and told him that's where all vital meetings were held in times of conflict, so he could only surmise it was back in use.

Suttor's injured head began to ache. "Juniper, I can't think of another thing," he said, rubbing between his eyes.

"Don't get discouraged, son. This is all intelligence we can use. As I said, the smallest thing can win the battle, and your knowledge of the War Room is no small thing."

Victor had gone to retrieve Suttor's brothers. "Ah, finally awake, I see," said Juniper. He grinned at the two young boys, both still groggy with sleep. "Boys, your brother has been helping us, sharing as much knowledge of the Kill Army as he can. Now, I know you boys weren't on active duty, but can you think of anything that might help us, anything that would assist us getting in or out of the Combs: a secret entrance, an escape route, anything at all?"

Duncan, still disheveled from sleep, his orange fur sticking straight up in various places, marched up to Juniper. He had a sure expression on his chubby face. "I can tell you something, Juniper.

The Kill Army kitchens," he stated plainly, as if Juniper should know exactly what he meant.

"What about the kitchens, Duncan?" asked Juniper, smiling at the plump rat. "What makes them so important?"

"Why, the chimneys, of course. They lead all the way up Topside. Can't you get in through there, late at night, when the kitchens are empty?"

Everyone at the table was taken aback. Then Juniper laughed out loud. "Yes, Duncan, yes, we can!" he said. "An attack from below *and* above. It's genius!" Juniper got up from the table and patted Duncan vigorously on the back. "My boy, how on earth did you figure that out?"

"High Cook allows me back in the kitchen from time to time. I asked her about the holes a long time ago, and she told me they're chimneys that go all the way Topside, letting out the smoke. She said they're lined with chicken wire to keep them from mudding up and the older soldiers scale the wire when they need to be cleaned. Cook lets me come back in the kitchen sometimes for a second helping of her creamed corn with bacon. It's my favorite. We talk a lot. I know she's kind of cross, but I like her all right."

"Duncan, I like her all right myself," said Juniper, slapping his paws together. "In fact, I like her very much at the moment. Virden, get word to Oard about the War Room. If it's next to Killdeer's den, they should be able to find it. Also, ask them to find the Topside location of the kitchen's chimneys."

Suttor thought of something else. "Juniper, once the kitchen is closed, no one guards it. There's no need. It's already within the Kill Army boundaries. Who would guard an empty mess hall?"

"You boys have no idea what help you've been!" Bostwick Hall was filling with smells of sausage and smoked fish. "Let's say we eat?" suggested Juniper.

"Oh, good," said Duncan, "I'm famished." Everyone laughed as they got up from the table.

Juniper put his arm around Duncan's shoulder and started walking towards the food line. "Well now, let's see what Lali has cooked up today. I cannot guarantee creamed corn with bacon, but we'll see what she can do. C'mon, everyone."

CHAPTER SEVEN
A City of Devils

CAUTIOUSLY POKING THEIR HEADS in and out of the many rooms surrounding Killdeer's sprawling den, Noc and Quip finally found the War Room. The High Minister sat alone, sifting through piles of tattered maps and blueprints. He couldn't fathom how his subjects were escaping so effortlessly. The Stipend intake was dwindling rapidly. Soon they would have to cut back on army rations.

The two worms pulled their heads back into the wall so they could speak. "Noc, how long do you think we have to wait here?" asked Quip, bored with listening to Killdeer's heavy breathing.

"I suppose as long as it takes. Hopefully, Billycan and his majors will be back soon enough, with information we can use."

"Wait! Do you hear that?" said Quip. "It sounds like footsteps."

"Quiet, now," said Noc. "I'd know that irregular gait anywhere. It's Billycan." They heard the War Room's door open. "Let's move closer. We can't afford to miss a word." The pair glided through the earth as Billycan and Majors Foiber and Schnauss entered the War Room. Noc slowly stuck his head out, blending with the dirt walls, unnoticed by the rats.

Leaving Killdeer alone had been done with purpose. Billycan suspected that if left to his own devices, Killdeer, no longer able to handle the stress of impending combat, would have retrieved a secret Oshi bottle. Had he failed the test, Billycan would have killed him right then and there. But it was obvious from Killdeer's countenance and the mess of documents he had been searching through that he was completely sober.

"Minister, we have news," said Billycan, sitting down across from him at the table. "We have deduced from our findings that the rats are digging out of their quarters, meeting up with Juniper's rats, and journeying on to Nightshade."

"Do we have evidence of this? I thought no noticeable disorder had been detected in the deserted quarters."

Billycan glared scathingly at the useless stack of maps, "Minister, someone is helping them clean up the mess. The floor in Mother Gallo's room was as smooth as glass, as if never walked on. She has raised three children, with many footsteps and sharp claws to scar that floor. In addition, every inch of the room is covered in a fine layer of dust, a dust one would only find after an intense dig. Rest assured they are getting help from traitors inside the Combs. Billycan will soon discover from whom."

Noc pulled his head back into the wall. "Quip, it will only be a matter of time before they pinpoint our tribe." They stuck their heads out once more and listened.

Killdeer had a plan. "Catacomb Hall is still set up for the Grand Speech, is it not? I've decided I will still give a speech—but only for the soldiers. We will assemble the entire Kill Army in the hall tomorrow night, at midnight. Leave one soldier at each security checkpoint. The others will go to the hall. No soldier is exempt, unless put on duty by one of us. Billycan, you and I will address them. I want every home in the Catacombs searched. I want every resident questioned, down to the smallest drooling child. We will find these conspirators. We can't afford not to, as our numbers grow thinner every day. The soldiers need to be trained in interrogation techniques. The senior lieutenants can each lead a unit, questioning our subjects one by one. They will scour the Combs until something is uncovered. Once we have suspects under lock and key, Foiber, Schnauss, you will take over the questioning. Billycan, emphasize the use of force. By the time it's your turn to speak, I'll have those boys eager to ring a few necks and knock a few heads. They'll think their very lives depend upon it. The questioning will commence directly following the speech. We'll tear our weary subjects from their beds, unsuspecting and unfocused, making it harder for them to lie."

Billycan sat and listened to the Minister. For once, he seemed to be making perfect sense. As he thought of what he would say to the troops, he noticed something out of the corner of his eye—something moving ever so slightly. It moved again, unnoticed by anyone but him. It was an earthworm. Springing from his chair, Billycan leaped in a lightning flash from the table and lunged at the earthworm, grabbing it by its head and flinging it with all his force against the War Room wall. The earthworm stuck to the surface for a moment and then slowly slid down the wall, dropping to the floor.

Killdeer and the majors snickered at the sight. "My word, how you despise those things," said Killdeer, his belly shaking as he laughed.

Billycan wiped his paw on his sash, recoiling from the moist feel of the worm's skin. "Earthworms are low, sickening excuses for life.

They do nothing but slink around the Combs, leaving their trails of filth behind them. There is no place for them in this world—no need."

"You know, majors," said Killdeer, "I've seen our Billycan kill hundreds of these worthless creatures. It's almost a pastime."

"I too have witnessed this exhibition many a time," said Schnauss. "It seems as though we finally know of something that unnerves our otherwise fearless High Collector and Commander." Schnauss, Foiber, and Killdeer rolled in their chairs in a fit of grunting laughter.

Killdeer snorted. "Someone call for a lieutenant to clean up this mess."

Noc was dead.

Quip flew through the soil, back to Nightshade. How would the tribe handle the news? The only comfort he could give them was that Noc had not suffered. He had died instantly. He would never forget the sound of his body hitting the hard wall and dropping to the floor. The way they had all laughed, as if Noc were nothing . . .

As he reached the threshold of Nightshade City, he stopped and lay still in the dirt. Had he eyes, he would have momentarily closed them. Noc had a family. He was Oard's second-in-command. The whole tribe was counting on him to secure their new home. Quip let out a whimper of despair and carried on to Nightshade.

He reached Bostwick Hall. He could hear Juniper, Oard, and the others discussing strategy and tactics. Oard was curled up on the main table, while Juniper, Cole, and the rest of the Council sat around him. The younger rats were all chattering together, getting reacquainted. Mother Gallo, Lali, and Clover were giggling, telling one another funny stories about Juniper and Cole. Quip heard Oard laugh his deep, genuine laugh at a joke Virden had told him.

"Oard," he called from the wall in a strained voice.

"Quip," said Oard throatily, "I'm glad you're back safe. What news do you and Noc have from the Combs?"

"I have something to tell everyone," he replied flatly.

"Quip, you sound peculiar. Where's Noc?"

The room went still. Everyone stopped talking and turned towards Quip. The worm trembled for a moment, and then spoke. "Noc and I found the War Room today. We received valuable intelligence, which I will report later. Just a short while ago . . . Noc's life was taken. Billycan spotted him as we were listening from the wall. He snatched him before Noc had time to react, throwing him against a wall, killing him instantly."

The rats' ears drooped. Their tails fell to the ground.

Hob walked up to Quip, who dangled from the wall. Hob stretched his neck up to see the worm. "You mean . . . Noc is dead?" he asked.

"I'm afraid so," he replied.

Hob's chin began to quiver. Kar walked over to comfort his friend as he had seen Juniper do. He put his spotted arm around Hob's shoulder.

Juniper was silent, overcome by guilt. He had gone to the earthworms for help, but he could not shield them from Billycan. His body shook. He let out a terrifying wail, startling everyone. "You see!" he cried. "You see how this so-called High Ministry values life? Be we rats or worms, we are of no value to the Ministry. We are nothing to them! Stipend holds more worth! All of you have lived under their regime. Stringing up rats in Catacomb Hall for all to see, swinging by their broken necks. Chaining so-called criminals to posts so you can watch them starve to death, so your children can watch them die!

When Noc died, they laughed, didn't they? Did they laugh, Quip? Did the leaders of the High Ministry grunt and cackle as Noc lay lifeless on the ground?"

Quip answered softly. "Yes."

Juniper took a deep breath as he unclenched his fists. He noticed everyone looking at him nervously. Walking over to Hob and Kar, he bent down and picked the boys up, one in each arm. Mother Gallo walked over and put a paw on Juniper's back, gently patting it. He looked over his shoulder at her and gave a cheerless smile.

"Oard," Juniper said, looking at his friend. Oard had not said a word, still sitting in his coiled position on the table. "We are truly sorry for your tribe's loss. Noc will be missed by us all, worms and rats alike. He *will* be avenged. All our loved ones will be. This Ministry has taken something or someone from everyone in this room." He faced the rats. "Heed me, now—Billycan's crimes will not go unpunished. He will answer for this and for every atrocity he has ever committed on any of the creatures that inhabit the Combs. He *will* pay."

Finally, Oard addressed the room. "Noc was a brave tribesman, my second-in-command, my brother, my friend. He knew the risks of what he was doing. With any revolution, death goes hand in hand. We have our first casualty of Nightshade City. Our first loss of life and, I'm sorry to say, probably not our last. I must go to Noc's family and tell them the sad news." Oard dropped off the table and moved towards the wall. "Quip and I will be back in a few hours. As Juniper said, Noc *will* be avenged. His death will have meant something." With that, he disappeared into the wall. Quip followed.

Juniper looked at the two boys still balancing on his arms. "Are you two all right? Did I frighten you?"

"Just a little, when you got loud," said Kar.

"Well, I'm very sorry, Kar. Sometimes our emotions get the better of us."

"It's okay," said Kar. "My brothers get that way too when they're mad, especially Suttor." Juniper mustered up a weak smile at the response.

Hob looked at Juniper and put his two small paws on the large rat's face. "It's okay to be sad, Juniper," he said tenderly. "My mother says if you hold all your sadness inside, it has nowhere to go and stays trapped inside you forever."

Juniper looked over at Mother Gallo. "Your mother is a very wise rat, far wiser than I."

Oard and Quip arrived back at Nightshade City as promised. The mood in Bostwick Hall was solemn. The two worms emerged from the wall and slowly dropped to the floor, making their way to the center table, each twisting up a leg. Oard coiled his large body in the center of the table, while Quip stayed off to the side, still rather shaken.

Juniper was the first to speak. "Oard, you didn't need to come back so promptly. We understand that you and your tribesmen need time to mourn."

Oard spoke so all would hear. "Juniper, you and I have been through a lot together. This has been a sad day indeed for our tribe, but when it's your time—it's your time. Noc was aware of the perils, but he knew those perils could not outweigh the hopes of fresh new soil for our tribe. We are not going to mourn Noc. We are going to celebrate him. Noc would want it this way. Do not feel pity for us. We knew full well the danger involved the moment you approached us. Now, as I just said to my tribesmen, no more sorrow. Am I perfectly clear?"

"You are, old friend," said Juniper.

"Good. Then let's get back to work," said Oard commandingly. "Now, Juniper, Quip has some important news for you, information that will change the entire scope of our attack. Quip, tell Juniper what you and Noc learned on your mission."

Quip reported what he and Noc had overheard: about the midnight speech in Catacomb Hall, and about Killdeer's plans to find Nightshade City. Juniper was troubled. "Foiber and Schnauss, those two ogres, are to interrogate every Catacomb rat? This is a witch hunt. Foiber and Schnauss mistake fear for deception, fidgeting for trickery. This will lead to bloodshed."

"There's more," said Oard. "We have found the Topside location of the kitchen's chimneys. They are easily accessible, with plenty of room for even a rat as large as you. You and your men should have no problem scaling down the chicken wire."

"Killdeer's speech forces us to speed up our plan. We can't allow these interrogations to happen. How many chimneys are there?"

"We located five in total," said Oard, "tucked away in the north alley of the Battery District's Brimstone Building, behind a green city Dumpster. If perchance the Nightshade rats tunneling in are discovered, whoever enters through the chimneys can quickly come to their aid."

The new strategy was to have half of the Nightshade rats enter the Combs through the kitchen chimneys, while the others would follow the original plan of entering through the abandoned quarters, ensuring that Catacomb Hall would be surrounded on all sides, with the Kill Army caught unaware, listening to the Grand Speech.

"All right, then, we make our move tomorrow night, just in time for this midnight speech. I will run the operation Topside. Virden, Cole, Suttor, Vincent, and Victor will each lead a group down one of the five chimneys. They will be the first to shimmy down to the kitchen. I will be the last, making sure everyone has gone down safely."

Vincent raised his brow, confused. "Juniper, you want *us* to lead?"

Juniper smiled. "Don't look so surprised, lad. No one in this room thinks you too young. Yes, indeed, we want *you* to lead."

The three boys exchanged glances, trying not to grin.

Juniper motioned towards the twins. "Ulrich and Ragan will organize the remaining rats who will be tunneling in from Night-shade. They'll lead groups into the Combs through the partially filled-in tunnels we have dug to the already-deserted quarters and meet us in Catacomb Hall. After we liberate them, the Catacomb rats will be directed down the tunnels and back to Nightshade."

"Juniper," said Vincent worriedly, "what if there are rats who don't want to go—rats who want to stay in the Catacombs?"

"Everyone has a choice," said Juniper. "If there are rats too afraid, or if, Saints forbid, they actually support the High Ministry, then they can stay put. The Catacombs are crumbling—no longer safe. If any rat wishes to remain after we arrive, they do so at their own risk. Our intentions are benign. No one will be forced to come with us."

One soldier at each checkpoint could be easily overpowered. Juniper suspected there would be few soldiers who would die in defense of the Ministry, but surely there would be some. He hoped that when it came down to it, these confused boys would realize that dying for the likes of Billycan and Killdeer was certainly not worthwhile.

The rats and worms worked late into the night, planning the particulars of the operation. Virden and Cole sat with Vincent, Victor, and Suttor, carefully going over their duties until all three had it right. They had only one chance for a crucial surprise attack. There was no room for error.

*   *   *

Following a long day of planning for his speech, Billycan sat alone in his bleak quarters, a paw under his chin, staring at the blank wall in front of him. He went over and over the speech in his head, fine-tuning his rhetoric. Someone in the Combs had to know where Nightshade City was. It would be pointless to send soldiers out to do a search of the Reserve—that was far too much territory for rats to cover. Billycan had to find the secret passageways to the city from within the walls of the Combs. Their subjects were in for a violent night, one Billycan thought they most certainly deserved.

The white rat had just consumed a tin of oily sardines and three slices of a tart yellow cheese. He needed sleep. Lieutenant Carn was scheduled to wake him at five o'clock sharp. He put his feet up on a small crate, folded his arms, and slouched down in a crooked horseshoe shape. With his nodular spine, the only way he could slumber comfortably was sitting up in a rigid wooden chair.

He stared at the wall, trying to clear his head. His mind drifted back to when he was young, alone in plastic cage 111 at the lab. He thought of Dorf, his first and only real friend. He called Killdeer a friend, but he knew that his portly associate would betray him without so much as a second thought. Sometimes he wished himself back in the lab, if only to see Dorf one last time.

Nightshade Passage was filled to capacity. Juniper and Cole were finalizing details. Everyone else had gathered into small groups. The rats that would not be going on the raid were sharpening weapons and adding to the ones already stockpiled. Their spears were not up to par with those of the Kill Army, but since the Kill Army soldiers had no idea of the impending ambush, they would probably be lightly armed, many not at all.

Mother Gallo was sitting with Virden, going over the standard protocol for Killdeer's speeches: how long they usually ran, where Killdeer and his officials stood, and so forth. Lali and Clover were once again running about, making sure everyone was fed.

Clover had begged to go along tonight, but Juniper would not allow it. Once she resigned herself to the idea of being left behind, her anxiety shifted to those who *would* be going, especially Vincent. The son of Julius Nightshade would make a prime target for the majors, the most brutal of the Kill Army throng. She glanced at him, took a deep breath, and kept working.

The Nightshade brothers and Suttor had roped off their own area of Nightshade Passage. They had put together a provisional fighting ring to show the less experienced rats how to protect and defend themselves. The rats gathered around them, forming a circle, as Vincent refereed a mock fight between Victor and Suttor. The spectators watched in awe as Victor and Suttor masterfully demonstrated their superior fighting techniques. Suttor was trained by way of the army. The Nightshades had learned in the corridors of the Catacombs, where fights for food were a common occurrence. Other young rats tried to steal often, not just to fill their bellies, but for fear of not having Stipend for Billycan. Vincent and Victor had learned early on how to defend themselves.

Victor was playing the loser in this round, acting out his part a little too well. He dramatically dropped to the ground when Suttor pretended to slice him in the jugular with his sharp metal rod. Victor grabbed his throat and gagged, shaking violently with fake convulsions and making a chortling sound as if blood were gurgling in his throat. The older rats laughed, while the smaller ones stared in horror.

"Victor, that's enough!" snapped Vincent. He shot a look at his brother, not wanting the inexperienced rats to be too terrified to fight.

"Sorry, sorry," said Victor, picking himself up off the floor, "just trying to make it more real."

"It will be real enough tonight," said Suttor firmly, handing Victor back his weapon.

"That it will," said Victor. He noticed some of the boys still staring at him, petrified by his realistic performance. "Don't worry, boys. You'll be fine tonight. Why don't you come over here and I'll practice with you? Trust me, if I can learn it, you can." The boys smiled feebly and scuffled over to Victor, who started showing them some simple yet effective moves.

"All right, then," said Vincent to the others, "remember, once we've entered the Catacombs, I want everyone to stay in packs of three. That way, if you're surrounded, you can form a triangle of sorts and fight from all sides."

Juniper had been listening in on their training session. It brought back memories of his youth—listening to Julius Nightshade and his big brother, Barcus, explain the ways of combat to him. Vincent was as natural a leader as Julius had been. It seemed as if they shared the same soul. Juniper desperately hoped they would not share the same fate.

Billycan jolted awake. He jumped from his chair and searched wildly round his darkened room. He grabbed his billy club, pointing it in front of him as if defending himself from an invisible foe. There was no one there.

The white rat's heart banged in his hollow chest—it had been only a nightmare. Dizzy, he collapsed back into his seat. His throat ached. He started to cough uncontrollably, spitting up froth and drool. Wiping his mouth with his paw, he noticed a metallic taste on his tongue. The spit on his paw was mingled with blood. The thick, red gel clung to his spiny digits.

He had dreamed he was being attacked. A large, shadowy figure had ambushed him in a dark corridor. The assailant pushed Billycan to the ground, easily overpowering him, and proceeded to strangle him. Billycan clawed at the unknown attacker but could not break free; his hold was too great. He yelled for his majors, but no one could hear him. As the rat applied more pressure to Billycan's throat, he began to gasp, his red eyes bursting from his skull. Seconds before the shadowy figure would have crushed his throat, he'd awakened, breathlessly hunting for his make-believe enemy.

He stared at his blood-stained paw. Was someone trying to kill him in his sleep? The albino rat did not believe in the supernatural. That was for the old ones, all their silly talk of the spirit world, their ancient incantations. It could not be Juniper. He was still alive. The living could not enter your dreams, but the dead, the ones whose lives were stolen by another, could enter at will, or so the old ones claimed. Billycan had scores of victims to choose from, including Julius Nightshade. Billycan sneered, thinking of Julius, the once blasted thorn in his side, always trying to defend his precious citizens. Julius was most assuredly dead; Billycan had seen to that, but it seemed his spirit was back to goad him one final time.

The Collector reached for his last oily sardine. He needed something to soothe his throat. As he came to his full senses, he started to chuckle. He realized how foolish he must have looked dancing about his quarters in his sleep, swinging his billy club wildly through the air. He must have nicked his throat on a fish bone. That *must* be it. He howled in laughter, realizing how comedic the whole scene must have appeared. He heard a knock at the door. It was Lieutenant Carn, there to wake him.

"Enter," he said, trying to stop his giddy snorting.

"Good evening, High Collector," said Lieutenant Carn. "It's five o'clock, sir."

Billycan couldn't stop his sniggering. "Lieutenant Carn, you're one lucky soldier. Had you shown up a few minutes earlier, you would most surely be dead!" He laughed heartily as he put the head of the remaining sardine in his mouth, then arose from his chair. "Don't look so serious, boy. Even Billycan can jest from time to time. C'mon, then, let's go. Billycan has much work to do, as do you. I'm starving. Off to the kitchens first."

Billycan took one last look round his quarters before shutting the door. No one was there. He shook his head at his foolishness, letting out a piercing shriek of laughter, startling the bewildered Lieutenant Carn as they walked down the gloomy corridor.

Juniper stood atop the platform in the center of Nightshade Passage. "All right, everyone, gather round, gather round," he called. "We are mere hours away. This is the climax of our story, resulting in a tragic conclusion or an illustrious first chapter in our great city's history.

"Our kind has never had it easy. We have toiled through the centuries to find a home of our own, away from predators, away from Topsiders. We were driven into the earth, into the shadows of the Catacombs. But guided by wise and courageous leaders, we didn't just survive those early days underground, we flourished. Each passing generation grew stronger and smarter than the last. We prospered. But our success inspired jealousy and greed, violence and evil. Our leaders were overthrown; our freedoms usurped. That is what brings us to this day. We fight to stay true of heart, to *never* become like those who capitalize on our misery, using our sons as shields and our daughters as slaves.

"Now, rats of Nightshade, we have a chance to let our founders, our ancestors, know that their good works will not stay buried with them." Juniper looked determinedly at the mass of anxious faces.

His voiced boomed off the vaulted ceiling of the hall. "It is time for our deliverance! Our weapons are sharp, our strategies sound, our hearts—sure. We are ready!"

The rats barked and howled, pounding their weapons on the dirt floor. The old ones called out the ancient war chants as the young ones cheered at the top of their lungs, climbing on one another's shoulders, screaming to be heard. Nightshade was ready.

Killdeer and Billycan sat at the head table in the mess hall, facing the Kill Army soldiers. The troops spoke in a jittery hush, quietly eating their surprise feast. They had never eaten in the presence of the Minister. It was Killdeer's idea to dine with the troops tonight. He would casually address them, making them comfortable, pliable, and easy to rally. He needed the soldiers to understand that *they* were the strength of the Combs, no one else. Their interrogations were *not* a punishment to the Catacomb rats but a means to protect them, and getting to the truth by force was not just acceptable, it was *necessary* to defend the Combs, to defend their home.

High Cook Longtooth and her servant girls had prepared the massive feast. She was instructed by Lithgo to use only her finest meats, cheeses, and fish.

Longtooth stepped out of the kitchen and peeked at Killdeer's table, making sure his plate was full. It looked unnatural for him to be drinking bitonberry juice instead of guzzling from a bottle of Oshi. The high majors had told her no ale or Oshi was permitted, so as much as she knew Killdeer enjoyed a nip, she dared not offer him any.

Killdeer spotted Longtooth and waved her to the table. She shuffled over, her aged hips creaking and popping with every step. She tried to make her craggy voice sweet, but only succeeded in making it grovel. "Yes, High Minister, what can I get for you?" she asked.

"Get for me?" said Killdeer warmly. "Why, nothing, Cook Longtooth, we are all feeling full and splendid. I simply wanted to thank you for putting out such a plentiful spread. As you can see by the mountain of empty plates, the soldiers surely appreciate your extra effort."

Longtooth melted, clasping her paws together in glee. "Oh, thank you, sir," she cooed. "Thank you very much indeed. It was worth the work to please the High Minister so." She smirked coyly at Killdeer with her jagged, brown-toothed grin, batting her sparse lashes. Killdeer smiled back, trying not to cringe as he locked eyes with her cloudy cataracts.

He moved from the table, ready to speak to the troops. He hesitantly put his arm around Longtooth, recoiling at the touch of her ashy shoulder, which seemed to have lost most of its fur. Killdeer grew a bit nauseated, feeling her gooseflesh under his paw, but continued with his address. "Good soldiers of the Kill Army, it is with great pleasure that the High Ministry brings you this sumptuous banquet before my midnight speech. Now, boys, let's all give a round of applause to tonight's chef, our own High Cook Longtooth." The soldiers started clapping; random whistles came from the back. Longtooth was embarrassed by the rare attention. She tried to cover her gawky grin with a paw.

"Now, Cook Longtooth," said Killdeer, gently trying to send her on her way, "why don't your kitchen girls finish the cleaning and you take the rest of the night off? You surely deserve it!" Killdeer motioned to the troops, leading their applause once more. Longtooth held the edges of her grimy apron and curtsied, scuttling back to the kitchen. She thought of her friend, Mother Gallo. She couldn't wait to tell her of Killdeer's compliments. How impressed she would be.

As the room quieted, Killdeer turned slowly in a circle, making eye contact with each section of the room. "All these faces," he said, as though in awe of the sight, "all this hope, all this possibility, sitting in this very room. For those of you who are older, you know all the trials and tribulations this Ministry has been through. You know what it takes to keep our Catacombs safe, our home out of harm's way. Most of you have lost your families entirely, orphaned by tragedy of one sort or another, but luckily our majors took you in, assuring me *personally* that each and every one of you were superior—well qualified to join my great army. Not everyone can be a member of my Kill Army. We've rejected many an orphan rat, sadly sending them Topside to look after themselves." This was wholly untrue, but the sheltered troops had no reason to doubt their Minister.

"Oh, yes," said Killdeer, in a woebegone voice, staring at the puzzled soldiers, "it's true. We have cast off many. The poor lost souls are wandering above as we speak, fleeing from predators and Topsiders—if not *already* dead. Simply put, they were not good enough. They weren't strong enough to be in this army. They were weak and undeserving lads of poor character, I'm afraid."

He walked up to a table of little ones barely able to manage their food, their military sashes falling off their sloped shoulders. He leaned down to their level, his voice softening. "Do you understand, young ones? *You* were chosen. *You* are the future leaders of the Catacombs. What's your name, son?" he asked a small, butter-colored rat, who trembled at the sight of the enormous High Minister. Killdeer knelt on one knee in front of the boy. "Don't be frightened, my boy. Now, what's your name?"

The boy answered meekly. "My name is Desmond, High Minister." He looked down at his plate, still shaking.

"Young Desmond," Killdeer said, looking him in the eye, "you and your counterparts are the future of this army. You are the lifeblood that holds us together." The child looked mystified. "I know it sounds silly to you now, but you have the power to be as great a leader as I am. One day, all this could be yours." Desmond's eyes widened. "Dear boy, I would not lie to you." He stood up and walked the room. "What I've stated is true for *all* of you." He pointed at various faces. "You hold the future of this Ministry. Boys, *you* are the power." His voice quickly grew to a boisterous shout. "Boys, let me hear you say it! 'I am the power!'" Sparked by their great leader's message, the boys yelled loudly in concert. "Now let me hear you scream it! 'I am the power! I am the power!'" Killdeer chanted the words enthusiastically until every last soldier did the same, jumping up from their tables, clanging their mugs and plates together, stomping their feet. Killdeer grabbed Desmond out of his seat and threw him on his shoulder. "C'mon, boy, let me hear you roar!"

Desmond shouted in his small voice, "I am the power! I am the power!" His fear turned to admiration. The noise from the mess hall was deafening. Every rat in the Combs could hear the chant booming all the way to Catacomb Hall.

Billycan stayed seated at the head table, still eating. He didn't feel the need to inspire the troops. Killdeer seemed to have that covered, a veritable master of manipulation. Billycan lazily chewed on a curried rib as he visualized his next meeting with Juniper Belancort. He thought about what it would feel like to carve out the other eye from the scruffy rat's head.

The Nightshade rats were lined up in the passage, just outside the hole leading into the Topsiders' brownstone. "Now, everyone, stay quiet, not a word," said Juniper sternly. As he looked behind him, the eyes of two hundred jittery rats stared back at him. Everyone had to get through the house safely and undetected. "Follow single file along the wall, and remember, not a word!"

Juniper looked at Mother Gallo. She had come along to see the

Nightshade rats off. Juniper asked her help in directing and reassuring the rats, as most of them were apprehensive about entering the Topsiders' home.

The rats skirted along the wall of the art studio, one in front of the other. As they reached the door leading to the foyer, Juniper held up his paw, motioning for all to stop. Everyone halted in his tracks. The rats stood in a line, patiently awaiting their next directive.

Cole and Virden were at the front of the line with Mother Gallo and Juniper. Once all the rats had safely entered the brownstone from the passage, Vincent, Victor, and Suttor joined them up front. Without hesitation, Juniper took his leave, squeezing under the door of the studio and disappearing. After what seemed like a long time to the waiting rats, he came back with news. "It's all clear, black as pitch. But the outer door and windows are locked tight; I'm afraid we'll have to break a window to escape. It's our only chance of getting to the Combs by midnight."

"Juniper," whispered Mother Gallo, "that's far too dangerous. We'll surely awaken the Topsiders, and it's a long jump down from that window. There could be injuries, possibly fatal."

Juniper sighed. "Maddy, I agree, you know I do; but I don't believe we have an alternative."

"But we do," she said calmly. "The boy."

Juniper and Mother Gallo climbed the staircase in silence. As they reached the landing, Mother Gallo stuck her nose into the air, picking up Ramsey's scent. She easily caught wind of the little boy, who smelled of chocolate and oranges. The twosome slinked down the hall, inaudible on the plush carpet.

Muffled voices murmured from the television, which gave off a ghostly radiance from under the door leading to the parents' room.

Despite the seriousness of their task, Juniper couldn't help but snigger a little when he heard the mother and father snoring. Mother Gallo gave him a stern look, swatting him on the arm. They came to Ramsey's door, decorated with pictures drawn on thick colored paper. Mother Gallo gasped.

"What is it?" Juniper said, searching the hallway for trouble.

"It's just . . . I think it's me," she said in amazement. She pointed to a crinkled piece of powder-blue paper taped at the bottom of the door. It was a child's depiction in crayon of a round, gray rat with a blue ribbon around its waist, holding a blob of yellow, which she assumed to be cheese. The rat had a smile on its face, more of a Topsider smile than that of rat, and Ramsey had even managed to draw a brown satchel on its shoulder. "See? Look, there's my sash, and your satchel. The child remembered everything."

Juniper looked at the picture. "It looks as though you have an admirer. You must have made quite an impression on the boy," he whispered. "Let's see if you can do it again." He pointed to the gap under the door.

"Stay out of sight," said Mother Gallo. "I don't want to scare him. A large, one-eyed rat like you might send him into a panic. Just stay out of sight till I say otherwise."

They squeezed through the gap. Ramsey's bed was in the center of the room, with a wooden chest pushed against its foot. On his nightstand he had a glowing red night-light in the shape of a rocket. Juniper waited by the door as Mother Gallo sank her claws into the bed's navy skirt and scaled her way to the top.

Ramsey was sleeping soundly, wrapped up in his comforter. She crept over to him and gently tapped him on the shoulder. He didn't move. She tried again, this time a little harder. Ramsey scratched his shoulder where she tapped him but did not wake. "Third time's the charm," she said, giving his shoulder a solid push. Ramsey yawned, rubbed his nose, and finally opened his sleepy eyes.

Mother Gallo stood in front of his freckled face. He squinted his eyes, then quickly sat up, gawking at her. Mother Gallo was afraid he might cry out. She leaped onto his nightstand and put a claw to her lips. Ramsey studied her from head to toe. He smiled, unafraid. Leaning in, he whispered, "Lady Rat, you've come back, just like you promised. I'm so glad to see you!"

Mother Gallo looked round the room. There were more drawings of her. She pointed to one tacked behind his night-light.

"You like my drawings?" Ramsey asked eagerly. She nodded yes. She pointed to a picture of her in front of a big brown door.

"The door—where we met," he said, smiling proudly. She pointed downward towards the floor. "You want to go down?"

Mother Gallo became excited and pointed to his window and then down again. "Oh," said Ramsey, "you want to go outside again!" She jumped up and down on his nightstand and clapped her paws.

Mother Gallo bounded over Ramsey to the foot of the bed and motioned for Juniper to come up. Ramsey watched guardedly as the woolly rat scaled his bed. Mother Gallo took Juniper by the paw and walked him over to Ramsey. The boy studied the violet rat.

Mother Gallo pointed to Juniper's bag, which hung across his chest, and then to Ramsey's drawing. The boy caught on. "This is your friend's bag, then?" he asked. Juniper smiled at the boy and bowed graciously.

Mother Gallo pointed to the window again. "Oh, yes," said Ramsey, "you want to go back outside."

Ramsey leaned in closer, now eye-level with the rats, and looked at them seriously. "My mother and father are sleeping. We mustn't wake them. I'm not allowed to roam the house after dark. So you both need to be very quiet."

Ramsey slipped out of bed and put on his slippers. He walked over to the wooden chest at the foot of his bed and carefully lifted the heavy lid. He reached in and pulled something out. It was a flashlight. He clicked it on. "Now, remember, be very, very quiet," he said, motioning to the door.

In the time it took for Mother Gallo and Juniper to rouse the boy, all two hundred rats had organized, scooting under the studio door, and were now waiting patiently in the foyer. One and all stood motionless, scared to even wiggle an ear or flick a tail.

Mother Gallo had explained to the Nightshade rats that a Topsider would be coming down and that he was just a child, no different from their own children, notwithstanding his size. He had helped her once before and, with any luck, would help them tonight. That seemed to put the rats a little more at ease, but child or not, a Topsider was still a Topsider.

A noise came from upstairs. All two hundred rats looked up apprehensively. They saw the light from Ramsey's flashlight bouncing down the staircase, followed by two small Topsider feet in crimson slippers. Mother Gallo and Juniper trailed quickly at his heels. The pair held their breath, not knowing how the boy would react to the mass of rats he was about to encounter.

Ramsey got to the bottom stair and shone his flashlight around the room. First he looked towards the kitchen. All clear. He then looked towards the front door. Everything looked fine at first, but on second glance he noticed a strange reflection coming from the floor. He slowly moved his light across it. There they were—four hundred tiny eyes gleaming like polished marbles. He just about dropped his flashlight to the marble floor below. All the rats held their breath as he fumbled with the light. When he caught it, a muffled sigh filled the foyer as all two hundred rats exhaled in unison.

Ramsey cautiously inspected the throng of rats, then slowly turned back to Mother Gallo and Juniper. He crouched down next to them on the bottom stairs. "I see you've brought your family with you," he whispered. They nodded yes. "Where are you going?"

Mother Gallo quickly jumped to her feet and started pointing to the numerous Saints' Day decorations adorning the home. Ramsey caught on. "Ah, you're going somewhere for Saints' Day. My father says lots of people travel during the holidays. I guess rats need to travel too." Mother Gallo nodded. Ramsey looked at all the eyes blinking back at him. "You know, you have an awfully large family, Lady Rat. You must be very proud."

Ramsey stood up. "All right, then, Lady Rat *and* Mr. Rat, I better get you out of here. Please make sure your family stays very quiet." The rats skittered out of his way. Most of them had never been so close to a Topsider, and they stared at the boy curiously as he tiptoed to the front door.

He pulled on the first door, which opened with a soft creak. He held it open as all the rats poured into the vestibule, their claws clicking against the cold tile.

The crowd of rats split in two, giving Ramsey room to make his way to the outer door leading to the street. He had trouble with the bolt, stiffened up with cold, but he eventually pried it open using all his strength. It gave way with a begrudging groan. A flood of icy night air filled the vestibule, stealing everyone's breath for a moment.

Ramsey crouched down and spoke to Mother Gallo. "Lady Rat,

happy Saints' Day," he whispered cheerily. "I'm glad you came back to see me." Mother Gallo hugged his ankle as a rapid current of rats poured out onto the sidewalk of Ashbury Lane.

Mother Gallo waved good-bye to Juniper, who paused as he watched her disappear back into the house and back to Nightshade City.

The rats headed to the Brimstone Building in the run-down Battery District of Trillium City, the location of the chimneys. Juniper led the pack as they twisted like spun taffy round the streets of the Reserve. Midnight was alarmingly close.

Killdeer, Billycan, and the high majors waited in the War Room, all donning their freshly pressed Kill Army dress sashes, with their coats groomed and shiny. Catacomb Hall was filling up with soldiers. As soon as the last seat was occupied, the speech would begin.

Killdeer held up his polished medallion and studied it. He would not meet the same fate as old Trilok. He would not be overthrown. He thought of Saints' Day, now so near, and how he had carved out Trilok's throat all those years ago, just like the Topsiders carved their roast suckling pig and stuffed fowl. He chuckled to himself, thinking the analogy rather funny. He turned to Billycan. "I do," he said bluntly.

"Minister?" asked Billycan, oblivious as to what Killdeer was referring to.

"What you said back in my den, when you so eloquently informed me of what a derelict leader I had become. The question you asked me—do I want to feel the glory again? I realize my answer is late in coming, but I'm telling you—yes, I do. I *want* there to be war. Never has my vigor been so strong. The last time I felt this high was the day

Trilok sucked in his last ragged breath. Just let those Nightshade mutineers attack us. Let them. I'll kill them myself and have the army burn their bloodied carcasses in Catacomb Hall! I'll have the High Cook boil their bones and make me a winter stew. I'll use Juniper's skull as my soup bowl!"

The majors laughed riotously. Billycan grimaced at the Minister's wit. As pleased as he was to see the Minister back to his old self, *he* would be the one to kill Juniper. Killdeer would not have that honor. He had not earned the right. Billycan ran his skeletal digits down the edge of his newly-sharpened blade hanging firmly on his hip, clanking against his billy club. He pictured the event. He would gut the troublesome rat end-to-end. The thought gave him a convulsive chill, which shivered up his spine. He smelled death. He jumped from his chair, knocking it to the ground, as the adrenaline took hold.

"My High Collector and Commander is ready, I see!" said Killdeer. "I can feel it too, Billycan." Killdeer bellowed down the length of the War Room, as they exited for the speech. "Death is forthcoming!"

Catacomb Hall was ready for the speech as soldiers gradually filtered in. The hall was set up with an imposing stage in the front, blocking Ellington's Tavern and the other businesses lining the horseshoe. There were numerous rows of seating, with a long ruby carpet trailing down the middle. The Kill Army colors of crimson and navy draped the stage and entrances, and long matching flags cut in the shape of a serpent's tongue hung from the ceiling, all decorated with Killdeer's three-pronged mark. Flickering torches lined the perimeter of the hall.

The Kill Army soldiers had no idea what the meat of the Grand Speech would be. Much gossip and conjecture had been offered up in the barracks, but for the most part the troops assumed it would have something to do with the kidnapped lieutenant and the Chosen One.

The Nightshade rats turned the corner, barreling into the north alley of the Brimstone Building. There it was: the green Dumpster, just as Oard had described. Juniper led the way, piloting the horde directly under the rusty container.

They spotted the five chimneys. The Kill Army had affixed copper flues over each chimney, allowing smoke to escape while still blocking out the harsh Trillium elements. Juniper, Cole, and Virden made quick work of the covers, easily ripping them off and tossing them aside, while Vincent, Suttor, and Victor started organizing everyone into five groups, one for each chimney.

The rats were ready to descend. The continuous moisture from the Kill Army kitchens had kept the soil of the chimneys pliable, easy to sink sharp claws into and scale down swiftly. Each rat had his weapon tightly bound to his back, ensuring it would not get tangled during the descent, should he accidentally fall.

From below, Ragan and Ulrich would be directing the Nightshade rats from the secret corridors dug from Nightshade City to the Catacombs. The earthworms had re-excavated most of the tunnels that led back to the Combs, all going into the deserted quarters of Catacomb rats who'd already fled to Nightshade. Each group of Nightshade rats would then wait in one of the empty homes until they heard the signal to move towards Catacomb Hall.

The hall was equipped with a bell, pilfered from a Topside academy. The bell was rung to signal the start of all High Ministry events. The deafening noise rang through every corridor, even to the farthest border. When the Nightshade rats heard the bell, they were to descend upon Catacomb Hall.

The Kill Army soldiers who were on guard would be bound, gagged, and placed in the abandoned quarters, guarded by Nightshade rats. Juniper anticipated little opposition from the lone soldiers, hoping fear would prevail over foolishness.

After the five groups were lined up in front of each chimney, Juniper and the group leaders met for one last time. They huddled under the Dumpster in a circle. "Everyone, bow your heads," said Juniper. "May the Saints be looking down on us tonight. May our hearts be strong and our aim true. On this night, so near to Saints' Day, may our enemies die with dignity and their souls be given the fate they deserve. Saints protect the innocent children of the Kill Army. May none of them meet their end by means of our blades." They all looked at one another for a moment, silently hoping that it would not be for the last time.

The group leaders motioned to Juniper and vanished into their designated chimneys. The rest of the rats descended, one by one, careful to keep an arm's length between one another. Juniper watched closely, making sure everyone entered the chimneys safely. Things were going smoothly, at least for now.

Barring the front rows, nearly every seat in Catacomb Hall was occupied by a Kill Army soldier. Only a handful of lieutenants were guarding the perimeters of the Combs, one per exit leading Topside. The High Ministry thought the speech too important to waste more than a few handpicked soldiers, already briefed on the proceedings and already bored as they manned their desolate posts.

Ragan and Ulrich were running the Loyalist operation from below, filling the reopened tunnels with Nightshade Rats and waiting patiently in empty quarters. When the bell rang, chiming throughout the Combs, the Nightshade rats quietly infiltrated their designated corridors. They then went about waking groggy Catacomb rats from their beds, telling them to stay quiet for their own safety and informing them that they were free.

At first, in their tired and fuzzy state, many of the rats were confused. The Nightshade rats explained that they were Trilok Loyalists—now led by Juniper Belancort, still alive and well! Catacomb rats shook, cried, and laughed. Some were frightened, not sure if they should believe their ears or trust these foreign rats. The Nightshade rats told them they could stay, but for what? Taking a chance on a new life, whatever that life may be, was far better than the tyranny they now endured. Most agreed. Parents quickly gathered their few meager belongings, clutched their little ones, and traveled down the tunnels to Nightshade.

Knowing that all the Nightshade rats would be needed at Catacomb Hall, Ragan sent a team of newly freed volunteer rats, guided by the earthworms, to the kitchen girls' cramped quarters to rouse them from their tiny beds. At first the girls didn't believe they could simply pick up and leave. It could not be true. They would be punished.

One of the volunteers, a mother, grabbed two of the girls and hugged them as hard as she could. "We are all free, all of us!" she exclaimed. "The rumors are true—Juniper is alive! The Loyalists have come to save us, giving us all a new home! You are free!" Some of the girls wailed in relief; others couldn't stop grinning. Sadly, many had no reaction at all, too numb from years of abuse. The mother spotted one of these girls, cheerless, a blank look on her face. She took the girl's chin in her paw and stared at her deadened expression. "You will wake up soon, you'll see. This has all been but a long and terrible nightmare. Our *real* life begins now."

The Kill Army quieted as the proceedings began. A lieutenant appeared at the base of the stage in front of the red carpet. He retrieved a trumpet hanging from his hip and blew a short, regal call, designating the arrival of the Kill Army majors and Ministry leaders. He left as quickly as he had arrived and took his seat on the sidelines.

The first to appear was the endless line of sector majors. They marched in formation down the red carpet, taking their seats in the front rows, just in front of the senior lieutenants.

After the sector majors came High Majors Lithgo, Schnauss, and Foiber. Lithgo stuck his snout in the air and sucked in his overfed belly as Schnauss skulked in behind him. Foiber eventually appeared, taking extra time as he dragged the cumbersome weight of his loose-fitting skin. The majors climbed the stage and took their seats facing the soldiers, behind the wooden podium.

The trumpeter stood once more and blew another royal number, signifying the entrance of Billycan and Killdeer. The soldiers rose from their seats and stood at attention.

Billycan walked the red carpet first, pushing out his concave chest and striding down the center of the army. The soldiers looked on apprehensively as he marched the length of the carpet. He swiftly jumped onto the stage and took his seat next to the podium, in front of the high majors.

There was a brief but purposeful pause in the proceedings. The soldiers looked anxiously towards the back of the room. Finally, Killdeer emerged at the edge of the red carpet. He walked the length of the carpet with an imposing swagger. The genial face he wore during the mess-hall feast had transformed into a stoic gaze, his jaw clenched, his brow furrowed.

Killdeer stood behind the podium, dwarfing it with his huge presence. He regarded the packed room. He sized up the Kill Army, his army. As he looked at the sprawl of soldiers before him, he pondered how far he had come to achieve all of this, this world—his world—he, once an exiled citizen, banished for his crimes, and now

High Minister of the Catacombs. "From criminal to king," he whispered to himself.

His voice resonated through the packed hall. "Gentleman, please take your seats. We are here today with a serious purpose in mind. We are here to discuss the future of the Catacombs—our home. It has come to the Ministry's attention that we have traitors living amongst us, pretending to be your friends, waiting for the right moment to stab you in the back." The soldiers looked cautiously at one another, wondering if a conspirator might be sitting right next to them. "We overthrew Trilok's Ministry so that you troops could have a better life, a better chance to realize your dreams, a place where honor and nobility are valued, but regrettably, there are rats who seek to ruin that for you—a whole city of them, in fact—a secret city." The entire army gasped in shock. Killdeer abruptly pounded the podium with his fist, growling at the thought of someone stealing what was his. "A city of devils—Nightshade City—or, as they should be called, *deadly* Nightshade, for they want to eradicate *you* and all that you have labored so very hard for, just like the lethal plant itself! Nightshade City wants me, your devoted High Minister, dead, but worst of all, my friends, my brothers in arms, my Ministry protectors, they want *you* dead. *You* are the ones they are most afraid of. If the Kill Army is destroyed, they can easily overtake the Catacombs. They plan to hunt each and every one of you down, heartlessly slaughtering you, perhaps where you sit right now, perhaps while you sleep in your warm beds." The soldiers shifted uneasily.

Slippery lies and half truths continued to spew from Killdeer's lips as two hundred Nightshade rats noiselessly entered the Kill Army kitchens. Hundreds more waited patiently, tucked away deep in the underbelly of the Catacombs.

CHAPTER EIGHT
Most Evil of Creatures

THE NIGHTSHADE RATS had organized into packs in the darkened kitchen, weapons ready. Juniper led them to Catacomb Hall, picking up several Kill Army prisoners on the way. The captured soldiers were bound, gagged, and deposited in one of the abandoned quarters.

Ragan and Ulrich's groups met with little resistance from the lone Kill Army soldiers posted to watch the exit corridors. As suspected, the captured troops went peacefully, an easy choice when facing the fatal end of a spear.

Only one soldier had tried to take a stand so far. A gangly rat about Victor's age, broken down by years of abuse from the Kill Army majors, had tried to attack Ragan. Ragan quickly subdued the startled lieutenant, giving the scared youth nothing more serious than a sprained arm. Tears streamed down the soldier's face. Ragan reassured him. "Don't worry, son, we're just restraining you boys till this is over. From now on, the only injuries you'll receive will be from roughhousing with your friends. Consider yourself retired from military service." The soldier looked at Ragan in confusion. Ragan grabbed the boy by the shoulders and looked him square in the face, giving him a firm shake. "You're free, boy, you're free!"

Killdeer had taken his seat. His opening speech had even the most hardened soldier squirming in his skin and wringing his paws. The Minister swore on his royal family, his beloved sisters, that the malicious rats from this primitive city were on a mission to massacre the Kill Army and take over the Combs. "Blackguards," he called them, lacking in morals and slow of mind, but thick with rancor and a monstrous lust for blood. He warned the soldiers that these degenerates would as easily kill them with their teeth as they would with a weapon, suggesting that the fiendish creatures would rip them apart and eat their still-warm remains, leaving the smallest recruits gripping their tails in terror.

Billycan took the stage, happy with the horror Killdeer had struck in the minds of the soldiers. His task would be easy. He slowly paced in front of the podium with his paws behind his back. His billy club knocked softly against his sword. He stepped behind the podium and spoke, his tone strangely humble. "Billycan can see the distress in your eyes. Our esteemed High Minister has frightened you, and rightly so. These demon rats, these cannibals—you should not just be scared of them, you should be petrified for your life's last breath. Billycan has looked into the face of these most evil of creatures, and it haunts me to this day. In fact, it *terrifies* me to my very core."

A hushed murmur came from the troops. Billycan feared nothing. "Oh, yes, it's true," he said calmly. "Even I am troubled by these unholy beasts. That's why it's so very essential that we find the headquarters of this wicked band of killers, this Nightshade City, lest they find us first." He took a moment and stared at a few faces in the crowd. The unlucky soldiers twisted in their seats, hoping his gaze would soon break. His shrill voice intensified. "These inbred heathens will show *no* mercy! They do not understand reason. The Topsiders call us rodents, vermin, but this hidden city of miscreants—they are the true vermin, a vile plague upon us! They think of us as mere farm fodder! Do you want to be their next victims? Do you want to be murdered by these savages, only to have your cold corpses used as their very food supply?" Billycan's body surged with glee as he fueled the soldiers' agitation, knowing that a fearful rat would be more effective, more eager to seek out a traitor, more apt to use extreme measures.

The soldiers whispered to one another, the little ones trying to hold back tears. Billycan smiled inside as he worked the boys into a lather. "Your leaders have a plan, a plan to ensure your continued survival, a plan—" Billycan paused. Cocking his head, he listened. "Silence!" he barked to the still-whispering troops. He heard what sounded like quick, heavy footsteps. His face contorted as he tried to detect where they were coming from.

Billycan scanned all the visible entrances to the hall; the beat of approaching footsteps grew stronger, causing the podium to shake. "Juniper," he muttered under his breath.

Suddenly, Catacomb Hall was flooded with weapon-wielding Nightshade rats pouring out of every entrance, rushing down on all sides of the seated soldiers, dirtying the red carpet with their muddy feet. The Kill Army soldiers sat confused and disorientated. The sector majors were soon surrounded, steel weapons pointed at their heads, throats, and bellies. They dared not move.

"Is that so?" asked a loud voice from the back. "Is that how you see us, High Collector and *loyal* Commander of the Kill Army?"

Cloaked in his filthy black shroud, Juniper walked dead center down the carpet. The Nightshade rats swiftly surrounded him, protecting him on all sides, weapons drawn. Some soldiers jumped up but promptly sat back down, realizing there was nowhere to go.

Billycan stood frozen at the podium, his face dropping, his mouth hanging open. What little color he had drained from his pasty skin.

Cole took the stage, followed by Virden, Suttor, and several husky rats, who surrounded Billycan, Killdeer, and the high majors. Billycan stayed silent as he eyed the metal blades pointed at his abdomen and head. Killdeer and the high majors had leaped to their feet but soon reclaimed their seats as the Nightshade rats stepped closer, close enough to puncture their throats and gouge their bellies with sharpened steel rods.

Juniper laughed at the sight on the stage. "Good boys," he said patronizingly. "Stay seated; that's right. I wouldn't want this to get messy. We must all mind our manners now." He pulled off the black cloak, tossing it to the floor. The hall gasped. The older soldiers, the ones who could remember Trilok's Ministry, echoed Juniper's name throughout the hall, whispering the legend of his supposed murder by Billycan to the smaller boys.

The whispers continued, repeating Juniper's name over and over, bouncing off the walls, invading Billycan's mind like phantoms. To see the rat he had thought dead—by his own claws, no less—there in front of him, pompous and arrogant, transformed his shock into unspoken fury as he contemplated his next move.

Juniper turned in a circle, while all the soldiers looked on as if a specter had risen from the grave. "Yes, boys, you're right. I am Juniper Belancort. Apparently back from a most untimely demise. You all thought your valiant Commander Billycan had taken my life during the Bloody Coup, but it turns out the only thing he managed to take was my eyeball!" Juniper snickered, lifting his leather patch, revealing the deadened hole.

A grin spread across Juniper's face as he caught Billycan in his sight, seemingly thunderstruck. "Why, High Collector," said Juniper, "you look as though you've seen a ghost. Did you think me Batiste, still searching for my lost sweets?" The Nightshade rats laughed heartily as Juniper turned back to the soldiers. " 'Murderous,' 'demons,' 'the most of *evil* of creatures': These are the words used by your leaders to describe the likes of me and my comrades, devoted friends of Trilok and patriotic Loyalists during the Bloody Coup. If anyone fits the description of 'murderous, evil creatures,' it is your righteous High Collector and your esteemed High Minister. Neither I, nor the rats I call friends, have ever taken a life that wasn't out to take ours first. Can Collector Billycan state the same? Can Minister Killdeer? After all, it was your revered High Minister who assassinated Trilok—was it not? And is it not Billycan who has brutally murdered countless rats, including children, over the years? You may have noticed that the sick fellow enjoys it—a good kill thrills your commander to no end. I am but a simple rat, no more significant than any of you. So, please, don't take my word for it. You boys make up your own minds." Juniper pointed at the stage, specifically at Billycan. "But what *he* has done to the Catacomb rats and to you boys, the scores of murders he's committed, *that* sounds like the deeds of a demon to me."

Juniper walked down the carpet, nearer the stage. "For those of you old enough to remember Trilok's Ministry and the Bloody Coup that ended it, I have some pointed questions." The soldiers remained silent, listening. "Do any of you remember your admirable High Collector starving youths in the middle of Catacomb Hall? Or perhaps cutting out a tongue or two for all to see, simply because a rat stole in order to feed his starving children?" Everyone looked at Billycan, who dismissed their stares with a frosty glare. "Do any of you remember your parents, all with the Saints now, telling you how different things used to be? How kind and generous the Mighty Trilok was? How much good he did for the Combs, before old Killdeer tore out his throat? You boys should be given toys, not weapons. You should be learning your letters, not how to kill one another.

"Now, let's chat a bit more about your revered High Minister, the *leader* of the Catacombs," scoffed Juniper. "Well, his story has changed entirely over the years. Maybe at one time he led the way—not what I'd call an honorable leader, but a leader all the same. Either through utter laziness or sheer weakness of character, your Minister keeps his venerated title in name only. He is nothing more than an overstuffed puppet, an empty vessel, used by our white-haired, red-eyed friend to convince you that this life, or more appropriately, this life sentence they have shoved down your throats, is the only life worth living."

Juniper started to pant, his emotion growing. "Don't be fooled by their words—the venom that seeps from their mouths, masquerading as sweet honey! Stand up for yourselves, for your departed families, for your future children! Stand up and take back what is rightly yours. Nightshade City awaits you. We don't want to defeat you. We want to *free* you! Now I ask you once more—all of you—do you remember what your parents told you? Do you remember how life was before these walking parasites leeched on to you, letting their warped notions soak into your brains like the deadly plagues of old—the plagues our kind is so famous for spreading? Does anyone remember?"

Senior Lieutenant Carn sat in the row behind the sector majors. He sized up the spear-brandishing Nightshade rats and rose from his seat. Victor, stationed closest, came at Carn with speed, his spear ready to thrust. Carn looked at Victor, not with militant rage, but with anguish. Carn gingerly reached for his dagger, holding it by its tip, and handed it to Victor. "I remember," he said quietly. Victor kept his weapon trained on Carn, who put his paws in the air. Juniper approached him, unable to forget the face of the senior lieutenant who had let them escape.

"By all means," said Juniper, "let this rat speak."

Carn kept his paws up and walked cautiously onto the carpet. As he lowered his paws, he looked at the other senior lieutenants—his friends, many of them playmates from before the Coup, now comrades in an army run by cutthroats and criminals. "I remember," repeated Carn to the soldiers. "I remember everything Juniper speaks of. I'm older than many of you. My parents didn't have to tell me what things were like and how good they were. I remember, because I was there."

Billycan shot up from his chair and screamed at him. "I suggest you shut your mouth and sit down, Lieutenant Carn, or I will shut it for you!" His rage towards Carn had finally given him back his voice.

Cole shoved his spear under Billycan's pointed chin. "I suggest *you* shut *your* mouth, High Collector," he sneered coolly. "Now, take your seat, or I'll put you in it myself." Enraged, Billycan stiffly took his seat. His eyes seared through Cole with contempt. Cole grinned back at him, pushing his spear deeper into Billycan's crusty skin.

"Continue, soldier," said Juniper to Carn. "Speak your mind. The floor is yours."

Carn briefly glanced at the still-seething Billycan. He cleared his throat. "Just like most of you, my parents and siblings were taken from me. They were murdered by Billycan." The hall gasped. "I was forcibly recruited by the Kill Army days later." Carn looked directly at Juniper. "Before that, I had a family. We celebrated the holidays. We ate together at our table—talking. Sometimes I laughed with my sisters till I ached. We loved each other as families do. But Billycan murdered them . . . and it was my fault."

"Son," said Juniper, "what do you mean *your* fault? You were but a child."

"Like you, my father also fought to keep Trilok's Ministry intact. Because he was away frequently, I was angry with him. I missed him. I deliberately disobeyed my mother, leaving our quarters in search of him, only to be snatched up by Billycan, who had managed to dismantle one of your traps. My father went searching for me. He came upon Billycan holding a knife to my throat. He told my father he'd let me go if he revealed your location, so my father reluctantly told him. I *knew* my father. I knew he thought that once I was free he could overpower Billycan, but instead, Billycan overpowered him, murdering him and then my family, keeping me as his aide—some sort of sick souvenir, I suppose."

"Bless the Saints," said Juniper. "Your name—it's different. I *knew* I recognized your face. You're Jacarn Newcastle—Jazeer's youngest son."

"Yes," said Carn.

"Jazeer was not a traitor at all. I *knew* we had to be wrong."

"No, my father was not a traitor," answered Carn. "*I* was. For eleven years I accepted my position serving under Billycan as just punishment."

"Lad," said Juniper, "you are *not* a traitor. You proved that already, and you are in no way responsible for your family's death—nor any of this." He motioned to the stage. "*They* are."

Carn looked up at Killdeer. He addressed his fellow soldiers. "Tonight our High Minister told us how we have to protect this '*good*' life he and his Ministry have provided. He told us we all are marked for death by this unruly group from Nightshade City. For those of you too young to know, this new city, Nightshade City, is named for our late, much-beloved Citizen Minister—Julius Nightshade. Do any of you remember Julius Nightshade? Do you remember our Citizen Minister? I know many of you must! He made sure every Catacomb rat was fed and families had decent, safe places to live. Does that sound barbaric to you? Is that the action of a murderous devil?"

Two soldiers, clearly brothers around the same age as Carn, stood up. "We remember too," said the taller one. "We remember Julius Nightshade. He made sure our mother had enough food for us when our father was killed in a Topsider's trap."

Carn's eyes brightened. The whispers in the hall turned into a low rumble. "Did Trilok or the Citizen Minister ever once ask your family for Stipend? Did they ever ask your parents to will you and your brother away to an army formed by criminals, once exiled for their despicable misdeeds against their fellow rats? Did they forcibly take your sisters and condemn them to a life of misery, serving the Kill Army majors and High Ministry day and night?"

The shorter rat answered. "No—never. No one ever asked us for anything."

Carn's voice grew desperate. "Then I ask you all again, who are the devils? Who are the true demons?" he shouted, spinning on the carpet, trying to see every soldier.

"Easy, Carn," said Juniper, trying to keep him calm. "We hear you. We all hear you, and you are right. That's why we're here."

It was too late. Carn could not be calmed. He shook his head, then faced the stage and pointed at Billycan and Killdeer. "It's them!" he yelled with all his vigor. "They are the devils. They feed happily off our suffering!"

Carn jumped on a chair. The room thundered with noise. Soldiers were shouting at the stage, growling and cursing. Someone threw a clump of dirt, clipping Major Foiber on his hairless head. Billycan glared menacingly at his sector majors in the front rows, urging them to take action. They complied.

A squat, thickset sector major in the middle of the front row jumped to his feet and threw his chair at the nearest Nightshade rat. The Nightshade rat and his comrades came at him with their spears, while the other majors stood behind their stout associate, brandishing their weapons if they had them and using their claws as blades if they did not.

Juniper grabbed Carn's arm, pulling him down from the chair. "Son, we didn't want another Coup! This will lead to needless bloodshed, bloodshed of the ones we came here to protect, to set free! This is not what we wanted!"

Carn looked at him bleakly. "This is not what anyone wanted."

A major came at Carn from the rear, wielding a newly-sharpened knife. "Carn, behind you!" blurted Juniper.

"Traitor!" shrieked the major.

Carn, much taller than the major, pivoted. With a laugh, he swiftly kicked the knife out of the major's paw, landed his foot squarely on the major's throat, and pushed his face into the ground. The other soldiers looked on in awe.

Carn grabbed the blade off the ground and pointed it skyward. He shouted, his words ringing through the hall, "Long live Trilok, long live Julius! Leaders of the true High Ministry—the only High Ministry! Let their deaths, my father's death, finally be avenged!"

The horde of soldiers, down to the smallest training lieutenant, bayed and hollered, breaking their chairs into crude weaponry, attacking the majors, whom they outnumbered twenty to one.

"So be it," grunted Juniper, as he hit an attacking major in the head with the back end of his spear, knocking him out cold. Five young lieutenants jumped on the fallen major, tying him up with a shredded tapestry and dragging him over to Ragan and Ulrich, who sat him on the ground among the growing pack of captured majors.

Juniper fought side by side with Carn. A gutless major had been hiding under his chair; he swiped at Juniper's ankles with a razor blade, hoping to slice the tendon to the bone. The major bawled pathetically as Carn plunged his dagger through the rat's paw, pinning it to the floor.

Cole, Virden, and Suttor kept their weapons trained on Billycan. He had been known to take out two rats at a time using nothing more than his claws. Foiber and Schnauss, daggers drawn, stood in front of Killdeer as the other sector majors tangled with the Nightshade rats. Major Lithgo was nowhere to be found. It seemed he had escaped.

More majors jumped in front of Killdeer, holding off the Night-shade rats. As Virden dealt with the pack of majors, Cole and Suttor tightly bound Billycan to his chair, while Killdeer followed Lithgo's lead and nimbly leaped off the back of the stage, creeping towards Ellington's Pub. If ever there was a time he needed a drink, this was most certainly it.

Victor saw Killdeer take his leave and motioned to Vincent, who had just skewered a major in the flank. Vincent watched as Killdeer slipped into the tavern. He quickly wrenched his metal spear from the writhing major, who wailed in agony. He and Victor ran behind the stage and into Ellington's Pub.

The tavern was eerily quiet. Killdeer had his back to the Nightshade brothers. Leaning over the bar, he searched for a bottle of Oshi, a keg of ale, any form of spirits. Vincent banged his bloodied spear on the ground, forcing Killdeer's attention.

The High Minister slowly turned. His face dropped as he saw the rat before him, aiming a menacing spear at his gullet. Victor stood just behind his brother, sneering at Killdeer, all teeth. It was evident the pair were siblings.

Killdeer looked Vincent up and down. "Well, as I live and breathe," he said glibly, "a green-eyed Julius back from the grave. I'd know that face anywhere. Come to kill me, eh?" Killdeer casually examined his nails, as if the situation were a typical one.

Vincent stepped closer, raising his weapon. "Something like that," he hissed coldly.

Killdeer was unnerved by Vincent's calm. He looked out the front entrance of Ellington's, hoping to spot one of his majors. He saw no one. "Listen, boy," he said coolly. "I'm well aware there is no love lost between my Ministry and your family, but you're wrong about me—dead wrong. I'm sure Juniper has filled your head with lies, telling you how evil I am. You think I killed your family, don't you? Why, it's written all over your face. He told you that—didn't he? A rat of great power, I'm quite used to being blamed for the crimes of others, but if you want my advice, I think you'd be wise to investigate Juniper. He always sought the limelight, and Julius was always the one to get it. Jealousy is a dangerous weapon. It can turn the best of rats into monsters."

"I don't believe you," said Vincent. "*You* murdered my family."

"Believe what you want, but if I were you, I'd watch my back. Clearly, you have the gift your father had, charisma, magnetism. You may not like it, but Julius and I were very much alike—you and I are very much alike—born leaders."

Vincent stepped closer, positioning his spear, ready to strike. Killdeer put both his paws in front of him, as if trying to calm a wild creature ready to attack. His voice softened. "You must remember, at the time of your father's death, we had just won. I had no further interest in killing anyone. I only wanted to form my Ministry. In fact, I wanted to give your father a title as a peace offering." Vincent did not waiver, unmoved by Killdeer's version of events. "Think about it, lad. Juniper could kill two birds with one stone. He murders your father in an envious fit, and then places the blame on me—shameful, really. I'm sure you already know what a great storyteller he is. He can weave a tale like no other, all the while treating you like the son he never had. Am I wrong? I'm sure he has built up your confidence, convincing you that I am wholly responsible for all that is wrong in our world—"

"Enough!" shouted Vincent, his rancor building with every word from Killdeer's lips. "You waste my time! You will not sway me. I am not a child, nor a frightened recruit of your army. I know the truth! I know my family was slaughtered by you and that white devil! All that time in the Combs, I should have been plotting my revenge on you, biding my time. Instead I feared you. But no longer! Sadly for you, you didn't kill my father soon enough. He taught me well. I know the ways of liars and killers. My ill will towards you knows no bounds!"

Vincent stepped closer, his brother trailing on his heels. Killdeer backed up to the bar, hitting it with his back, as Vincent prodded his soft belly with his spear. Killdeer swallowed nervously. "Now, listen, boy, you're starting to put me a bit on edge," he said, delicately reaching for a half-filled bottle of Oshi left on the bar from the night before. "Now, I'm just going to have a little drink while we talk this out. I need to calm my nerves."

Killdeer pulled off the cork with his teeth, spitting it on the ground, eagerly guzzling the contents of the bottle. "Ah," he said, exhaling, "that's better." He held out his thick paw. "See? Steady as a rock."

Vincent pushed Killdeer's belly with the spear, purposefully trying to goad the Minister. "You know," said Vincent, "my father said your kinship with alcohol would lead to your downfall. If you'd like more, don't let me or my brother stand in your way. Every rat deserves a drink before dying."

"You have your father's intellect and Juniper's sharp tongue, a dangerous combination for a young rat," said Killdeer. "This conversation grows tiresome. Now, once and for all, boy, I did *not* kill your father or your family. Neither myself nor the High Ministry had anything to do with it. They are dead, and tragically so, but not by my claws!"

Victor had been listening silently. He finally spoke up. "Vincent, I thought Father died in the flood. You said so yourself. You said our entire clan drowned. Didn't they?"

Vincent kept his eyes trained on Killdeer, not daring to turn his back. "No, Victor. They did not die in the flood. That's what the High Ministry wanted everyone to believe, a way to keep the peace and still carry out our family's killing. The Great Flood provided a perfect cover for murder. Juniper told me the truth. I didn't think it right to tell you, not until you were ready. I suppose you're ready now. Maybe you always have been. I swore Juniper and the others to secrecy. I'm sorry."

Victor came forward, stepping next to his brother. "You should have told me, Vincent." His eyes started to burn. "There is no right or wrong in what you did. Had I been the older one, I would have done the same. The only wrong you've done is to yourself, in keeping the burden on your shoulders. Had we been with our family, I'm sure Billycan and his majors would have us dead and buried next to our brothers and sisters. You and I, we are all that's left. We are together in this."

Victor stared at Killdeer, who struggled uncomfortably against the wooden bar. "You gave the orders, didn't you? You wouldn't want to get your own paws soiled, now, would you? So how was it done?" He sobbed as grief mingled with rage, then swallowed, and said, "Did your soldiers hold them down while Billycan slit their throats? Did he cut out their tongues and watch them bleed out one by one, as he so likes to do? Did he bring my father's head to you on a silver platter?" Tears ran down Victor's face, leaving small wet trails in his black fur.

"Victor, is it?" asked Killdeer. "Victor, I may be a hardened rat. I may be everything Juniper says and more, but I would never murder a family—never children."

Victor ignored him. "What has made you so depraved, so vile? What evil burns inside you? What force lives in your heart, breeding such malevolence? I just want to understand. I *need* to understand you!" He stared at Killdeer, bewildered.

"Greed, gluttony, lack of conscience," said Vincent. "There is nothing for us to understand. You and I will *never* understand the workings of his twisted soul."

Victor started to shout. "My family, you killed them all! My mother, my father, brothers and sisters I never had a chance to know! I barely remember them! I *don't* remember them!"

"Now, boy, calm down. This is all a misunderstanding!" barked Killdeer. "Victor, I'm not the bad rat you think me. I'm *not* a killer! It's Juniper. He's the reason your family is dead!"

Victor looked at Killdeer with disgust. Without warning, he ran at Killdeer, charging him, shoving his steel spear clean through the dazed Minister's shoulder, the force so great it threw Killdeer over the bar, pinning him to the back wall of Ellington's, as bottles of Oshi fell like missiles, smashing on the hard dirt floor. The spear lodged in the wall. Killdeer tried desperately to pull it out but couldn't get a grip on the blood-slicked metal. Victor dug his claws into Killdeer's neck, anchoring himself solidly to the Minister. Vincent tried to pull his brother off. Blinded by rage, Victor accidentally kicked his brother in the head. Vincent fell to the ground, unconscious.

Killdeer writhed in pain as blood surged from his neck and shoulder, turning his gray coat a thick, matted crimson. With his free paw, Victor pounded on the Minister's face, striking him again and again, crushing the socket of his eye.

Killdeer reached behind his head and grabbed a bottle of Oshi. He shattered it against the side of Victor's skull. Victor hung loosely to the Minister, temporarily stunned. Killdeer was losing blood rapidly, his wits fading. He laughed as blood gushed from Victor's ear. Frothy red spume gurgled from the Minister's mouth as his raucous laughter carried through the empty tavern.

Vincent awoke to the sound of Killdeer's freakish laughter. The deranged cackle sent a shiver through his body. He sat up and grabbed his throbbing head. His vision returning, he saw his brother still clinging to Killdeer, still striking him, his blows growing weaker and weaker. Killdeer laughed louder as he slowly lifted his uninjured arm and made a tight fist, aimed at Victor's head.

Vincent rushed to his brother, who seemed trapped in some hypnotic frenzy. He jumped over the bar, pushed in underneath, and wedged himself between Killdeer and Victor. He grabbed hold of Killdeer's silver medallion. He thought of his father as he wrapped the chain around his fist and elbow, winding it tighter and tighter around the Minister's ample neck. He twisted the chain until it felt like it might snap. Victor weakly threw punches at Killdeer in a mechanical motion, his strikes no longer effective.

Killdeer's fist suddenly unclenched and his arm fell limply, slapping the back wall of Ellington's. He stopped laughing and grabbed for his chain, now a silver noose, desperately gulping for air. His eyes bulged, and he coughed and gasped as red foam bubbled out his mouth. Killdeer suddenly went silent.

Vincent yelled to his brother, trying to rouse him. "Victor!" he pleaded. "Victor! Wake up, please! Look at him—Victor, look!"

Victor finally heard his brother's calls. He stopped punching. He looked down at Vincent, still clutching the silver chain. He looked at Killdeer, unrecognizable, a mess of blood and bruises. The great rat did not move—his face expressionless and his eyes dull.

"It's over, Victor. It's over. He's gone."

Victor wrenched his bloodied claws from Killdeer's neck. He threw himself backwards onto the bar top and lay flat on his back, looking up at the tavern's stained ceiling. Blood seeped from his ear. "Vincent," he said as his eyes started to close, "Vincent, we won."

A pack of sector majors, including Lithgo, had escaped Topside. Foiber and Schnauss, too old to put up much of a fight, had been captured along with over two hundred sector majors, all now shackled and being led back to Nightshade's detention corridor. Their fates were yet to be decided.

Very few soldiers fought against the Nightshade rats; those who did were killed or maimed in the mayhem. Although many Nightshade rats were bruised and scratched and a few seriously injured, not one had lost his life. Juniper's original theory rang true. The Kill Army was no army at all, merely a pack of lost boys. After the Kill Army leaders had been captured, many of the former soldiers excitedly ran back to their barracks, collecting the few possessions they had, ready to start a new life in Nightshade.

Billycan sat tethered to his chair, still sitting atop the stage. Cole, Virden, Suttor, and several other rats guarded the High Collector, encircling him like a gang of vultures, not daring to let him out of their sights.

Billycan stayed silent, all four paws, even his tail, securely bound. He did not try to break free. What was the point? He did not yell out in rage, nor did he spit profanities. He did not scream treason in the name of the High Ministry or the Kill Army. He did not even acknowledge the Nightshade rats. He did nothing. Billycan slumped back in his chair, a bored expression on his face. His reign was over. He hoped Juniper would have enough hatred to put him to death, but he suspected that would not be the case. Juniper and his accursed goodness would not feel justified in killing even him, the rat who most undoubtedly deserved that fate.

Billycan had never been afraid to die. He didn't believe in the Saints. He didn't believe he would rise above the clouds of Trillium, going to some brilliant world in the afterlife, nor plummet down to a hellfire pit deep within the underworld. Dead was dead. As he sat on the stage, watching the surreal scene, he couldn't even pray for death. Since he had no faith in the Saints, praying would be utterly ridiculous. He laughed at the idea.

In spite of his hatred for Juniper, Billycan respected the rat. He knew Juniper would have him imprisoned in a tiny cell till the end of his days, a much greater punishment than the finality of death. Billycan had to agree with the theory, although he enjoyed killing too much to follow the practice. As he sat thinking, ignoring the happy clamoring of the Nightshade rats and the newly freed Kill Army soldiers and Catacomb subjects, he noticed the mood had unexpectedly changed.

The hall had fallen totally silent. No one moved. Every rat, friend or foe, stood stiff, looking towards the red carpet bordering the front of the stage.

Vincent and Victor trudged in front of the stage, dragging what looked like a possum behind them. But it was no possum. Billycan watched as the two black rats each dragged a foot of the bloodied and bloated High Minister.

Billycan tilted his head in curiosity, examining the oddity, his leader, his comrade, the reason all *this* had started—dead. It was time, he thought to himself, and better by their claws than his. Killdeer's eyes were lackluster—staring up at him vacantly. *So many vices,* he thought. Killdeer's pitiful self-indulgences, drink, food, females, his inflated ego, his brazen vanity. Killdeer spoke of the Saints, but Billycan never knew if he truly believed in them—in their retribution for sins. For Killdeer's sake, they had best not exist.

Juniper came forward. Both boys were crusted with dried blood. They looked down at the ground.

Juniper finally spoke. "Boys, are you all right?" He inspected Vincent, then Victor, examining the blood that had erupted from his ear. "Thank the Saints you're both alive," he said, holding Victor's head and tilting it back. "Virden, come and look at this ear." Virden jumped off the stage and took Victor to a nearby chair.

Juniper studied Vincent's grim face. "Vincent, what happened? What led to this?"

"Victor found out what really happened to our family, that Killdeer had ordered their deaths, and went mad with grief. Like some sort of switch had been pulled. I got between them before Killdeer could . . . "

Juniper put his paws on Vincent's shoulders and looked into his eyes. "I see," he said. "Vincent, I'm sorry it was left to you and your brother, but there has to be a reason for this. There always is. I don't think the Saints would have had it any other way."

"I suppose you're right," said Vincent, "but I should have told Victor the truth sooner. Then maybe he wouldn't—"

Juniper would not allow him to finish. He spoke firmly. "I *know* I'm right. You did no wrong. All your life you've protected your brother—just as you did tonight. You are true of heart, no shame in that. You are not to blame for this outcome. Justice comes in many forms."

Vincent exhaled, smiling a little, relieved it was over, relieved by Juniper's words. Walking over to Killdeer's body, Vincent knelt down and released the silver chain from the deceased Minister's neck. "Here," he said, handing it to Juniper. "I think this belongs to you now."

Victor called from his chair. "Juniper, put it on!"

Cole nodded in agreement from atop the stage. "They're right, old friend. Put it on."

Everyone stared at Juniper, holding the weighty medallion in his hands. He looked around Catacomb Hall, then hesitantly put the chain over his head. The medallion rested comfortably on his chest. It felt strange.

Juniper looked out at all the anxious faces. He stood in front of Killdeer. His voice ripped through the silent hall. "The Ministry is no more! Everyone—you are free!"

Thousands of voices thundered in Catacomb Hall. Rats chanted and stomped.

"Juniper!" shouted Cole from the stage, his alarmed voice cutting through the clamor. Juniper looked up at the stage. "Juniper, he's gone!"

The white rat had disappeared.

CHAPTER NINE
Home

I{T WAS SAINTS' DAY}. Bostwick Hall was full and then some. Mother Gallo and Clover directed everyone to seats and tables as several large rats brought out platters filled with piping-hot sausages, dried beef, and mushroom stew. Lali dashed around at her usual pace, placing baskets of her bitonberry muffins and butter biscuits on every table, specifically requested by Juniper and Vincent.

Juniper, Vincent, and Victor sat at the center table along with Suttor, Carn, and the Council. Ulrich had broken his arm in two places when a frightened soldier bashed him with a wooden chair. Lali made sure he had an extra mug of ale to ease the pain. Suttor's little brothers and Mother Gallo's boys sat at a smaller table right next to them. They kept staring over at the older boys, awed by their brave efforts.

The new young residents of Nightshade City sat with their friends, laughing and joking like children, not soldiers. The freed Catacomb rats were quickly adjusting to their new surroundings. As the generous portions of food and ale were being passed around, it was hard to fathom a life of plenty, a life without ever having to pay Stipend again. It was like waking from a long nightmare.

Juniper looked down at his chest, still feeling the weight of Trilok's medal. He picked it up and turned it towards him. He looked at Duchess Nomi's face. It made him think of Maddy. He scanned the room, spotting her as she passed out muffins to a table brimming with little girls, once slaves to the Ministry, now just girls, giggling and playfully teasing one another. He smiled as he watched Maddy laugh merrily, walking round the table. Soon, he thought, soon he would have an important question for her.

Vincent and Victor looked at each other and grinned. Victor nudged Vincent on the arm as he caught him staring at Clover, who smiled back as she refilled mugs of ale.

Victor whispered to Vincent. "Do you think now's a good time?"

"As good a time as any," replied Vincent, setting down his third muffin.

Vincent brushed the crumbs from his paws and climbed atop his seat. Victor clanked his mug against his plate, signaling for attention. The room quieted. Vincent spoke. "New citizens of Nightshade City, may I have a brief moment of your time?"

Juniper looked up from his plate, and Vincent gave him a wink. Juniper glanced across the table at Cole, who shrugged his shoulders in bewilderment.

"Now, then," said Vincent, "it has recently come to my and my brother's attention that we have just become an extremely large city." The hall quaked with laughter. "We are a new city, a thriving city, yet still a city without a proper leader. At least," Vincent said, looking down at Juniper, "officially. That being said, my brother and I have come up with a suggestion. A suggestion we were hoping you can all adopt or reject this very moment. We think we need some *elected* officials—no more self-proclaimed High Ministers. Victor and I would like to officially nominate Juniper Belancort and Cole Kingston to lead us as Chief Citizen and Deputy Chief Citizen of Nightshade City!"

The hall rumbled with applause. "All right, then," shouted Vincent, "are there any more nominations?" The room hushed. Vincent waited patiently, but no one spoke. "Then let's put this to a vote. Everyone in favor, stand now!" Every rat got up from his or her chair or stool and stood in silence, looking round the hall, searching for anyone who was not on his feet. The old ones, too aged to stand, held up their paws in endorsement. Victor and Suttor joined Vincent atop their chairs, inspecting the room for anyone still sitting. The only ones not voting were the two dazed nominees.

"It's unanimous!" yelled Vincent. "Congratulations, Chief Citizen Juniper and Deputy Chief Cole!" The hall exploded with noise. Juniper and Cole stood up from the table as well-wishers came in droves to hug them and shake their paws.

Juniper pulled Vincent down from his chair and put his arm around him. "You," he said to Vincent, "you will one day lead this city, and you will lead it well. I have no doubt."

"Thanks to you, my father's dream has been realized," said Vincent. "As for myself, maybe one day I *will* lead this city, but for now, there's much I need to learn—from you."

Smiling, Juniper patted Vincent's back. "Then I'm glad to teach it, son."

Mother Gallo rushed up to Juniper. "I'm so pleased for you!" she said.

Juniper pulled her near. "Be pleased for *us*, Maddy. We couldn't have succeeded without you."

Lali ran over to Cole, kissing and hugging her husband till he was dizzy.

Clover crept up behind Vincent and kissed him on the cheek. "You are a brave rat," she whispered. Vincent's head started to spin and his chest began to ache. He grabbed the edge of his chair so as not to stumble in front of her, and gazed at her with a silly grin.

Virden suddenly jumped onto the table, rattling the utensils. "Silence, everyone, silence!" The commotion was quickly brought to a standstill, and all eyes stared up at Virden. "Now, let's do this by the book, shall we?" Virden held up his glass of Oshi. "Let us toast this momentous night—this Saints' Day is a day of jubilation for those of us here and for all those long departed. May our brave new city honor their memory and may we, their heirs, now hold our heads high once more. To Nightshade!"

Glasses clinked and clanked. Everyone toasted in unison, "To Nightshade!"

"Now," said Virden, his face aglow, "let's celebrate!"

As the clamor and laughter resumed, Vincent turned back to Clover. "Clover," he whispered in her ear, "you kissed me!"

"Why, yes. Yes, I did," she replied.

Vincent suddenly grabbed Clover round her waist and twirled her in a circle. She giggled in surprise as her feet left the ground. Taking in a deep breath, Vincent caught the lemony scent of Clover's fur. He closed his eyes, listening to the sounds whirling around him: the cheerful voices, the singing, boys and girls laughing wildly, especially his brother—especially Victor. He opened his eyes and smiled contentedly at Clover. Vincent at last knew the feeling his father had spoken of—his old world had ended and a new world had begun, all in the same breath. He was home.

Nightshade City finally felt whole. Mother Gallo, with the help of Juniper and the Council, assigned the citizens, former soldiers, and servant girls to the available quarters of the city. They had only so many rooms ready for occupancy, so the new residents would be crowded together for a while. No one seemed to mind, especially the young ones; it was nice to have someone to look after them.

In the following months, vast growth and change took place within Nightshade. Juniper and Cole stepped right into their roles within the new democracy of Nightshade City. Among the other elected officials, Mother Gallo served as Citizen of Education. Virden was elected Citizen of City Planning. Ragan, Ulrich, and former lieutenant Carn became Tri-Citizens of Security and Intelligence, and lastly, Vincent and Suttor were selected as Co-Citizens of Youth Advancement.

Victor was glad it was decided he was too young to be elected as a city official. For now, he was content to have as little responsibility as possible. His main concern was the next time Petra's parents would let her out of her quarters to see him. Luckily for him, her parents found him hard not to like. Thanks to Killdeer, Victor had permanently lost the hearing in his left ear. Virden had stitched his outer ear back together the morning after the battle. At first, Victor detested the ugly scar, but he quickly changed his mind when Petra told him she thought it made him look quite distinguished.

Vincent and Suttor seemed to grasp the world of politics with ease. Together they worked on Nightshade youth agendas, giving the young a voice they had never had. Vincent easily balanced his position with his time with Clover, as she had been granted a position as Youth Citizen Education Adviser, allowing them to work side by side.

Clover had decided to move into her own quarters but ended up with quite an unexpected roommate. Sweet but slow Texi had had nowhere to go. Her sisters had fled Topside, where she never would have stood a chance. Mother Gallo suggested the two girls move in together. Texi was nothing but kindhearted, and Clover could use some kindness after her ordeal.

Texi helped Lali, now Nightshade's Chief Cook, as well as the busy mothers of Nightshade in taking care of their growing broods. After they met during her security interview, Texi began spending time with Ulrich. He found her truthful and gentle; it was hard to comprehend that she was related to Killdeer. Best of all, she adored his stubby tail.

As for Cook Longtooth, she gladly retired her greasy apron in exchange for helping Texi with the many new babies of Nightshade. The once-crusty culinarian transformed into a tender and patient caregiver, enamored with the infants she cuddled, who smiled brightly at her mangled grin.

Cole, now Deputy Chief Citizen, had taken well to his new

station. Lali was instrumental in making sure all the displaced Kill Army children were moved in with loving Nightshade families, who happily volunteered their homes and hearts to the orphan boys and girls. Cole had become like a father to Suttor, and he and Lali had taken in Suttor's younger brothers, as well as Desmond, the timid little boy who could tell all his friends that he had sat atop Killdeer's royal shoulder on the night of his demise. The once-quiet Kingston home was now overrun with noisy, rowdy boys. With their new family and demanding positions, Lali finally got a full night's sleep and Cole's mood never darkened again.

The captured majors would be facing trial soon. Ragan, Ulrich, and Carn had interviewed citizens who had resided in each major's sector. Carn provided a wealth of information in this department, as did the other senior lieutenants. After gathering witness accounts, it turned out that some of the sector majors had had no loyalty to the fallen High Ministry. They were simply doing what they were told, trying to survive. The many majors who did prove to be vicious, the ones with a true bloodlust, were locked up in Nightshade's detention corridor, forced to live out their days in tiny, dank cells: a far better fate than the ones they had given their victims.

Major Lithgo had been found a month after the battle, hiding in the storage area of Killdeer's compound. He had tried to fight his way out, attacking a Nightshade rat and biting through his neck. The Nightshade rat survived; Lithgo did not.

As promised, the earthworms finally got their sanctuary, deep within the rich soil of Nightshade. Juniper gave Oard and his tribesmen a huge chunk of earth, which was never to be disturbed by the rats again. A metal plaque was forged in Noc's honor, placed on the single rat entrance to the tribe's new home. Rats were granted entrance only by approved request. To date, no rat had ever been refused.

In the months after his disappearance, rumors abounded as to Billycan's whereabouts. Some heard he had boarded a cargo ship on its way to exotic Tosca Island, hidden in a crate of waterchip root, an ironic fate for the rat who loathed the root's putrid smell. Others said he had jumped a fuel tanker headed to the deep south and had joined up with an ancient colony of big brown bats. The old ones still swore that the singular white rat was supernatural. They were sure he had vanished into thin air that night by his own will and would reappear when the time was right.

The Chief Citizen considered all the rumors. The earthworms had headed Topside the night Billycan made his escape, but the only news they discovered was that he did indeed go south, which said nothing about his current whereabouts. He could be anywhere. The former High Collector was unquestionably a threat, much more so than Killdeer would have been. Juniper had his best trackers cover every inch of the Combs and Nightshade. They found nothing, not even a lone white hair.

One more story still made the rounds—one that Juniper considered most unsettling of all. Many said Billycan had dug under Nightshade, deeper than any Trillium rat had ever gone. Living the life of a hermit, patiently biding his time, he waited for the right moment to return to enact his bloody revenge—one final showdown with Juniper Belancort. For everyone's comfort, the earthworms patrolled under Nightshade regularly. Thus far, no trace of life had been uncovered, but the story still haunted the residents of Nightshade City, who swore Billycan had dug himself so deep that he would never be found.

Juniper settled into his recently finished quarters. He had made a pair of rocking chairs for himself and his new bride, and he thought today would be the perfect afternoon to try his out. Mother Gallo had taken all the boys but one to visit Suttor's younger brothers for the afternoon.

Upon the discovery of Major Lithgo deep within the confines of Killdeer's compound, the Nightshade rats had come across a skeletal infant rat, wrapped in a tattered cloth, nearly dead from hunger. He was found hidden in a corner in the quarters of Killdeer's sisters. Texi knew nothing of the child and assumed that her sisters had hidden it from her, worried she might accidentally reveal the birth to her brother, who strictly forbade his sisters from consorting with males.

Mother Gallo missed having a baby in the house and begged Juniper to take the foundling infant in. Begging was not necessary. Juniper happily accepted his new ward, hoping that one day the boy would call him Papa.

Juniper sat in his chair next to the fire. He held his son in the crook of his arm, rocking him tenderly. Juniper drifted between reality and dreams. His cloudy thoughts shifted to Billycan and the night the white rat had whittled out his eye as a gruesome souvenir. He fell asleep.

Juniper slept like the dead, his infant son curled next to him, murmuring peacefully. The boy's miniature tail and feet were snugly tucked under Juniper's dense winter fur. The fire smoldered softly, infusing the room with a warm caramel glow, the ideal setting for a midday nap. Juniper had earned his rest. The battle was over, and for the first time in a long time, life underground was calm.

A noise interrupted Juniper's sleep—a dull scraping against the planking of his chamber door. "Who is it?" he called out. Juniper sluggishly looked up from the rocking chair, hoping that the anonymous knocker would go away and that his much-needed nap could continue. He listened for a reply; no answer. It appeared that the stranger at the door had given up. Letting his muscles once again relax, Juniper settled back into his slumber, his substantial arm cradling the tiny boy.

A low, raspy voice whispered, "Juniper. Juniper, wake up."

Juniper half opened his eye and for a second time looked towards the door, now a bit bothered. "Whoever is there, please come back tomorrow. I'll be more than happy to talk to you first thing in the morning. I promise you will have my undivided attention." He waited for a response; again no answer. The stranger had gone. "Thank the Saints," Juniper said. The room was silent, apart from the baby, who squeaked softly as Juniper shifted in the chair and once again drifted off.

"Juniper!" railed the voice, jolting him from his tranquil state. Juniper bolted from his chair, and plucking up his son, he reached into the fire pit for the hot poker, but it had vanished. He looked frantically for a weapon, quickly grabbing a knife off the table. Trying to follow the voice, he blindly swung the dull blade into the shadows.

There was a crash. Juniper jerked around. His leather satchel had been ripped from its hook and had fallen to the hard dirt floor, its contents sprawled everywhere. Unable to see in the hidden corners, Juniper spun wildly in a confused circle. He hollered angrily into the dark. "Come out! Come out and face me, coward! I *know* why you've come!"

Finding a match, Juniper swiftly lit the wall torches, illuminating all things unseen, and still clutching his sleeping boy, he scoured the room.

No one was there.

Confident his quarters were secure, Juniper gently stroked the boy's long snout and spoke to him softly. "It's all right, son. You are safe with me."

The fire had faded. Juniper found the blanket Mother Gallo had made for the baby and swaddled him in it. The baby briefy woke, giving a soft little squeak. His eyes opened for just a moment, revealing a bright flash of fiery red.

"There, there, Julius," whispered Juniper as the infant's eyes once again closed. "Papa's here." Feeling a draft, he pulled up the child's blanket. All that could be seen from its woollen folds was the baby's snow-white nose.